A STRICT SEDUCTION

by

MARIA DEL REY

CHIMERA

A Strict Seduction published by
Chimera Publishing Ltd
PO Box 152
Waterlooville
Hants
PO8 9FS

Printed and bound in Great Britain by
Omnia Books Ltd, Glasgow

A STRICT SEDUCTION

Maria del Rey

A Strict Seduction

Patti pulled the shower curtain back slowly so that she could get a better look at herself in the full-length mirror on the other side of the bathroom. Her black hair was slicked back, a glossy mane that seemed to shine under the soft glow of the lights. She stood straighter, pushing her shoulders back so that her breasts were pushed forward, the dark tips of her nipples jewelled with droplets of water. She looked at herself critically, wondering how she really compared to Sarah's sleek frame.

The doorbell took her by surprise. Tom was early! A frisson of fear passed through, making her heart beat faster and her hands shake a little. She stepped out of the shower quickly, water pouring onto the tiled floor, dripping from her hair and body to form puddles around her feet. She stepped to the bathroom door and poked her head out. For a second she was afraid it was Sarah, back from work unexpectedly early, but the doorbell rang again right on cue.

'I'll be there in a second!' Patti called, hoping Tom could hear her.

She snatched a towel quickly and wrapped it around herself, looking once more in the mirror as she did so. Her face and body were flushed slightly by the hot shower, a touch of pink added to her pale skin, in contrast to her black hair and brown eyes. The towel was up under her arms and reached down to her knees, a chaste image despite the fact that she was naked under it. She half smiled to herself and lowered it slightly, revealing the swell of her breasts whilst still keeping her decent.

The doorbell rang again, its impatient tone demanding

attention.

'Just a second!' she called once more, padding out of the bathroom hurriedly. She just hoped that Sarah was going to be as late as she said she would be. There was no longer any doubt in her mind that it was Tom at the door, no one else would be that demanding.

She slipped the security chain on and then opened the door a fraction of an inch. She looked up, her dark eyes wide with apprehension.

Tom seemed surprised to see her, but a warm smile still stretched across his face. 'I seem to have caught you at a bad time,' he said apologetically.

Patti looked down at herself and then back at him. Did he like what he saw? His smile was always there for her, even when he was only popping by to pick Sarah up, but was there something more to it?

'I'm sorry, Tom,' she said, releasing the chain on the door and then making way for him to enter the flat she shared with Sarah.

He stepped inside and waited for her. She closed the door quickly and then turned to face him, her hands reflexively reaching for the towel. 'I'm so sorry,' she said, making a face, 'but I was supposed to call you earlier…'

Tom sighed audibly. 'Let me guess,' he said wearily, 'she's working late again.'

His tone was more than one of plain resignation, there was a hint of irritation there, something beyond plain acceptance of the facts. Patti flashed him a sympathetic smile. 'I'm sorry,' she whispered. 'It's my fault. Sarah tried to call you but couldn't connect. She phoned me an hour ago and I promised I'd ring and let you know.'

He was still standing in the narrow hallway, as though waiting for an invitation into the rest of the flat. Patti held her towel tightly around her chest, her wet hair clinging coldly to her shoulders. 'It's cold out here,' she reminded him.

It was his turn to apologise. 'So, what great excuse did she offer this time?' he asked, heading into the sitting room.

Patti slicked her hair back again, and then followed him, wondering whether she should take a chance and relax the hold on her towel. 'She said something came up urgently,' she explained, 'something about a report she needs to deliver by tomorrow.'

Tom stood in the middle of the room to take in the news. He was a tall man, good looking, authoritative, and with a smile that melted Patti's insides every time. Sarah was crazy, there was no way Patti would let a man like Tom hang around.

'Did she say how long she'd be?' he asked, glancing at his watch.

A wave of panic swept through her. 'No, not really,' she said quickly. 'Look, why don't you sit down,' she suggested, 'let me put something on and I'll get us some drinks.'

She hoped that the suggestion sounded innocent, there was no way she wanted Tom to get the wrong idea. He looked at his watch again. 'I'm not sure… If she's going to be much later then I might as well get going.'

'No, no, I'm sure she's not.'

Tom looked at her and smiled. 'You sound pretty certain. Did she say what time she'd be home?'

'No, not exactly,' she said, 'but she said she'd ring to let me know.'

He sighed once more and then sat down. 'Okay then,' he agreed, 'I'll have whatever you're having to drink.'

He was going to stay! Patti felt a nervous thrill run through her.

'I won't be long,' she promised, and then headed straight back to the bathroom before he could change his mind.

She dried herself hurriedly, running the thick pink towel through her hair and over her skin. She let it drop and stood naked before the mirror once more. Sarah was tall, blonde, leggy and very sexy. Beside her Patti always felt dowdy and unsexy, despite the fact that there seemed to be no shortage of men who found her curvy body, pale skin and dark eyes a distinct turn-on. She reached for her silk robe and slipped it on, cinching it tight at the waist. The silky garment reached down to mid-thigh, revealing slim, attractive limbs which drew the eye naturally. Around the chest it was tight, the fullness of her breasts moulded to the shiny fabric.

She skipped barefoot to the kitchen, aware of the coolness of the air in the flat. She was almost naked, her body hidden by the flimsy garment and nothing else. 'A glass of wine okay?' she called from the kitchen, her heart pounding so hard she could almost hear it out loud.

'That'd be great,' Tom called in reply.

Patti poured a couple of glasses of red and then stopped. A sudden doubt took all her resolve away. Sarah, ten years older and a good deal wiser, was her best friend. Did she really deserve what Patti was doing? The answer was no, but then Patti thought of Tom's smile and the allure in his deep blue eyes and she knew that she couldn't resist.

She loosened her robe a fraction and reached inside. Her nipples were already hardening and she stroked them with her fingers, teasing them to erection and letting the pleasure flood through her. She was breathing hard and the excitement was like fire in the pit of her belly. When her nipples were hard she tightened the robe once more, haloes of light shimmering where her full pert breasts were wrapped in silk.

Tom looked up as she came into the room, his eyes registering surprise at what he saw. Patti smiled nervously as she walked towards him, carrying the glasses of wine and trying to affect a nonchalance she did not feel.

'Thanks,' he said, taking the proffered glass and fixing his eyes on her. He was sitting in the middle of the big three-seater sofa which dominated the room. Patti hesitated for a moment, not sure whether to risk sitting next to him or not. The dilemma was resolved for her, Tom shifted over to the left and made way for her.

She sat down beside him, tucking her legs up under her, and smoothing her robe down so it covered her thighs. She still felt nervous, half afraid that Sarah would return home unexpectedly, or else afraid he'd rebuff her advances. Both the possibilities were frightening, but still Patti felt something other than fear stirring inside her.

'We don't often get a chance to have a proper chat,' he said, taking a sip of his wine.

It was true enough. Sarah always seemed so jealous of any attention Tom might give to Patti. Who didn't Sarah trust? Patti or Tom? The question made Patti lose her tongue.

'You're not going out this evening?' Tom asked a moment later.

'No, not tonight,' Patti confirmed. In fact, she'd planned on going to the cinema with a couple of the girls from work, but once she'd got the call from Sarah she'd changed her mind.

'It's a Saturday night,' Tom responded, cocking an eyebrow questioningly. 'I would have thought a pretty girl like you would have been out on the town.'

Patti averted her eyes shyly. What could she say? 'No, I felt like a quiet night in,' she lied.

'Really? Isn't there someone special at the moment?'

She shook her head and smiled sadly. 'No, there isn't,' she sighed. Her robe fell open a little at the chest, revealing soft white skin against the silk. She was aware that his eyes were on her but she made no move to cover herself up, even though she could feel the first flush of embarrassment.

The ringing of the phone startled her. She turned instinctively and reached over the arm of the sofa to grab it. Even before she spoke she knew it was Sarah on the line.

'Patti? Is Tom there with you?' Sarah asked briskly.

'Yes, he is,' Patti admitted softly.

'Let me speak to him,' Sarah snapped angrily.

As Patti turned she became aware that her robe had ridden up high and that most of her bare thigh was on view, not only that but it had become loose at the top and was affording Tom a good view of her breasts. Her face coloured as she wrapped the robe around her again and passed Tom the phone.

'Hi, Sarah,' he said, his deep voice sounding relaxed and at home, with no trace of the annoyance that Patti had heard earlier.

'Another couple of hours…? Can't you make it any sooner? No… Of course… Forget it… No, I'll probably be gone by the time you get here… Yes, of course… Okay, I'll call you tomorrow.'

Tom passed the phone back and Patti replaced it in its cradle, this time taking more care not to expose herself. The conversation between Tom and Sarah had been brief but she had gathered the gist of it. Sarah was going to be late and so Tom was going to go home, another wasted evening to put down to experience.

'How about another glass of this?' Tom suggested, lifting his half empty glass in the air.

Patti smiled. 'Sure, why not,' she agreed.

She stood up and took his glass, secretly thrilled that he wasn't going to disappear immediately. The fact that Sarah was treating him in such an off-hand manner seemed to make things easier. As she walked the front of the robe opened a little and this time she made no move to cover herself up. Tom was looking at her long bare thighs and it felt good to have the attention.

She refilled the glasses in the kitchen and then decided to take the bottle with her too. She clutched it to her chest and then carefully walked back with a glass in each hand.

Tom's smile was anything but innocent as he watched her returning.

'Let me take that,' he said, leaning forward to take the bottle wedged between her arm and her chest. She leant forward and her robe parted completely, exposing her nakedness once and for all. She held her breath, partly shocked by the accident and partly wondering what his reaction would be. There was a silence for a moment and then their eyes met.

'I've got it,' he said quietly, taking his glass and the bottle from her.

She straightened up, her face burning red with embarrassment. She tucked her robe quickly, covering herself up hurriedly.

'I'm sorry,' she whispered.

He looked at her, a serious expression on his face, his sweet blue eyes unreadable. 'I don't think so,' he said quietly.

She was still standing in front of him, holding her robe in place with one hand, her other hand shakily holding her glass of wine. Now that it had come to the crunch she felt embarrassed. Seducing Tom had been a fantasy that she'd enjoyed for so long, now that it was becoming reality she no longer felt certain of anything.

He reached out and tugged at her robe gently, forcing it from her grasp so that it fell open once more. She felt frozen into place as his eyes tracked her slowly, his gaze travelling from her bare feet, up her long silky thighs, over the dark triangle covering her sex, up over the gentle curve of her tummy and the fullness of her breasts, to her open mouth and the look of shock in her eyes.

'Sit here,' he suggested, his voice low, almost a whisper that she felt deep inside her.

Shakily she did as she was told, sitting beside him on the sofa. Her breasts were framed by pale silk which contrasted with the darkness that tipped them. She could

11

not look at him, suddenly all of her confidence was gone and she felt nothing but fear. Sarah was her best friend, and here she was parading naked in front of Sarah's boyfriend.

Tom took her hands and pulled her towards him. She did not resist, and when his mouth met hers she accepted the invasion of his kiss. His tongue slipped between her lips and her breath was sucked away violently. He held her tightly, keeping her on the edge of the sofa while he explored her mouth with his tongue. She gasped for breath, shocked that things had moved so far so quickly.

He released her suddenly, letting her hands go and withdrawing his mouth from hers to leave her wanting more. She opened her eyes, aware that she was almost naked before him, the loose robe barely covering her breasts, and that her sex was partly visible through the folds of silk.

'How old are you?' he asked her, a slight smile playing on his lips. She looked into his eyes for a moment, then looked away. He seemed to be amused by the situation, the sparkle of desire she saw was more than matched by the expression of bemusement. It was a strange question to ask given the circumstances, and she felt angered by it. What difference did it make how old she was?

'Old enough,' she replied, covering herself up quickly. In her fantasies the long, first kiss was supposed to give way to something more, not a bout of questioning about her age.

He smiled indulgently. 'Are you twenty yet?' he asked, putting his hand on her knee.

'Yes I am!' she snapped, brushing his hand away.

He shook his head. 'No,' he said quietly, the low rumble of his voice touching something deep inside her, 'we don't stop now.'

It sounded as though she had no choice in the matter, adding to her growing feelings of anger. 'Look, Tom, I think this has been a mistake…'

She tried to stand but he wouldn't let her. He gripped her by the wrists and pulled her back down to the sofa. 'You misunderstand,' he whispered, drawing her closer towards him. His grip was tight around her wrists, it was almost painful, and yet there was something about his confidence that excited her. If he kissed her she knew she would not be able to resist. 'What do you think Sarah would say if she could see us now?' he asked quietly.

Patti didn't want to answer the question. She didn't even want to think about it any more. In fantasy it had all been so different; questions of right and wrong, loyalty and betrayal, had never intruded on the images inside her head. 'Please, Tom,' she whispered, looking into his eyes in the hope that he would relent, 'I'm sorry this ever happened. Can't we just forget it?'

He held her wrists with one hand and used the other to slide up her thigh slowly, as though enjoying the feel of her smooth flesh under his fingers. She held her breath, startled both by the sureness of his touch and by the thrill of desire that passed through her. 'No,' he replied finally, 'we can't just forget it.'

She closed her eyes as he touched her again, his hand travelling from her thigh and up over her tummy. Her nipples were already hard and when he grazed them with his fingers she inhaled sharply. He cupped her right breast in his hand, enfolding her flesh, her nipple trapped between his fingers. This time there could be no denying the pleasure that surged through her, it felt as though there was a line of fire that connected her breasts and the heat between her thighs.

When she opened her eyes she realised he'd released her hands, that she was free to stand up and leave if she wanted to. He cupped both breasts with his hands, squeezing her soft flesh gently, flicking his thumbs over the hard nipples so that she sighed despite herself.

'This is wrong…' she sighed, still struggling with her feelings.

'I know,' he said, half smiling. He leaned forward and kissed her nipples gently, his mouth flicking wet caresses over each hard nub of flesh in turn. His breath was hot against her skin, enticing and arousing and impossible to resist. She moved closer, suddenly offering herself to him, wanting his mouth to tease and bite the most sensitive parts of her breasts.

He took her hands and placed them on her breasts, folding her fingers into place so that she cupped her breasts for him, offering herself wantonly, feeding her reddened nipples to his voracious mouth. She moaned softly, the pleasure pulsing through her as he suckled softly, his tongue working back and forth, building up the sensation so that each movement of his mouth on her breast was magnified in pleasure. She was wet, wetter than she had ever been before. Somewhere in the back of her head a voice was telling her that what she was doing was wrong, but that voice was growing faint and the only effect it had was to add to her excitement.

'Here,' he said, pulling her astride his lap. She moved across him, sitting over his knees as he sucked and stroked her breasts. He used his lips and teeth to rouse her still further until she could feel the moisture escape from within her. She cupped her breasts, squeezing her flesh tight so that her nipples bulged into his hungry mouth.

He held her by the waist, keeping her in place over his lap, her thighs wide, opening her sex to the slight breeze that passed through the room. She was breathing faster and faster, the fire burning uncontrollably as he teased her breasts. She wanted him, she wanted him desperately yet he made no move to touch her sex. She murmured wordlessly, driven beyond endurance by the way he toyed with her nipples.

'Please, Tom…' she whispered, trying to pull away from

his mouth, trying to escape the attentions on her breasts so he could begin to explore her elsewhere. She was so wet, she could feel her pussy lips opening, blossoming with pleasure, dappled with her slick juices and desperate for his touch.

He slapped her hard on the back of the thigh, an unexpected burst of pain that momentarily confused her. She glanced down to see the redness imprinted on her pale creamy skin, the mark of his displeasure expressed vividly on her skin. It had hurt, yet she felt nothing but renewed pleasure.

His hands strayed down, at last, moving down her back and over the curve of her bottom, which was still stretched across his lap. His hands massaged her backside, his fingers pressing against her skin, surveying every inch of her curves. He sat back a little and she looked down at her breasts, still offered up to him. Her nipples were red and glistening, tiny bite marks edged here and there, and when she stroked her fingers over them she shuddered with pleasure.

He began to massage the inside of her thighs, his hands exploring her, tracking the naked expanse of flesh, moving back and forth, unhurried and possessive and making her restless once more. Her desire was at a peak, she needed him inside her.

'Please…' she urged him, unable to control herself. She'd never been turned on so much, her desire was immediate, urgent, physical, and yet he would not be hurried.

At last his fingers stroked against her pussy. She gasped. The fleeting touch made her stomach somersault and her body stiffen. Her breath was coming in gasps and she knew that she was teetering ever closer to orgasm. She leaned forward and kissed him hotly on the mouth, lifting her bottom slightly so he could stroke her pussy from behind. His tongue explored her mouth just as his fingers began to explore her sex. Her clitoris was hard, wet and aching for his caress.

'Like this?' he teased, sliding his fingers along the wet groove of her body. She moved with him, sliding herself back and forth across his hand, mewing softly like an animal each time her pleasure bud brushed against his fingers. They kissed hard and then he was sucking her breasts again, his lips clamped tight over a nipple while his tongue lashed it back and forth with the same maddening rhythm that he used on her pussy.

She was lost to everything but pleasure. She could think of nothing but the reality of his fingers in her pussy and his mouth on her breast. The tension in her thighs and in the pit of her belly was tight, a coil waiting to unleash as he drove her closer and closer to pure blind release. He moved his other hand round and she moved with him, lifting herself unexpectedly so he could press a finger between her bottom cheeks. He wet it with the slick honey from her sex and then pushed it against the tight rear hole. She gasped once as he penetrated her behind, and then she fell against his shoulder and cried out as the orgasm took her with a force so strong she could do nothing about the scream that tore from her throat.

'I haven't finished with you yet,' Tom whispered a few moments later. Her breath was still ragged and she still felt weak. He eased her back up to a sitting position and smiled. She looked into his eyes for a second and then looked away, suddenly embarrassed at the way she had screamed her pleasure. She had been powerless, there had been no way she could control herself, no way she could resist the pleasure he had given her.

'On the floor,' he told her, moving her off his lap. She obeyed without question, a little dazed by it all. He had her sit on the carpet, there down between his thighs. Her eyes fixed on the impression of his hard cock bulging in his trousers. She had been desperate for it, and yet he hadn't even allowed her to touch him. Now, as she watched with renewed excitement, he unbuttoned himself to reveal his thick hard flesh.

'Isn't this what you need?' he asked, a slight, taunting edge to his voice.

She nodded, transfixed by the sight of his hardness, the rigid flesh tipped with a purple dome that made her belly flip once more. He held himself, his fingers lost in the mass of hair at the base.

'Here,' he whispered, urging her forward.

'Can't I…'

He shook his head. 'I want your mouth,' he told her, and there was no disputing his desire. She crawled forward, her eyes fixed on the spearing flesh. She kissed it tentatively, half afraid he would deny her even that pleasure. Her breasts swayed slightly, her nipples still erect and sensitive as she moved. She kissed harder, and then opened her lips to his erect cock. She closed her eyes as she suckled on him, delighting in the feel of his hardness deep in her mouth. He held her head in place, wrapping his hand in her long wet hair, and then thrusting rhythmically deeper and deeper. He was so hard, so forceful, the deep masculine scent of him adding to her pleasure.

He moved her back so she was on all fours while he fucked her hard in the mouth. There was something wonderfully flagrant, almost animal about the way he used her. She sucked harder, wanting to give him the pleasure he had given to her. He fucked her powerfully, pushing his prick deep into the back of her throat so that her face brushed against his abdomen. Somehow his cock seemed to grow bigger, harder, an iron rod that pushed deeper into the soft envelope of her mouth. At last he gasped and clamped her head into place, forcing every inch of his manhood into her mouth as he jetted thick waves of jism down her throat. She struggled for a second, choking on the deluge of his come, and then he released her.

She sat back, a trail of his seed leaking from the corner

of her mouth. She had swallowed most it, welcoming the warm, sticky fluid as it slid down her throat.

'All of it,' he told her, reaching out to touch the smear on her chin. He scooped it up on his finger and then offered it to her. She looked up at him and saw he was waiting. Her face was already red with shame, but she did not disappoint him. She lapped up the spunk from his fingers, and then moved forward to suck up the last droplets leaking from his subsiding cock.

He waited for her to finish before speaking. 'You'd better get dressed,' he told her softly. The commanding edge had gone from his voice, and now he sounded concerned for her. Her emotions were haywire; she felt too many things and all of them at once. What had she done?

He stood up and walked to the bathroom to fix himself up. She wrapped her robe around herself again, covering herself up as though denying that anything indecent had happened.

'Listen,' he said, when he returned a few minutes later, 'I'd better be going.'

She nodded numbly. What else could he do?

'Don't worry,' he told her at the door, 'Sarah doesn't need to know about this.'

Tears welled up in her eyes. What had she done? The pleasure had been more intense than anything she'd ever experienced. But now? Now that it had finished? She watched Tom go, and felt the weight of the world descend upon her shoulders.

Patti spent the next few days trying to avoid Sarah, and each time they came into contact she was certain that the other woman would somehow divine the truth. Sarah was almost ten years older and seemed much more a woman of the world. It felt as though she had seen and done everything, and that she would take one look at Patti's guilt-ridden expression and leap to the truth. However, as the days dragged on and Sarah said nothing the fear lessened considerably, though the idea of being discovered still made Patti's heart jump like crazy.

The phone call from Tom came almost ten days later, while Patti was at work. She was surprised that he had her number, and for a split second she was convinced he had called to say that Sarah was onto them. In fact he seemed quite calm and was calling merely to check that she felt all right. The sound of his voice, and his evident concern, touched something in her. By the end of the conversation her mind was full of the images of what they had done together. It excited her still to think about it. She imagined the feel of his fingers in the wet heat of her pussy, the sensation of his mouth and lips on the hard nodes of her breasts, and the hardness of his cock as it pushed into her mouth.

When he called again the next day and suggested meeting for lunch she agreed without hesitation. His charm and her imagination conspired against her natural caution, and though she felt nervous about it, they were nothing compared to the tremors of fear she had experienced in the first few days.

She was late arriving at the little restaurant he'd chosen, but if he was annoyed he showed no sign of it. He rose from the table as she arrived and kissed her lightly on the cheek. 'Patti,' he said, 'I'm glad you could make it.'

She smiled nervously and sat down at the secluded table in the corner. The kiss on the cheek, although a friendly gesture, seemed to mean more. 'God, I'm not used to this,' she explained after the waiter had gone.

'If it's any consolation,' he replied, 'neither am I.'

The conversation stopped and started fitfully during the meal, but on more than one occasion she looked up to find him looking at her intently, his deep blue eyes fixed on her. She could see the desire in those eyes, and despite her best intentions she could not help but respond to it.

'What time do you have to be back?' he asked her over coffee.

She glanced at her watch, suddenly realising that she'd lost all track of time. 'I'm late already,' she said.

He smiled. 'Don't worry,' he told her calmly, a sly smile forming on the lips that had greedily bruised her nipples.

She could feel herself flushing red, her face burning as she recognised the undertone to his voice. 'How can I not worry?'

'Just leave it to me,' he assured her, waving over the waiter to ask for the bill.

'By my boss's going to hit the roof if I'm any later than this.'

Tom's smile broadened. 'Let me handle your boss,' he stated calmly.

'But…'

'No buts,' he insisted. 'Come on, you've got the rest of the afternoon off.'

Patti shook her head. 'No,' she said, determined to resist whatever it was that Tom had planned.

He looked at her again, his eyes drilling into her, forcing her to look away. 'It would be better if you let me do this,' he said, his voice low, a sharp, commanding edge to it. Patti knew he wasn't about to brook any arguments.

'Do what?' she whispered.

'Come back to my place,' he stated. There was no question there, rather it was a foregone conclusion that Patti could not avoid. Her heart was already beating hard and the tone of his voice seemed to connect to something deep inside her.

She tried to say 'okay' but could only mouth the word in silence. Her hands were trembling as they left the restaurant and walked back to Tom's big black car. She glanced about nervously as she slid into the passenger seat, afraid that she'd be seen by someone from work, or else by Sarah or one of Sarah's friends. Tom showed no qualms as he accelerated away from the kerb, his commanding hands on the wheel, an intense silence about him.

They arrived at Tom's flat a few minutes later. It put the place she and Sarah shared completely in the shade. The place reeked of money and power. As soon as she was inside and the door was closed she knew that she would do whatever she was asked. She was in his domain now, in his territory, and there was nothing she could do to resist him. The idea made her head swim with fear and excitement in equal measure.

The lounge was a spacious, airy room, with big square windows that let in lots of natural light that bathed the room in a soft, summery glow. A big leather sofa sat under the windows, a dark, brooding presence rather than a piece of functional furniture. He threw his jacket onto a chair near the door and then settled down into the dark embrace of the sofa.

'What's your boss's name?' he asked, picking up the phone that nestled on a small table to the left of the sofa.

'What are you going to do?' Patti asked, standing nervously in the doorway of the room, hardly daring to enter.

He looked at her for a moment before answering. 'I'm going to make sure you spend the rest of the afternoon here with me,' he told her bluntly. 'Now, what's his name?'

'Her name's Amanda Jeffries,' Patti reported quietly.

Tom dialled immediately and asked to be put through to her. Patti listened silently while Tom spun Amanda a convincing pack of lies. His tone was sombre, but still there was something charming about him. By the end of the call it sounded as though he had convinced Amanda that Patti had witnessed a serious traffic accident during lunchtime and that she had helped one of the victims to hospital and was required to give a full statement to the police.

'I'll never be able to keep all those lies up,' Patti told him when he had finished.

Tom smiled. 'You will,' he said, 'because you have to. Now, why don't you come into the room? Are you afraid of me?'

Patti considered her reply and then nodded. That made him smile.

'It's not me you're afraid of, is it?' he told her.

She hesitated for a moment, and then walked fully into the room. He was right, of course, but that made it no easier to handle the situation. 'Aren't you afraid of Sarah finding out?' she asked, stopping directly in front of him. She looked down at him, all relaxed and in control of the situation, his dark grey suit contrasting with the blackness of the sofa.

He took her by the hand and pulled her down into the space beside him. 'What the eye doesn't see the heart doesn't grieve,' he whispered. He looked into her eyes and she saw the intensity of his desire, a desire that was powerful and frightening and irresistible.

'That's such a simple answer,' she said, lowering her gaze. Her heart was pounding and she could feel her skin flushing. His desire was hard, physical, commanding. And despite herself she was responding; his desire reached out to something inside her.

He took her chin in his hand and lifted her face, bringing her lips closer to his. He kissed her immediately, pressing his mouth against hers, his tongue pushing her lips apart, stifling the protest she felt she ought to make. And as he kissed her, long, slow and sensuous, his other hand slipped under her short skirt to stroke her stocking-clad thigh.

When he released her she remained close to him, her body pressed against his, yielding to him wordlessly. The hand sliding up and down her thigh was insistent and possessive, the fingers gliding from silk to skin and back again. He kissed her again on the mouth, and then down across her throat while his hand slipped between her thighs. She sighed softly, parting her thighs slightly so his fingers trailed across the warmth of her panties, pushed hard into her sex.

She shifted round, reaching out to put her arms around him, but he pushed her arms back with his free hand. She was not to touch him, not to hold him, and somehow that made her feel even more excited.

'Can we go to the bedroom?' she whispered.

'No, I want you here,' he replied. He put his hands on her waist and moved her off the sofa to the floor. She knelt down in front of him, unable to hide the disappointment she felt.

He bent down and kissed her again and then pulled away slowly, forcing her to reach up to him, to sit up on hands and knees to kiss him. He stroked her face as they kissed, his fingers exploring every inch of it, as though to see her was not enough and he needed to feel her too. She began to unbutton her blouse, knowing it was what he wanted, but he slapped her hands hard.

'I'll tell you when,' he whispered sternly.

Again she felt a mingling of disappointment and desire. It seemed she was to have no say in what they did. She was there to please him, to accede to his demands. The idea repelled and excited her. She was already wet, her panties were moist and she could feel the heat of desire flaming inside her. This time she wanted his cock, she wanted it hard inside her, deep in her pussy and not just in her mouth.

He unclasped her skirt and tugged it down over the taut curves of her bottom. She wriggled out of it and then pushed it away, glad to be free of it. She glanced down at herself and saw the dark band of her stockings contrasting strongly with the pale white of her thighs, and the high cut of her silky black knickers revealing much of her bottom. It turned her on to see herself and the pleasure was redoubled when he began to unbutton her blouse, exposing the lacy bra which pushed her breasts up and which bulged delightfully at the nipples.

He put a hand on her back, and with the other he explored her body, stroking her thighs, moving across the flawless expanse of her back, tracing the inside of her thighs and gently squeezing her breasts. Each caress was heaven. Never had she felt so desirable and desired. She kissed his fingers as they touched her mouth, lapping quickly and then sucking them into her mouth.

'You're so perfect,' he said quietly, and she shivered with delight.

He took her head in his hands and guided her between his thighs. She quickly unzipped him and took his hardness in her hands. The glans was already wet, weeping a silver tear of fluid that she took into her mouth immediately. She suckled him gratefully, taking his length and sliding her tongue over it. She closed her eyes and pictured herself on hands and knees, clad only in her underwear and deliriously mouthing his hard cock.

He unclasped her bra and let it fall to the floor. His fingers sought her hard nipples and the pleasure she felt was electric. He teased her flesh, exciting the hard points so they stood out, sensitive tissues that tingled under his touch. He tugged at her hair and she pulled away from his cock, looking up into his dark blue eyes pleadingly. He kissed her hard and she opened her mouth to him.

She sat up on her knees and he took her by the waist. She cupped her breasts and he sucked on each in turn, making her sigh desperately as the pleasure grew more and more intense. His hands strayed from her waist to her backside, moving in parallel to stroke her bottom cheeks. She wanted to pull her panties down, to expose her backside to him, to let him see and feel her sex which pulsed with desire, but she couldn't bring herself to take her breasts from his mouth.

He stopped suddenly. She sat back on her knees and watched him undress. His body was toned, muscled, masculine, the body of a man who kept in shape. Her eyes feasted on his body as his had done on hers. No wonder Sarah desired him so much, she thought, a twinge of guilt surfacing suddenly.

He took her by the hand and pulled her to her feet, embracing her immediately, pressing the silky hardness of his cock against her tummy. They kissed quickly and then he led her to the bedroom. She hardly had time to take in the spacious room, as airy and filled with light as the other. He sat her down on the edge of the large bed and pushed his hardness to her mouth. She kissed the bulb of his cock gently, then opened her lips to it once more, happy to close her mouth around him, to feel him slide his erect flesh into the tight warmth she created for him. He held her face and fucked her with long, slow strokes that made him gasp softly.

They lay back on the bed and he began to kiss her breasts once more, biting harder this time, exciting her so that she moaned softly and clutched him tightly. He slid one hand down her back and under her panties, stroking her gently so that her wetness ran freely from between her pussy lips. He teased his fingers into her sex and the sensations of having her nipples sucked and her pussy touched became indistinguishable; a single continuum of pleasure that she murmured wordlessly. Her panties were pulled down slowly, eased from her bottom, which he explored with wet fingers. She gasped when he stroked her rear hole, his wet fingers lingering for a moment before he bit hard on a nipple and made her cry out.

He flipped her over on her tummy unexpectedly and she lifted her backside instinctively, offering him her sex from behind. He stroked her back with both hands, moving them down in parallel to her waist and then to her bottom cheeks. He parted her behind gently, opening her to gaze longingly at her pussy lips and the dark jewel of her anus. His fingers sought her wetness again and she responded by arching her back, lifting her bottom still higher, opening herself wantonly to his desire. He kissed her there, his hot breath felt on the membranes of her sex, his tongue delving into the pool of her juices. He licked her slowly, taking up her wetness on his tongue, and then moving a fraction higher to spread her juices around the tightness of her rear opening.

The sensation of having her bottom tongued was pure pleasure, one that had her panting softly. She wanted him now. She was so close to orgasm and she needed to feel his hardness inside her. She needed to feel her pussy tighten around his hard, male flesh as she bucked and writhed at the peak of her pleasure.

'Do you want me now?' he whispered hotly, kneeling over her, his hands holding her bottom cheeks apart.

'Yes… Yes, fuck me now…' she sighed.

She felt him take his hard cock in his hand and push it down between her thighs. She closed her eyes as he stroked his hardness between her pussy lips, teasing the moisture of her arousal onto his flesh. She pushed back impatiently, wanting to feel him enter her.

The scream of pain tore from her lips. She bucked uncontrollably and tried to get away from his cock as it entered her rear hole. It felt like fire, as though she were being burned. He held her down and pushed his cock into her behind, sliding it in slowly, taking pleasure in penetrating her even as she screamed. And then, when he was pressed down on her with his penis deep between her bottom cheeks, she stilled.

He reached under her and found her pussy, still wet, still aching with want. He kissed her gently on the shoulder, his lips trailing back and forth as he fingered her sex. The pleasure was still there, and despite the unexpected pain and the shock, she began to move. He bit her on the neck as he began to move inside her, fucking her anally as his fingers fucked her pussy. There was pleasure there too, although it felt strange to have his cock in her bottom; she had never been fucked like it before. Soon they were moving together, entwined as he thrust in and out of her, his fingers and hers playing with her pussy bud. He released her and held her by the waist, fucking her hard as she frigged herself closer and closer to orgasm. At last she cried out and her body shook as the wave broke. A moment later she felt him thrust deep into her backside, and then she felt her anus clench tightly around his throbbing cock as he spurted his come into her.

'Will we do this again?' she asked later, when she had showered and dressed again.

'Do you want to?' he asked casually, pouring her a drink.

Her body tingled all over, from the tips of her nipples bruised by his mouth, to her pussy to her backside. He had taken her from behind, violating her anally, brutally almost, and yet the memory of it made her feel nothing but excitement. 'Yes, I want to,' she admitted quietly.

'What if I want to fuck you like that again?'

She lowered her eyes guiltily. 'If that's how you want me…'

He smiled and passed her a drink. 'That's how I want you,' he told her. 'I want to take you in every way I can.'

'What about Sarah?'

He shrugged. 'She'll not find out,' he assured her.

She nodded, accepting his word. She alternately felt guilty and excited. The two sides of her character were in conflict and yet the sense of excitement, the pure animal desire inside her, was growing stronger all the time.

'Have you dressed as I told you?' Tom asked as Patti slid into the passenger seat beside him.

She half smiled and nodded. His instructions were becoming increasingly precise, and yet it excited her to comply. He twisted round in his seat and looked at her. 'Show me,' he suggested calmly.

'Tom! Not here,' she said, shocked at the idea. The car was at the kerbside in a street full of people.

'Show me,' he insisted.

She glanced round at the busy street, and realised he wasn't joking. People were rushing by, some of them only inches from the car, and any one of them could see into it.

'I can't,' she said softly. Her heart was beating fast and she could feel the first flush of red touching her cheeks.

He reached across and lifted her short skirt. Her face coloured instantly and she hardly dared to look down at herself. She was wearing black high heels, black stay-up stockings, and nothing else under the short grey skirt. It had been bad enough waiting in the breezy street, half afraid that a sudden gust would lift the skirt and reveal her nakedness to everyone. Now he held her skirt up and gazed at the triangle of hair around her pussy, and at the join of dark stockings and pale flesh.

'Good,' he said simply, seemingly satisfied with what he saw. 'And up top?' he added, releasing her skirt.

She smoothed down her skirt quickly and pulled open her jacket. Underneath she was wearing a simple white blouse and nothing else. Her breasts were almost visible through the translucent material; her nipples, already hard, were impressed on the tight fitting garment. She was almost naked, there for him to use and display as he liked. The thought made her feel aroused, making her nipples harden and her sex moist.

He smiled and then started the car. 'Are you wet?' he asked, steering it into the long slow line of traffic.

'Yes,' she admitted softly.

'I like that,' he said, 'you know how much it turns me on to know that you're wet.'

'I've been wet all day,' she said.

The traffic lights ahead turned red, and as soon as Tom stopped the car he lifted her skirt again. Her discomfort was obvious, and it seemed to do nothing but spur him on. He stroked her pussy, touching a finger to her wetness and then trailing it across her thigh. She stared straight ahead, afraid that others would see what was going on, and yet she felt unable to resist. All morning she had dreamed of him, all morning she had been fantasising about what they would do together.

As soon as they drew up outside his flat she was out of the car. He came round and took her by the waist and pulled her closer to kiss her forcefully on the mouth. His hands slipped under her skirt and he held her there, out in the street, her naked backside almost on display.

'Does that excite you?' he asked hotly.

She could not say the word 'yes', so she nodded. He laughed and took her by the hand to lead her into the lobby. They rode up in the lift in silence, she standing with her legs apart while he eased his fingers between her pussy lips. The doors opened and she looked up suddenly, her heart racing with fear, but there was no one there.

Once inside his flat they kissed again. She opened her lips to him, let him take her there with his tongue the way he did with his cock. His hands explored her freely, caressing her behind, her thighs, her breasts and her pussy. Each touch of his fingers was pleasure that added to her arousal. He opened her blouse easily and took possession of her breasts, closing his fingers tightly over them so that her nipples were pushed out. He licked them in turn, wetting them in preparation, and then he whispered that she should go to the bedroom.

She removed her jacket and top but kept her skirt and her stockings on. She sat on the bed and waited, a knot of nervous fear in her tummy. Each time they met it was in secret, and each time he pushed her further, making her act ever more outrageously, ever more wantonly. He once asked if there were any limits, and though she was afraid of it, her answer had been a simple, solemn 'no'.

He joined her a moment later, already naked, his thick cock jutting forward obscenely. She knelt down on the floor and looked up at him pleadingly, her eyes wide with desire, her lips parted in anticipation. He stroked her face gently, almost tenderly, and then took her by the arm and lifted her to her feet.

'Not now,' he said softly, kissing her on the mouth and throat. He held her close, his hands travelling up and down her smooth back.

They stood by the side of the bed and kissed again before he took her by the hand and led her towards the window. She tried to cover her breasts but he lowered her hands. 'I want the world to see you,' he told her, kissing her once more before turning her to face the window.

She closed her eyes and tried to turn away, but he took her face in his hands and forced her to look. They were within view of half a dozen buildings, flats and offices, some of them so close she could make out people sitting down at work or moving around their homes. And, she knew, just as she could see them they would be able to see her at the window, naked from the waist up. He kissed her from behind and then gently pushed her against the glass, pressing her face against it, and then her chest. Her nipples puckered at the contact with the cold glass, making them even more visible.

He reached down under her skirt and began to stroke her pussy, his fingers sliding up and down the wet groove, grazing maddeningly against her clit with each circuit. She sighed and opened her mouth to gasp as he bit her shoulder. He kissed and bit her there, his desire violently voracious as he finger-fucked her pussy. She moaned and cried out, all the time pressed flat against the glass, on display as she was violated. He lifted her skirt at the front and pressed her tummy against the glass so that her sex was also visible.

'Look,' he said, lifting her chin so she could follow his direction.

Patti looked across and saw the unknown couple staring at her from one of the windows in the block opposite. They stared at her as though she were some strange, inhuman creature writing at the window. She closed her eyes and trembled violently as she orgasmed suddenly, her pleasure screamed under glass.

At last Tom allowed her to step away from the window. She turned and collapsed into his arms. He kissed her tenderly and helped her to the bed, where she lay on her back, breathless. It took a moment before she realised she was alone. She sat up on one elbow and saw that the bedroom door was slightly ajar.

'Was I good?' she asked, when Tom returned a moment later.

'Very good,' he said quietly.

'Yes, very good,' Sarah added, striding into the room.

Patti jumped up, the shock so sudden it took her breath away. She reached for her top but it had been taken away. She curled up at the top of the bed, covering her breasts, her face white with shock.

Sarah glared at her angrily. 'So,' she said, an air of menace about her, 'this is how you repay my friendship.'

Patti could not bear to meet Sarah's cold, accusing eyes. She looked beyond her to Tom, but he said nothing and his blue eyes gave nothing away.

'Well?' Sarah demanded, 'haven't you anything to say for yourself?'

'I... I'm sorry,' Patti whispered weakly.

'Oh, you will be,' Sarah warned coldly. 'How long has this been going on?'

Patti shook her head, trying to dispel the image, hoping it wasn't true, that it wasn't really happening.

'Answer me!'

'Not long,' Patti replied hurriedly.

'You lying bitch,' Sarah cried angrily. 'And to think that I trusted you...'

'It's not my fault...'

Sarah snorted derisively. 'Do you really think I'm that stupid? Don't you know I can see what a slut you are?

31

You've done everything you could to get Tom, haven't you? Come on, tell me you haven't been parading the streets with nothing on this morning. Tell me you haven't been acting the slut for him!'

'It's not like that…' Patti sobbed, unable to hold back the tears that poured from her eyes. It wasn't like that at all…

'It's too late for that,' Tom said, his voice as cold and hostile as Sarah's.

'But Tom…'

He marched across to her and grabbed her by the arm. 'Sarah knows everything,' he hissed.

Patti looked at Sarah and sobbed again. Things had gone so badly wrong… She had never started out with the intention of hurting her best friend, but somehow things had developed too far and too quickly.

'Punish her!' Sarah snapped angrily.

Tom showed no hesitation. He sat on the edge of the bed and pulled Patti across his lap. His strong arms moved her into place, and then he pulled her skirt up over her waist to expose her backside.

'This is what you deserve,' Sarah told her, standing closer, her shiny black heels cracking down hard on the floor.

'Please… please…' Patti begged.

Tom lifted his hand high and brought it down in a wide arc that ended with a crack of sound that filled the room. Patti screamed at the impact of his hand against her bottom. The searing red pain burned through her and she bucked up, but that only lifted her bottom higher for the second stroke which hissed down through the air. She squealed and struggled but he beat her hard, his hand coming down alternately on each bottom cheek, spreading the red flush of heat and pain across the taut curves of her behind.

Sarah knelt down in front of them and took hold of Patti's shoulders, holding her down while Tom continued to spank

32

with harder and harder strokes. Tears poured from Patti's eyes, but there was no let up. The rain of hard smacks came down all over her punished buttocks and the top of her thighs.

At last the spanking ceased and Patti lay across Tom's lap, her bottom raised high, patterned red and smarting terribly. And yet there was something else there. She could feel Tom's hard cock pressing into her hip, and his excitement was echoed inside her. The searing heat of punishment touched her pussy, the tingling pain subsiding into a wet heat of desire.

Sarah reached out and stroked her hand from Patti's shoulder down to the punished flesh. Her fingers travelled up and down slowly, moving from the reddest parts of Patti's bottom and then down towards her sex.

'She's wet,' Sarah reported softly, a note of surprise in her voice as her fingers slipped into Patti's sex.

Patti closed her eyes and sighed. It was true, embarrassingly so. She felt aroused, excited and unable to deny the evidence that oozed from her pussy lips. Involuntarily she lifted her bottom higher, opening herself to Sarah's probing fingers.

'Does that feel good?' Sarah asked softly, pressing her wet fingers up against Patti's hard clit.

Patti nodded. She had no words to speak with, the power of speech had gone and all she knew and understood was the power of her arousal. She looked round and Sarah's mouth was there, ready. They kissed once, softly, tentatively, and then again, stronger, hungrier. Sarah's tongue pushed into Patti's mouth just as her fingers pushed into Patti's sex.

Tom parted Patti's bottom cheeks with his hands and eased his fingers into the wetness too. He joined with Sarah to touch and stroke, tease and toy, and then he used his wet fingers to press against Patti's rear hole. She responded immediately, moaning her encouragement as his fingers entered her from behind. She closed her eyes and felt herself to be nothing but pleasure.

She was carefully eased to the floor, on all fours. Tom's fingers were insistent, slipping in and out of the tight rear opening, fucking her there while Sarah's fingers did the same between Patti's pussy lips. Sarah's kisses, exciting and passionate, moved from Patti's mouth to her breasts.

Sarah lay back on the floor and pulled her skirt away, revealing black panties pulled tightly between her pussy lips. She pulled them to one side, roughly exposing her sex which glistened with juices. She touched herself, wetting her fingers, which she pressed to Patti's mouth. Patti licked them clean, eager to taste her friend's pleasure. She understood what it was she needed to do. She knelt lower, lifting her bottom higher so that Tom could wet her anus with her own juices, and then she touched her lips to Sarah's pussy.

Tom's cock pressed against the ring of muscle between her bottom cheeks. She tensed momentarily, but then relaxed as he moved his erection into her. She closed her eyes to enjoy the feel of him entering her, pushing deep into the forbidden opening of her body. His body pressed against her backside and he was within her, his cock buried deep and her anus tight against the thick base of his hardness. She opened her eyes to gaze adoringly at Sarah's pussy, excited by the thought of what she was to do. She licked at it gently, knowing that she was to give her friend the pleasure she had stolen from Tom.

The taste of pussy filled her mouth, and it made her head swim with delight. She licked and sucked, exploring the folds of Sarah's sex, seeking out the wetness from within and rewarded with the sighs of pleasure that Sarah moaned. At the same time Tom was fucking her hard in the backside, his erection thick and strong and filling her completely.

They moved in unison, three bodies united in pleasure, Sarah moaning softly and playing with her own nipples while Patti fucked her with her mouth, and Tom holding Patti by the waist while he thrust his hardness in and out of Patti's tight anal hole. Sarah cried her orgasm first, shuddering as she climaxed into Patti's mouth. A moment later Tom climaxed, pumping his jism into Patti's backside as he clawed at her reddened, punished bottom. Finally Patti screamed her pleasure, her body an electric glow of ecstasy that seemed to radiate through the room.

Later, as Patti lay naked on the bed drifting in and out of sleep, she heard voices. The door to the bedroom was still ajar. She sat up weakly, her body still tingling with the afterglow of her orgasms, and listened.

'You see,' Sarah was saying, 'I was right, wasn't I?'

Tom's reply was indistinct.

'From the moment I first set eyes on her,' Sarah continued, 'I knew she'd be the one.'

Patti lay back, confused. The conversation continued but none of it made any sense. But it did not matter, she decided, because now she knew that Sarah and Tom would always be there.

Family Fortune

The window was open and the slight breeze parted the net curtains, letting the unfiltered light flood through the room. Stephie stood at the window, biting back the tears, her mood in stark contrast to the pureness of the summer day. Outside the sunlight sparkled on the silver blue of the pool, beams of light reflected back from the unbroken surface, dancing with the light ripples from the breeze. Beyond the pool were the grounds, beautifully arranged gardens, fountains, gravel paths through the shrubbery and then, right at the end, the heavy border of trees that marked the high walls that enclosed the estate.

In every way it was the ideal country mansion, at it's very best in the still afternoon light of a perfect summer's day. So fine, and yet at it's heart something rotten. Stephie turned away, dazzled by the light that flashed so vividly from the pool. She turned and found that her stepsister, Ariana, was standing in the doorway, watching her closely.

'Don't look so unhappy,' Ariana said softly, her own voice tinged with unhappiness. She wore a very simple white cotton dress, and in the sharp light it was clear that she was naked underneath; her nipples were dark disks against the thin cotton and the join of her thighs marked by a dark crease.

'Why shouldn't I look unhappy?' Stephie demanded, her voice quivering with hurt. Her dark eyes flashed angrily, and then she felt the tears well up, ready to cascade down her pretty face.

'Is it so bad?' Ariana asked, taking a step into the room. 'Is Timothy so repulsive?'

Stephie looked at her sister uncomprehendingly, as

though seeing for the first time a new side of her character revealed, a side that was dark and nasty. 'He's your husband,' Stephie cried, 'don't you think it wrong that he wants to make love to me? Do you really see nothing wrong in that?'

Ariana turned away for a moment. 'Don't make it sound so awful,' she whispered. 'He's an excellent lover, you'll enjoy it, you both will.'

Stephie ran across the room and threw herself on the bed, sobbing her heart out. She had never wanted Ariana to marry Timothy, no matter how long his family tree or no matter how big his fortune. There was something corrupting about him, as though he were consciously trying to live up to the image of a decadent aristocrat. His latest idea, bedding wife and sister at the same time, was one of a long line of such escapades.

There had been the time when Stephie and Ariana had walked in on him and the gardener, a tall muscular Spaniard. Timothy had merely smiled and invited them to join in, though as his prick was deep between the Spaniard's backside it wasn't exactly clear what he had wanted them to do. Stephie and Ariana had backed away, red-faced and embarrassed, but later that evening Timothy had regaled them with the story of his seduction of the Spaniard. Stephie could still see the smile on his face as he explained that the Spaniard could suck cock better than any woman could, though he added that he had no objection to Stephie trying to better him.

It would not have been so bad if he was more discreet, but he seemed to get an extra kick out of flaunting his sexuality as much as possible. At one family party he had managed to bed one of his own cousins, a shy young Lady who fell for his charming manner and classical good looks. He had made love to her in the master bedroom, with the window open to the balcony, so that the sighs and moans of her orgasm had floated across the lawn like an early morning mist. Poor Ariana had to pretend that nothing had happened, and the pitying looks she got from her family and friends were like an elixir for him.

'Please don't cry,' Ariana whispered helplessly, putting her hand out to Stephie. She leaned over and kissed Stephie's shoulder, her lips cool and soft against her skin.

'Go away, leave me alone...' Stephie cried, burying her head in the pillow, wanting to blank out everything. She felt horror, disgust, shame, and most of all pity. She felt so sorry for Ariana, and yet there seemed to be nothing she could do. Ariana left the room, her face a picture of defeat.

Stephie's tears carried her to a dark dreamless sleep, through the humidity of the afternoon and into the coolness of the evening that settled slowly over the great house. When she awoke, hours later, it was as if the ugliness that had spoiled the perfection of the summer's day had not happened. The house was still, at rest after basking in the heat, the silence heavy and melancholic.

Stephie rose and bathed quickly, the coolness of the shower refreshing her spirit somewhat. She tried not to think of Timothy and Ariana. Instead she wandered through the house alone, enjoying the building that had yet to be served up to the public. She loved the house, it was the only thing that tempted her to return time and gain to visit her sister and her errant husband. She walked the corridors like a thief, lost in silent admiration of the treasures it contained. So many rooms to explore, so many surprises to discover. Timothy's family had made their money in the New World, alert to the possibilities of trade, while most of the other great families of the age had slumbered through the seventeenth century. It alone explained the fact that the family had been able to keep the house private, and to prosper when others had been forced to seek alliance with the rising class of merchants and bankers.

'You wouldn't have liked great uncle,' Timothy commented, startling Stephie, who had been gazing at one of the immense family portraits that glared down from the wall of one of the many chambers in that wing of the house.

'Wouldn't I?' she asked sullenly, looking at him sharply.

'No, he didn't like wilful girls like you. He'd have had you strapped by one of his slaves before having you for himself,' he smiled, the idea obviously appealing to him too. 'And if you were still stubborn he would have handed you over to the slave to give you a smidgen of the New World experience.'

'That isn't even funny,' Stephie said. She turned and walked across the chamber, certain that he would follow.

'I don't think it was meant to be funny, Stephanie darling. He was a humourless old bastard really, no sense of fun at all. It's said that once one of the tenants on the estate had complained that the master had taken the virginity of his, the servant's, daughter. In actual fact the master had taken the man's daughter, mother and grandmother, and no doubt he would have taken his daughter's daughter in turn if he'd lived long enough.'

'Is that why you want to have sex with me and my sister?'

Timothy laughed. 'I see, you think I'm trying to emulate the old bugger. Well, that's an idea, isn't it? Only thing is that the old boy didn't bother to marry the tenant's daughter to have her. They did things with greater style in the old days.'

'I suppose you think that's funny,' Stephie sniffed, leading the way down the central staircase to the main dining hall.

'Yes, I do actually,' he smiled. 'Now, have you and darling Ari worked anything out yet?'

'No, not at all,' Stephie replied bluntly.

'How tedious this all is,' he mumbled under his breath, loud enough for Stephie to hear, although she made no comment.

The dining hall was an oak panelled delight that would have pulled in the American tourists by the coach load; high ceiling, intricate workmanship, coats of arms wherever you looked. It was the perfect setting for a medieval banquet, which is what it had been once, and Stephie had heard that it was on Timothy's wish list too. He was a man that took his desire seriously, he liked to expound on the things he wanted to do, almost as much as he expounded on the things he had already done. Sometimes he'd pause in the middle of an episode to glance at Stephie, who always listened to his adulterous goings on in stony silence. Ariana on the other hand had long since accustomed herself. She even enjoyed adding the odd detail to the story, just so everyone knew she wasn't the martyred wife, but a willing participant in all his sexual adventures. It was an act, and everyone knew it was an act, except Ariana herself.

Dinner passed off peacefully, conversation was light and inconsequential, and at the close of the meal Ariana was glowing, her face lit up by the simple happiness of it all. Timothy had been a charming host, Stephie a grateful guest, and Ariana herself so happy to have the two people she loved the most acting with pleasant civility to each other. She could ask for nothing more.

Stephie was reading a book, her window was open to the welcome breeze of the night, and when she heard a gentle knock on the door she froze. For a second she feared it was Timothy, but then Ariana's reassuring voice whispered from behind the door.

'I just wanted to talk,' Ariana said apologetically.

'Where's Timothy?' Stephie asked suspiciously.

'Preparing for a trip down to the City,' Ariana assured her, walking across the room to sit on the very edge of the bed. She was still wearing the same simple white dress that she had earlier. Cool and loose, it did nothing to conceal the gentle curves of her body, from the fullness of her breasts to the swell of her backside.

'What do you want to talk about?'

'Why can't you and Timothy always be like you were

tonight? Why can't you just be friends?'

Stephie sighed. 'Because he wants to be more than friends. Come on Ariana, you were there when he asked, no he demanded, I suck his cock. Didn't that mean anything to you?'

'But there's nothing wrong with it,' Ariana insisted. 'Why have you turned into such a prude all of a sudden? You never used to be like this... Have you really forgotten what we used to do?'

'No, I haven't forgotten,' Stephie said softly, lowering her eyes. 'But that was different, that was...' she searched for the word but couldn't find it. 'That was different,' she repeated firmly.

'That was worse,' Ariana smiled. She leaned across the bed and took the book from Stephie's hands. The sister's looked at each other for a second, melting into each other's eyes. Stephie made the first move, moving forward, parting her lips for the kiss that she longed for. They kissed long and hard, mouths duelling, breath shared, tongues exploring. They parted and looked at each other again, faces flushed red and eyes sparkling with desire.

Stephie reached out and stroked her sister's breasts over the thin covering of virginal white cotton. The nipples soon stood hard and erect, pressing against the softness of the material, the colour dark against the whiteness. They kissed again, fingers exploring softly, flitting touches against breast and thigh and face.

'Make love with me,' Ariana breathed, an aching whisper escaping from her red lips.

In a moment Stephie was naked and wrapped in Ariana's arms, her mouth sucking furiously at Ariana's nipples, still clothed in thin white cotton. Her own nakedness was caressed by the butterfly touch of the night breeze, she opened her thighs, guided Ariana's fingers to the heat of her sex. She was wet, the nectar slick between her thighs. Ariana's touch was sure, a knowing caress that teased her

41

sister's clitoris exquisitely.

Stephie responded instinctively, opening herself, letting herself go to the waves of pleasure that pulsed from her hot sex. Her nipples throbbed while they were suckled, teased with teeth and tongue until Stephie could hold back her cries no longer. She arched, threw her head back and felt the shuddering ecstasy of orgasm.

'Well, well, this is a nice little family gathering, isn't it?'

Stephie froze, Timothy's voice draining the pleasure away from her. She opened her eyes and saw him standing before her, one hand on Ariana's shoulder, a possessive gesture that was not lost on either woman.

'I knew you two were close,' he continued, a sick smile stretching the features of his face to make him look hideous.

'How long were you watching?' Ariana asked softly.

'Long enough. My, Stephie darling, what a passionate young filly you are. And there was I thinking you were a frigid little bitch. Or is it that you're frigid with men but a real nympho with the gals?'

'You wouldn't understand,' Stephie spat angrily, sitting up on the bed but making no attempt to hide her nakedness.

'Oh, but I would. You've taken my wife from me. This is adultery in the grand manner, isn't it? Do you know, I can just see the headlines now. Think of the scandal.'

'You wouldn't,' Ariana whispered, thoroughly appalled by the idea.

He smiled. 'Oh but I would, dearest. It would make such a change to see your name dragged through the mud as well as mine.'

'You can't do this to us,' Stephie cried, her eyes wide with alarm.

'Don't tempt me,' he murmured darkly.

'Please, Timothy...' his wife begged, her eyes filling with tears.

'What do you want?' Stephie demanded, looking at him

42

sharply.

'So businesslike,' he complained. 'You know what I want. You turned me down earlier today.'

'How do I know that will be the end of it?'

'You won't Stephie, darling. But don't worry, you have my word as a pervert and a lecher that I just want to fill that lovely little mouth of yours with come, just this once. Is that too much to ask for?'

'Please, Stephie,' Ariana pleaded, holding her sister's hands tightly.

'I have no choice,' Stephie agreed coldly, flashing Timothy a look of pure hatred.

'Good. Before we begin, however, my darling wife has to be punished,' he smiled to her wickedly. 'Can't have you throwing yourself into bed with every close relative that visits, can we now?'

'But... Please Tim...'

There was no deflecting him. Reluctantly Ariana lifted her skirt to reveal her naked backside, her full round buttocks showing perfectly, the bulge of her pussy displayed to perfection when she bent over. He unthreaded his belt slowly, flexed it once, and then brought it down hard on her pert bottom. She squealed, forced her mouth shut, and suffered the half dozen strokes in silence.

At the end of it the top of her thighs and her arse cheeks were flaming, her skin tanned a deep red were the leather belt had touched her so forcefully. She started to get up, but he pushed her down and forced two fingers into her pussy. She groaned, sighed, her body collapsing into a heap as he frigged her to climax with a few quick strokes.

'She loves the belt, though not as much as the riding crop,' he commented cruelly to Stephie, revelling in the shame on his wife's face. 'You can go now,' he ordered, and silently Ariana walked away, deliberately avoiding her sister's eyes.

'Did you have to beat her?' Stephie asked after Ariana

had left.

Timothy laughed. 'You know she loves it, Steph. Why shouldn't she get some pleasure tonight as well?'

'You are just so devious,' she said, lying back on the bed, her pussy tingling with excitement. The way he beat Ariana had excited all three of them, and now she couldn't wait to get his long hard prick between her thighs.

'Years of breeding, darling,' he said, stripping off quickly. 'Did I ever tell you about my ancestor that liked to...'

'Enough of that,' she interrupted impatiently. 'I've been waiting for your cock all day, I can't wait any longer. Fuck me nice and dirty,' she sighed, 'nice and dirty.'

Our Little Secret

I was certain that she was doing it deliberately, and in that certainty I found nothing but confusion and indecision. That certainty was reinforced when I looked up and saw Nicole coming into the room. She beamed me a smile and then carried on through the room to switch on the television. I half smiled back, trying to fathom the look in her dark brown eyes that seemed to be at once so innocent and yet so knowing. My eyes scanned her quickly, she was wearing a very tight T-shirt, the shape of her firm young breasts impressed on the cotton, her nipples protruding slightly, and a short skirt that revealed just how long and smooth her thighs were. She flicked the television on and then sat down on the sofa, directly opposite to where I was sitting.

'What time's Jim getting home?' I asked her, forcing my eyes from the view of her shapely thighs, displayed to perfection by her tight skirt.

'He said he'd be late again,' she said with a sigh, for one moment an expression of sorrow clouding her eyes. She turned back to the television, perhaps wanting to hide her true feelings from me.

At first I had been sure it was my imagination. After all, I was probably spending more time at home with Nicole than Jim, who seemed to be putting in more and more hours at work. It could have been imagination, but slowly I grew certain that Nicole was flirting with me. No, it wasn't flirting exactly; it seemed to me that she was playing a little game and enjoying every second of it. First it was her clothes: very short mini-skirts, skin-tight tops, low-cut blouses. Then it was more obvious: the bathrobe that would fall open accidentally, affording me a split second view of

45

her finely shaped breasts, her nipples cherry-red against the whiteness of her skin, or the bedroom door left open so I'd see her as I walked past.

Never a word was said, never a hint of anything untoward, not even a silent smile of complicity. On the surface everything was entirely innocent, and I'm certain that Jim had no idea that anything was going on. And perhaps there really was nothing going on. But then again, every glimpse of her body, every look that was so innocent and so knowing, would set my heart pounding and body responding. Damn it, Nicole was a beautiful young woman and I found her presence very arousing.

'Are you watching this?' she asked, turning to me and breaking my train of thought.

'No, not really,' I mumbled, aware that she had been talking to me and I had been so wrapped up in my thoughts that I hadn't even noticed.

'Daydreaming again, Paul,' she sighed, a sad shake of the head transforming into a friendly smile.

'Sorry, I was miles away,' I told her, smiling back, all the time wondering what was going on in her pretty head. Her smiles could mean a million different things, always open and friendly, but occasionally I thought I detected something else, something much deeper and more dangerous.

'Do you mind if I turn this over?'

'Not at all. Is there anything else on the other side?'

She shrugged. 'Isn't there a film on tonight? Have you got the paper?'

I pointed to the magazine rack beside the television. Where was Jim? Such a pretty girl and yet he was neglecting her again, spending time at work or with his mates in the pub rather than with her. I couldn't understand it. He and Nicole were the same age, just under twenty, half my age, and yet they were worlds apart in personality. She liked nothing better than to cuddle up close to him, or for them to go out dancing, whereas he had plainly decided that his career was number one.

Nicole dutifully dragged herself off the sofa and walked across the room to the magazine rack. My eyes widened as she bent over to retrieve the newspaper. She was standing with ankles together, bent over at the waist, her skirt rising up at the back so I could see the full length of her gorgeous thighs. She flicked idly through the thick pile of papers and magazines, and as she did so she swivelled round slightly, making her skirt rise even higher. I could see the muscles of her thighs pulled taut, every inch of her silky smooth skin displayed, and at the top of her thighs the curve of her backside, the slight bulge of her buttocks. Her panties were a thin white strip of cotton that had been pulled tightly between her rear cheeks.

'Can't find it, you sure it's here?' she called, glancing round. I nodded silently, my eyes fixed on that rear view of her.

Was she doing it on purpose? I didn't know, and yet she was surely driving me insane. So sexy, so desirable, but still very distant and definitely hands-off.

As she read the newspaper I caught her sneaking looks in my direction, furtive little glances over the top of the pages, and then a guilty smile. Or did I imagine that?

'There's nothing on,' she announced after a few minutes, as though that were a surprise to either of us.

'So, you don't know what time Jim's getting back tonight?' I asked her.

'No, I just know he'll be late. I'd better put this back,' she said, getting up to walk back to the magazine rack. She looked over her shoulder at me again, caught my gaze and smiled. I couldn't keep my eyes from her. She bent over very slowly, her black skirt rising inch by inch over her thighs until I could again see the faintest outline of her white panties pulled tight into her crotch. She held the position for a few moments, wriggling from side to side to force the paper back into the overloaded rack, and incidentally allow me a good long look, and then she straightened up.

She looked at me again, her eyes sparkling with excitement. This time there could be no pretence. I had to say something. 'Doesn't Jim mind you wearing those mini-skirts?' I asked, managing a note of admonition.

'No, why should he?' she responded, smiling a smile of sweet innocence that made my prick throb dangerously.

'Well, they're so short,' I explained.

She laughed. 'They're supposed to be, silly. That's why they're called mini-skirts.'

'Of course,' I agreed, smiling. Damn it! The moment had gone. I had been certain that there'd been something beguiling, something alluring in her smile, but now that was gone and all I could detect was that childlike innocence I found so effective.

'There's nothing on the box tonight,' she remarked, 'but you couldn't do me a favour, could you?'

'Sure, what is it?'

'Well,' she said excitedly, 'Jim has promised to take me out to a club tomorrow night and I don't know what to wear. If I try on a couple of outfits, would you tell me which one you like the best?'

'Me? I have the dress sense of... I don't have any dress sense at all.'

She giggled. 'It doesn't matter. You're a man, you know what you like. Please, will you?'

She was pouting, and she knew I couldn't resist that. I drew breath sharply and nodded my agreement.

'Great!' she shrieked, and jumped across the room to plant a big wet kiss on my cheek, her breasts bulging against her tight top. She was so obviously excited that I hardly had time to react before she bounded up the stairs to her room.

Nicole may or may not have been intentionally flirting,

but my reaction was physical and I knew I would end up making a pass at her. I was brooding on this when I heard her coming downstairs, high heels cracking hard on the stairs.

'Well? How do I look?' she asked anxiously, walking into the centre of the room.

I could hardly believe my eyes, and my astonishment must have been clear to see as she paraded and twirled around in front of me. She was wearing a short black dress that seemed to have been sprayed on. It left nothing to the imagination. It was cut low so that her pert breasts were almost fully displayed, the nipples threatening to pop out at any moment. The dress was very short too, even shorter than the skirt she'd been wearing earlier, and barely managed to cover her backside. Added to which it was so tight that I could see the full rounded shape of her posterior and the slight bulge of her belly.

'You can't go out dressed like that,' I whispered, my eyes focusing on her breasts. The nipples had become erect little points that bulged against the tight low-slung neck of the dress.

'You don't like it?' she asked, advancing towards me, every step reflected in the bounce of her firm round breasts. She stopped in front of me, legs slightly apart, the shape of her limbs emphasised by black high heels. Was she enjoying my discomfort? I couldn't tell. All I knew was that she had never looked sexier, and the bulging of my prick was a painful reminder of the effect she was having on me.

'It's so revealing,' I tried to explain, my eyes travelling over her body only inches away from me.

'What about my scent?' she asked, suddenly leaning over me, offering her slender throat so I could breathe her perfume. It was an aphrodisiac, making me feel almost dizzy, my eyes only inches from her breasts offered so temptingly close.

'A lovely perfume,' I agreed, aware that her nipples were

such hard points against the tight velvet of her dress.

'Jim bought it for me,' she informed me, stepping away again, almost skipping across the room like an excited schoolgirl.

'But the dress...' I reminded her.

Suddenly she dropped the velvet purse she'd been holding, the perfect accessory for her dress. I watched as she bent over to pick it up, keeping her legs straight as she moved over at the waist, the tight dress parting her bottom cheeks before riding up sensuously over her skin. As I had thought, she was wearing no panties, and for one tantalising moment I was treated to a glimpse of her bare bottom, the dark hairs around her bulging sex visible from behind. Before I had time to react she was standing again, looking at me with pursed lips, as though unaware of what I had seen and deep in thought as to what to do next.

'Maybe you're right,' she finally decided, 'perhaps this is a bit too showy. Let me show you the next one, then you can decide.'

I didn't have the power to object. I merely nodded my agreement, and followed her with my eyes as she left the room. Damn it, I knew she was playing some strange game, flaunting her lithe young body, parading herself and enjoying my feelings of discomfort and excitement.

I stood up and walked to the drinks cabinet, adjusting my trousers, glancing down to see my cock etched against my clothing. She had to have seen that; there was no way that even a casual glance would have missed my erection. My hands were shaking as I poured myself a neat scotch and gulped down the amber drink. I closed my eyes, trying to block out the image of her breasts, trying to forget the image of her bent over, legs parted and set straight – trying but not succeeding.

'Paul, Paul!'

I sighed, wondering what new torture she had decided to inflict on me. She was calling from her bedroom, so I went to the bottom of the stairs to find out what she wanted.

'Could you just have a look at something for me?' she called, a pleading note to her voice.

I kept calm as I climbed the stairs. Her bedroom door was open and I just went in, vowing to keep cool no matter what she wanted. She was standing by her wardrobe, dressed only in a lacy bra and a short red mini-skirt, just as short as the dress had been. The wardrobe door was open, a mad jumble of clothes inside it. She smiled in a good-natured sort of way, that naïve smile she reserved especially for me.

'Could you reach up there for me?' she asked, pointing to a sports bag lodged on top of the wardrobe. The bra was almost see-through, a frilly black lace thing which lifted and parted her breasts, and barely covered her hardening nipples. It was a tease, but she was acting as though nothing untoward was happening.

'What's up there?' I said, sighing, looking from her breasts to her eyes, and realising just how much she was enjoying my attentions.

'I've got a matching skirt and blouse in there, I'd just like to try them on.'

'How did you get the bag up there?' I complained.

'Ah... Now I remember,' she exclaimed delightedly. She reached for the vanity chair in front of the dressing table and positioned it by the wardrobe. 'Jim held the chair while I just shoved things up there,' she told me. 'I'd forgotten.'

She skipped up onto the chair and I saw how unsteady it was. I did as instructed and bent over to hold it steady while she stretched up and grabbed the bag. She hadn't been lying, the bag was stuck, and as she struggled to pull it away I was treated to another view of long thighs, and this time a flash of black where she'd put a pair of panties on. At long last the bag was free and she stepped down, though not before she'd seen me eyeing up her long legs.

'Here it is, tell me what you think,' she giggled excitedly.

I watched her unzip the bag and produce a long dark skirt, the longest skirt I'd ever seen her have. Before I could make a comment she unclipped her red mini and let it fall in a bundle around her ankles. She faced me in her underwear, lacy black bra and matching knickers, with not a trace of shame on her face.

'What the hell do you think you're doing?' I demanded angrily, driven beyond endurance by her brazen exhibitionism.

'What do you mean?' she asked innocently, her eyes widening.

'What is it, girl? Are you enjoying this silly game of yours?' I bellowed, unable to control my anger any more.

'Paul, what is it?'

'You, that's what it is. Why are you parading yourself like this? Showing off in front of me, are you enjoying embarrassing me? Is that it?'

'I'm sorry, I hadn't realised this was embarrassing,' she sniffed, pouting sulkily.

'Don't act the little innocent with me,' I warned her, 'or I'll have to teach you what happens to girls that misbehave.'

Her eyes seemed to perk up. 'What does happen to girls that misbehave?' she asked, her mocking tone contrasting to the excitement I saw in her eyes. Her nipples were hard points of flesh, and I couldn't help but notice that her backside was reflected in the mirror behind her.

'They get punished,' I replied. 'And parading around in your knickers, or parading around without any knickers on at all, is a sure way to get punished.'

'But I wasn't parading...' she started to complain.

'Don't push your luck, madam,' I warned her coldly.

'I'm sorry,' she replied softly, averting her gaze guiltily.

'Tell me the truth, were you deliberately leading me on?'

There was a lengthy pause, and then she nodded. 'I could see you were getting turned on,' she admitted. 'And I sort of enjoyed it, and the more I did it the more I enjoyed it.

I've been very silly, haven't I?'

It was my turn to pause. I knew what I wanted to do then. 'I think I've every right to punish you for that, don't you?'

'I suppose so,' she mumbled.

'How do you propose I do that, young lady?'

She shrugged her shoulders. 'I don't know, I suppose you deserve to get your own back. How do you think I should be punished?'

I took a deep breath. 'You deserve a sound spanking,' I told her, exhaling slowly. 'I think the way to ensure you keep your knickers on and hidden from view is to smack you so hard on the behind that every time you sit down you'll remember.'

There was no surprise on her part, no look of horror. Instead she nodded to herself, as though she understood the justice of it all. 'Here?' she asked nervously.

'Yes, here and now.'

I pulled the vanity chair over and sat down, positioning myself so that I was comfortable. The wardrobe door, with its inside mirror, was open, and that in turn was reflected in the mirror on the dressing table. I motioned for her to step forward and she did so, glancing at me nervously.

'Across my knee, young lady,' I explained, pulling her towards me. She made no reply but knelt across my lap, reaching out to stop herself falling. In seconds her bottom, still clad in thin black panties, was presented for my delectation. She could see herself in the mirror, and the reflection of her backside too, an infinitely receding view of herself ready for punishment.

I raised my hand high and brought it down hard, the slap of skin on skin resounding around the room. My fingers stung lightly, but that was nothing to the sting she must have felt on her pert round behind. She made no sound. Instead she bit her lip and looked up at me appealingly. I raised my hand again and brought it down firmly on her other bottom cheek, gratified to feel her jump when my hand landed so firmly on her taut round buttock. Again and again, six quick strokes in succession, turning her pale and delicate flesh first pink and then a deeper shade of red. Soon Nicole was squirming and moaning, her body responding to the searing heat of punishment that rained down on her posterior.

'Stand up now,' I commanded, my breath coming hot and fast as I enjoyed my task of punishing Nicole's backside.

'Oh, it hurts,' she complained, pouting her full red lips.

'It's supposed to,' I told her gruffly, noting at the same time that her nipples had grown even more erect. I could see that the excitement was still there in her eyes, and I guessed our little session had yet to run its course.

'But I wasn't such a bad girl,' she protested, pushing out her chest so that she was flaunting herself again.

'Right, there'll be more for that.'

'More for what?' she demanded defiantly.

I grabbed her and pushed her against the bed. She fell across it, face down and bottom out. There was a black hairbrush on the dressing table and I picked it up and weighed it in my hand.

'Please, not that, Paul,' she wailed, her eyes open wide with horror when she saw me with the brush.

'I'm going to teach you a lesson, young woman,' I told her. In moments her pretty lace panties were around her ankles and her backside, patterned red by my hand, was fully exposed. Her bottom cheeks were slightly parted, and I could see the dark bud of her rear hole and the puffy lips of her sex. She looked delightful, so exposed, so vulnerable, her punished body exuding a kind of raw animal sexuality.

The first impact of the brush on her bottom cheeks echoed around the room, accompanied by her yelp of shock and pain. I reached out and smoothed my hand over her buttocks, able to enjoy the heat that flamed on her skin.

She moved back, pushed her bottom towards me, enjoying being touched and caressed on the seat of her punishment. Her correction had yet to end, and soon her cries of pain were a constant refrain as I let go with half a dozen hard blows with the hairbrush. I moved round and smacked her again, each time landing the brush precisely on her lithe young body.

Her behaviour changed subtly. Her cries were deeper, breathier, and she was lifting herself, offering me her rear for every blow. I made sure that I tanned her body evenly, smacking her hard on the buttocks, at the top of the thighs, and even between her thighs.

Her strangled cry of pleasure as she climaxed suddenly brought me to my senses. What had I done? I looked down on her reddened posterior, at her writhing body, at the look of sweet pleasure that marked her face. I had punished her for sure, but much to my surprise she had found pleasure in her pain.

'Are you all right?' I whispered, letting the brush fall to the floor.

She opened her eyes and looked at me. 'That was so good,' she sighed. 'That felt so different; it hurt me but I enjoyed it too. I don't know why...'

'You'd better get dressed,' I told her. My eyes travelled down over her body, her bra had fallen and her breasts were patterned pink, her rosy nipples so enticing. Her sex was wet and pink where the brush had touched her. As for her buttocks and thighs, they were deep red and had never looked so good.

She nodded. For once she had nothing to say, as though the pain that was smarting on her pretty little backside had robbed her of the power of speech. I watched as she covered herself up, wrapping a red robe tightly around her body, looking quite chaste compared to the way she normally flaunted herself in front of me.

I went downstairs for another drop of scotch and left her

55

standing awkwardly in her room, her eyes lowered and her face quite pale. The drink tasted good, I savoured every drop as I waited for her to come downstairs, knowing she would have found the experience thoroughly disorientating. I wondered whether it had been the first time she'd ever been chastised. Certainly there had been none of the shock and horror I would have expected.

'Paul...' I turned and saw that she was standing in the doorway, her dark soulful eyes looking at me nervously.

'Back to say you're sorry?' I asked her sternly.

'Sorry? But you're the one that punished me,' she whispered softly.

'Will it be the last time?'

'It stings,' she complained, neatly avoiding a reply to my question.

'Show me,' I demanded, setting my tumbler of scotch down on the counter and advancing towards her.

'But... but I haven't got anything on under this robe,' she told me breathlessly, her face colouring slightly.

'It's a pity you weren't so modest earlier, isn't it? Now, show me.'

'No, I won't show you,' she told me defiantly, her lips twisting into a smile. Her eyes were burning again, with an intense glow of excitement.

I strode across the room and grabbed her by the arm, pulling her towards the armchair. She struggled but her heart wasn't in it, her squeals and complaints were empty and passionless. I positioned her beside the armchair and lifted the back of her robe, exposing her beautiful backside, which was tanned a deep pink that contrasted with the white skin of her thighs. I could still make out my handprints on her flesh, but stronger than that was the array of oval marks that the hairbrush had imprinted. I stroked her buttocks and she winced, her punished flesh warm to my touch.

'It's a shame that one session hasn't been enough,' I told her, shaking my head sadly.

'What do you mean, Paul?' she asked, her eyes brimming with tears.

'I mean that your wilful behaviour hasn't changed.'

'You can't mean...'

I knelt down and slipped her dainty slipper from her left foot and then straightened up. She gave a wide-eyed look of horror when I flexed the rubber sole, testing its mettle before deciding it was a good enough paddle for her posterior.

'Ten strokes of this,' I explained, 'and any nonsense and you'll get extra.'

She bit her lip and nodded, then, without prompting, she bent over the thick padded arm of the chair. Her position was perfect, backside nice and round, pink and inviting, her thighs very straight, her breasts rubbing softly against the seat of the chair. I raised the slipper and brought it down swiftly, retribution laid against her pert young buttocks. She tried hard not to cry out as the first smack burned on her behind. I touched her, felt the heat of impact with the tips of my fingers. The second and third strokes were on the same buttock, spreading that heat evenly. The fourth stroke I switched target, and when it landed heavily on her right bottom cheek she let out a howl that goaded me on for strokes five and six.

'How many have you had?' I asked, pausing for a second, wanting to keep the suspense and raise the tension further.

'Seven, Paul,' she whispered miserably.

'You'll get extra for that lie,' I whispered.

I cut off her complaint with a hard stroke of the slipper, aimed between her thighs. She cried out, but this time I noted the sigh of pleasure mixed in with the pain. Again, another stroke that brushed the underside of her thighs and touched her sex. It was happening again, she was stealing pleasure from her punishment. She was pulling herself down and sticking her bottom out, forcing herself into the stroke, accepting it eagerly. She shuddered as I dealt the last hard blow between her buttocks, a sharp stinging lick from her slipper.

'Stay there,' I warned her.

I waited for a while, relishing the view of her punished backside, of her twin globes blazing red and pink. I wondered whether she was getting off on being exposed, after all, there was no doubt about her exhibitionist inclinations; that was what had got her into trouble in the first place.

'Did you enjoy that?' I asked casually.

There was a long pause before she answered. 'Sort of...' she admitted hesitantly.

'Do you want more?'

'No!' she cried at once, without hesitation at all.

I nodded to myself. She found pleasure in her chastisement all right, but it was punishment all the same: painful, humiliating and to be avoided at all costs.

'Stand up and face me,' I instructed. 'You can forget about covering yourself up too,' I added.

Her eyes were lowered, and I was pleased to see that her face was as red with shame as her bottom was red with punishment. Her breasts were ripe and attractive, her hard nipples pointing out enticingly. I noted that her skin was flushed, with that radiant afterglow of orgasm.

Without warning I raised the slipper and brought it down sharply on her right breast. She squealed with shock, but the red imprint on her flesh made her nipples stand out even more. The left breast got the same sharp treatment, a spanking with the slipper that made her cry out.

'You can go and get dressed now,' I told her at last, satisfied that her punishment was complete.

'First this,' she said softly. She knelt down and crawled forward and touched the outline of my cock, impressed on my trousers. In seconds she had loosened my clothes and released my aching erection.

'You are such a naughty girl,' I told her tenderly, sighing

as she stroked my hardness with her slender fingers.

'You can always punish me...' she whispered, and then closed her luscious red lips around my helmet.

It was heaven, admiring her punished backside while she mouthed and sucked my cock. She knew what she was doing. I had never felt so much pleasure. She teased and caressed until I thought I would be the one screaming. And then I felt myself explode, filling her lovely mouth with wave upon wave of thick creamy come.

'You'd better clear up,' I told her later, kissing her mouth and stroking her hair.

'Sure,' she agreed lazily, 'Jim will be home soon. Let this be our secret, our little secret.'

I nodded, that was what it was exactly, our little secret. The last thing I wanted was for my son to find out what I'd been doing with his girlfriend.

Marianne

Stephen stood up and went to the window. The sky was a uniform milky grey, leeching the colour from the day and leaving everything dull and flat. He stood for a moment, looking out across the fields to the thin line of trees on the horizon, the thin green plumes pointing to the hazy white disc that was the wintry sun.

'If we're going to do this then we have to do it properly,' he had said earlier in the bar. She had agreed readily but had avoided his eyes, looking instead into the roaring flames crackling in the brick fireplace.

The air felt heavy, the atmosphere was already very tense, filled with an expectation that was almost tangible. He returned to the desk and buzzed Marianne, jabbing a finger forcefully at the intercom.

'Yes sir,' she responded breathlessly. He could imagine her sitting on the edge of her seat, waiting for his call, her legs crossed so that the tight skirt revealed the perfect shape of her thighs.

'I want your personnel file please,' he said clearly, managing to conceal the tremor of emotion with an air of cool formality.

'My file?' she asked with a note of genuine surprise.

'Yes please,' he said, and cut the phone off, her quizzical note still hanging in the air. He leaned back, sinking into the welcoming comfort of the leather chair, and waited for her to come in. The Sullivan account file lay on the desk in front of him, the buff folder containing the full details of the most important account the company had. It was the first file he had asked for when they had both arrived that morning. He remembered the nervous look in her eye as she handed it over, as if she wasn't sure that she wanted him to see it. But the account had been lost and he had to see the file.

Marianne entered and smiled coolly. It was an efficient smile that managed to conceal whatever feelings she had, yet managed not to look false. 'My file,' she said, carefully handing him the blue folder with her name neatly stencilled on the cover.

'Thank you, Marianne,' he said, deliberately placing it next to the Sullivan file.

'Is there anything else?' she asked, hovering in front of the desk nervously.

'No, thank you.' He looked down at her file, not bothering to wave her away. She hesitated for a second, standing in front of the desk, one leg crossed in front of the other, hands together, fingers locked tight. It was only when she turned to walk away that Stephen looked up again. She was wearing a smart navy skirt and jacket, with black seamed stockings and black high heels with butterfly bows on the heel. Her skirt was tight and her hips swayed slightly with each step, emphasising the constraining tightness of the skirt and the elegant curves of her body.

She lingered at the door for a moment and he felt sure she was going to say something, but if she was she changed her mind. She closed the door gently and he felt a sigh of relief. These situations were always so difficult, so very tricky. He skipped through her file, flicking through the pages, not even pretending to read through it. He knew all he had to know, but he was stalling for time, wanting just those few extra moments to think things through. He leaned back in his seat once more and looked around at the comfortable office, at the framed certificates on the wall, at the book-lined shelves, at the painting by the door, at the drinks cabinet in the corner. Success – everything reflected the success of the company, and of the people who worked there. Until now.

He buzzed Marianne again. She responded too quickly, her voice just a little too loud and a little too eager. 'Marianne, I'd like to see you for a moment, please,' he said, as calmly as he possibly could. His heart was thumping and his throat had gone impossibly dry.

'Yes, Stephen,' she said when she came in. Her smile was more nervous than it had been a moment earlier, as if she realised that things had finally come to a head.

'This is going to be very difficult,' he said, playing with a pen nervously, finding it easier to look at that and not at her. 'Very difficult,' he repeated softly, 'for the both of us. You've been with us a long time now, and sometimes that's not a good thing.'

'It's about the Sullivan account,' she said quietly, barely whispering, her sharp blue eyes suddenly full of tears.

'Yes. The Sullivan account.' He paused, exhaled heavily. 'But that's not the first time, is it?'

'But it wasn't my fault,' she whispered, her lips trembling.

'I'm afraid it was,' Stephen said softly but firmly, hoping she wouldn't make a scene. 'You were late with the tender documents. We missed the deadline for the contract and they lost the job. They lost a major contract because of us, and it was our fault. Your fault. They were our biggest client and now they've gone. This was the third time Marianne, the third. We've given you chances before, too many perhaps. We just can't go on like this.'

'Please, I'm sorry,' she said, the anguish etched miserably on her face. Her skin was pale, making her red lips more prominent, pouting, alluring.

'I'm sorry too,' he said, closing her file and pushing it towards her.

'Please Stephen, I'll do anything...'

He shook his head sadly, exhaled slowly. 'I'm sorry,' he repeated, looking up into her eyes for the first time.

She looked at him, eyes wide, her body trembling. Then

she looked away. 'Please...' she whispered.

'What else can I do?' he asked reasonably. 'You've been warned before. You've been given chances. What can we do? It's as if harsh words aren't enough. Sometimes I think there's only one thing you'd respond to. Sometimes I want to...' He stopped, suddenly aware that he'd said too much, gone too far.

'What? Do what? I'll do anything, you know I would,' she said earnestly.

He looked at her. She was beautiful, even the tears in her eyes and the anguish on her face were seductive. His heart was racing. He had said too much, letting the tension and the emotion get the better of him. 'Nothing. Forget I said anything,' he said apologetically.

'Please Stephen, what were you going to say? It's not fair, you can't do this to me. You owe me more than that.'

He nodded. 'I was going to say that sometimes I think you'd only respond to being properly punished.'

She looked up sharply. 'What do you mean?'

'I mean treated like a naughty child. Punished with more than just sharp words.'

There was a moment of tense silence and he regretted ever opening his mouth. It hadn't been a smart thing to say and it was going to make a difficult situation impossible.

'Yes. Maybe you're right,' she said very quietly, her face flushing pink. Her eyes were fixed on the floor, avoiding his own questioning look.

'Pardon?'

'I said, maybe you're right. Maybe I do need to be punished.'

'No, I don't think you understand. I meant punished as in smacked on the backside and told to behave.'

'Yes,' she agreed quietly. 'That's what I thought you meant. Perhaps I do want to be punished like that.'

Stephen breathed deeply, his hands trembling. 'Remove your stockings,' he said, his voice almost hoarse.

63

Marianne's face was burning red, her embarrassment clear to see, yet she obeyed. She turned her back to Stephen and pulled her skirt up at the front. She reached under and fiddled with her suspenders. Stephen stood up and walked round to the front of the desk, his eyes fixed on her long elegant thighs. She looked away from him but made no effort to cover herself. Her stockings were dark against her soft white skin, and when she rolled them down he felt the heat rising within him. It was like a dream, something he could hardly believe was happening. She slipped her shoes off and pulled the stockings off completely.

'Bend over the desk,' he said, putting a hand to her shoulder to stop her picking up her stockings. She stepped back into her high heels and then went to the desk. She bent over at the waist, pressing herself flat against the smooth leather-topped desk, pressing her face against the cool surface, her hands up by her face.

Stephen stood behind her, enjoying the sight of her skirt pulled tight over her backside, pulling the buttocks apart slightly. Very gently he took the hem of her skirt and lifted it high, up and over her waist. Her long legs were smooth and straight, the knees locked tight so that every muscle and sinew was stretched tight. Her snow-white panties were pulled tightly between her thighs, deep between her rounded bottom cheeks. The darkness between her thighs was unmistakable, the outline of her sex clearly visible.

'I'm going to smack you six times,' he said, his voice trembling. 'I don't want you to scream or cry. If you do I'll punish you for that as well. Is that clear?'

'Yes,' she said, her voice as nervous as his. 'Yes, sir,' she added, twisting round to look at him, her eyes sparkling with fear and excitement.

Stephen hesitated, eyeing her lovely long legs and beautiful rear. He reached over to the desk, to the photograph of happy laughing children, and turned it over.

The first smack echoed in the room, a sharp sound of

flesh on flesh. Marianne moaned softly, her hands pressed hard onto the desk, her eyes half closed. Stephen waited a second then smacked her again, a hard slap on the other buttock. He stopped to admire the imprint of his fingers, marked deep red on the soft white flesh of Marianne's backside.

'Does it hurt?' he asked softly.

'Yes, it stings horribly,' she replied quietly, her eyes still half closed. She was breathing hard, though Stephen couldn't tell how she was reacting; her feelings were closed off from him, obscured by her silence and her half closed eyes.

He spanked her again, two quick strokes in rapid succession. Each time she tensed and then exhaled slowly, the breath escaping from her glossy red lips like a sigh.

'Oh, it stings. It's like a fire spreading...' she whispered, as if talking to herself, telling herself what it was like.

Stephen's prick was hard, throbbing. Marianne's beautifully punished backside was the most erotic thing he had ever seen. He wanted to stop and touch her, to slip his fingers under her panties, to part her buttocks and stroke her there, to press a finger between the inviting lips of her sex.

Marianne moaned again. She was opening and closing her eyes slowly, breathing hard and deep, almost gasping for breath. He saw that her panties were damp, and that the wet heat was spreading. The look on her face seemed to hover between pleasure and pain, her lips parted, half smiling, half scowling. He smacked her again, a hard stroke directly between her gorgeous arse cheeks.

'Oh Jesus...' she moaned, her body tensing momentarily, her eyes flaring open. Another hard smack in the same place and she cried out, an animal cry that could only be interpreted in one way. She had climaxed powerfully, the heat from her reddened backside spreading deep into her sex.

'Don't move,' Stephen ordered sharply, stepping away from her.

Marianne opened her eyes and twisted round to look at him, but he had retreated to the back of the office. He poured himself a drink from the glass cabinet and then turned back to her. He could see that her skin was patterned red with his finger marks, that even the white panties couldn't obscure the evidence of punishment. But it hadn't been enough. She had found pleasure in the pain, joy in her punishment and finally release.

'Don't move, not until it's over,' he warned.

'Yes sir,' she responded, so softly that he hardly heard her. He downed his drink and then stripped off quickly. It wasn't what she was expecting, but then neither had he expected her to climax while he spanked her.

'What...'

'Quiet!' he snapped, banging the bottle of whisky down in front of her. 'You haven't been very honest with me,' he said grimly.

'I don't know what you...'

'Quiet! Now I'm going to punish you properly.'

Marianne screamed when the heavy leather belt fell across her buttocks. She tried to move away but he held her in place and beat her again with the belt, striking hard at the top of her thighs. The office resounded to the rhythm of the belt and Marianne's cries of pain and moans of pleasure.

'Oh please... please...' she whispered, sounding close to hysteria.

'Please what?' he asked coldly, his own nervous feelings swept away by the wave of excitement.

'Fuck me! Hit me with the belt and fuck me...'

Roughly Stephen pulled her soaking panties down to her knees. Her sex was hot and wet. He felt her respond when he pressed his fingers into the sticky heat.

He raised the belt and brought it down swiftly between

her arse cheeks and she climaxed again, arching her back and crying out deliriously. He picked the bottle up and poured the amber fluid over her smarting skin, watching it cascade down between her thighs, droplets glistening like jewels in the raw pinkness of her sex.

At last he took her by the waist and pressed his raging hardness into the velvety heat of her pussy. She was hot and receptive, raising her punished backside up to meet the hard thrusts of his cock. She rode with his rhythm, moving with his body, eyes closed and a look of ecstasy etched on her face. She was beautiful, sexy, the most fantastic lover he'd ever had. He fell over her, covering her body with his own, pumping hard, crying out with her, sharing an explosive climax as one.

Marianne was waiting when he emerged from the office. She was trying hard to look cool and composed, but her eyes were glowing and she still looked a little dazed. He knew that her bottom must still be smarting, it would be marked for days, an eloquent reminder of her punishment.

'Thank you,' she said quietly, counting the money at the same time.

'Will we ever do this again?' Stephen asked hopefully.

She shook her head. 'I think not,' she smiled.

Stephen nodded sadly. That was how it was. He had known all along that it would never happen again, but in the shared excitement he had hoped that Marianne would change her mind. He took the money from her and stuffed it into his pocket. They shook hands and then she disappeared back into the office. Stephen waited a second in the Saturday morning silence, hoping she would relent. He looked at the door for a moment, at the name plate that said 'Marianne Hughes, Managing Director', wishing it would open, but there was no point. He shrugged, then turned and left.

Coincidence

It had begun innocuously enough I suppose. Alan and his wife moved down from Doncaster to London when he was transferred to my office. Although technically I was his superior, we were close enough in age and outlook that we functioned better as a team than as competitors. He was a good worker, not afraid to get involved, and not afraid of putting in any extra effort either. I liked that about him, and I suppose that matched my own temperament and way of working. Moving down from Yorkshire to London was a big step for he and Madelaine to take, especially as she had already made one move from Scotland to Yorkshire to be with him.

Neither of them had friends or family down south, so it was natural that I felt a bit protective about them both. He was a good friend, and I didn't want to lose him as a colleague either. So, once they had moved in I took them under my wing a bit and made sure that they met my friends, made friends of their own, and generally settled down quite comfortably. It hadn't been difficult, especially as they were such a nice couple. He friendly, quiet, intelligent, she a bit bubblier, very attractive and a warm personality.

As I said, I liked them both, and when Alan told me the date of Madelaine's birthday the coincidence seemed quite fitting. We shared the same birth date it seemed, and once the two of them found out they insisted that they take me out for a special birthday treat. I wouldn't hear of it, but of course they twisted my arm, and when she gave me that special coy smile of hers I gave in graciously. As the day approached I can remember the two of them sounding me out as to what I wanted as a present. I was adamant that a night out was more than enough, but they wouldn't listen. Here I did not relent, and I was scrupulous about not giving them any clues as to what I might want.

The restaurant they had chosen was perfect. Excellent food, waiters that didn't patronise, service that was exemplary, and an atmosphere that could not have been bettered. As the wine flowed, as well as the conversation, I thought to myself just how lucky Alan was to have a pretty young wife like Madelaine. The two of them were so obviously in love that it hurt just to look at them. It wasn't lovey-dovey and sickly sweet, which always makes me immediately suspicious, no; theirs was more relaxed, more genuine and spontaneous.

She looked good too. There was something a little bit vain about Maddy, but given that she was so pretty anyway we could all forgive her that. Dressed in a little black dress, high heels and black stockings, she looked the sexiest creature on earth, and drew more admiring glances from the waiters in the restaurant than all the other women put together. Alan noticed of course, and we both took great pleasure in teasing her about it, which made her blush and us laugh.

'That was, without a doubt, one of the best meals I've ever had,' I sighed, waving over the waiter.

'We should do this again,' Madelaine laughed, leaning back into Alan's arms. They were seated opposite me, and she was nestling up under his arms, wrapped around her in a loose, protective hug.

'It's on us...' Alan began to say, but before he could complain the waiter was marching off with my credit card.

'Hey! That's not fair!' Maddy complained, sitting up, a look of consternation in her dark brown eyes.

'Fair or not, I've had a great time and I don't want to spoil it with any arguments,' I told her, smiling. She smiled back and then looked away shyly, as though embarrassed by the way I was looking at her.

'In that case,' Alan decided suddenly, 'I think you ought to come back to our place for a nightcap.'

'If you think I'm going to argue, then you're mistaken,' I laughed. Maddy smiled again, glancing up into her husband's eyes quizzically. Something was going on between them, though I had no idea then what it might be.

The blast of cold air as we emerged from the restaurant into the street was bracing, a sharp jolt of sensation that cleared the mind instantly. Alan had parked his car a few streets away, and now in the sharp cold I could see that Maddy was in no mood to walk all that way.

'I thought you Scottish girls were used to the cold,' I joked, winking to Alan, who laughed.

'No,' he replied quickly, 'she can't stand the chill, which is why I have to warm her up every so often.'

'Alan! Please!' she exclaimed, stamping her heel on the ground angrily. Her face was bright red, and she hardly dared look me in the eye.

'Tell you what then,' Alan said, his voice still full of good humour, 'you two wait here while I go and fetch the car.'

'Sure, we'll wait,' I agreed. We watched him march off, bracing himself against a sharp gust that cut through the street.

'Does he warm you up often?' I teased, enjoying the flush of embarrassment on her cheeks. Her dark eyes were intense, and I knew that I was intruding on some private joke between the two of them.

'You should have let us pay,' she said softly, deftly trying to change the subject. 'You've been good to us, this was our way of saying thank you.'

'There's no need,' I assured her, touched by the earnest tone. She was changing the subject though, and I was more than a little intrigued to find out what the two of them were going on about. 'It was worth every penny just to see the way he teases you,' I added.

'I knew you would,' she whispered. 'You two have so much in common...'

'We're common now, are we? I'll tell him that when he gets back!'

'Oh, you! You know what I mean,' she giggled.

The car washed thick beams of light over us as it came to a slow halt at the kerb. 'What are you two laughing about?' Alan asked, pushing the passenger door open.

'Your wife's just accused us of being common,' I reported, sliding into the rear passenger seat.

'I did not,' Maddy protested, getting in beside her husband. Her dress rode up and I was treated to a glimpse of black stocking top against smooth white thigh. She looked gorgeous, and Alan was watching me watching his lovely young wife.

'Lovely legs, don't you think?' he asked me, lowering his voice a fraction.

'Alan! Stop that!' she cried, wriggling in her seat as she smoothed her dress down. It was no good, a dress like that was designed to flatter, designed to show off, not to hide.

'Lovely legs,' I agreed, delighting in the look of shame that made her face redden even more.

'Sorry, Maddy, it's just that we're so common,' he explained, straight-faced so that we didn't know if he was joking or being serious.

'That's not what I said,' she insisted, obviously believing that Alan was being serious.

'Is that or is that not what she said?' he asked me.

I hesitated, tried to measure the look in his eyes. 'Yes, exactly what she said,' I agreed finally.

He nodded, as though it was the answer he wanted to hear. Without warning he put his foot down and we sped off. The unexpected jolt of acceleration threw us back against the seats and temporarily silenced any further conversation. The atmosphere had changed, and where I had been comfortable before, I now felt more than a little confused.

Their flat was not too far from the restaurant, and at the speed that Alan was driving we were there in a matter of a few minutes. He parked quickly and efficiently and cut off the engine before we'd even realised we were home.

'That's not what I said,' Maddy repeated, her voice low and indistinct. She was pouting, her lips pursed and kissable, red lipstick making her mouth look glossy and seductive.

'Well, I'm a common sort of guy, perhaps I misunderstood,' I said, wondering how to get the atmosphere back to the way it had been in the restaurant.

Alan ignored her and turned to me. 'A drink?' he offered, as though nothing unusual were going on. There was a look in his eye that I couldn't decipher, but I nodded.

'A drink sounds like an excellent idea,' I agreed.

We walked from the car to the flat in total silence, though I caught the worried expression on Maddy's face. Her heels smacked hard on the pavement, drawing attention to her long, stockinged legs, covered imperfectly by her short black dress.

'I hope Maddy's not ruined your evening too much,' Alan remarked apologetically, showing me into the living room.

'Listen, that was just a gag,' I whispered, glad that she'd not followed us straight into the room.

'You're a good mate,' he responded instantly, 'and you deserve better.'

'No, you don't...' I began, but stopped as Madelaine wandered into the room, looking thoroughly downcast.

'I'm sorry,' she mumbled to me. 'I shouldn't have said what I did. I'll understand if you never want to see us again...'

'She's right,' Alan added. 'I'd understand if you felt insulted.'

'A drink?' I suggested, feeling thoroughly out of my depth.

'Get the man a drink, girl!' Alan snapped angrily.

Maddy jumped. She crossed the room and began to shakily pour two beakers of scotch, only she was pouring more of it onto the floor than into the tumblers.

'Look what you're doing!' Alan scolded her.

'Sorry, sorry,' was all she could think of saying. She put the whisky tumblers down and then looked at the pool of scotch on the floor. Taking her hanky from her bag she knelt down to mop it up. As she did so Alan and I were treated to another display of her elegant thighs, stocking tops and soft pale skin. The shape of her backside was impressed against the tight black material, leaving little to my feverish imagination.

'Enough of that,' Alan told her promptly.

'I'm so sorry,' she whispered, sounding on the verge of tears.

'You've been sorry all evening,' he said coldly. 'I think it's time you really had something to feel sorry about.'

If I was tempted to intervene the threat in his voice, and the responsive look on her face, made me bite my tongue. For a moment it seemed I had been forgotten about, that I was an intruder on some private domestic argument. Then Alan looked at me, the harsh look on his face not matched by the excitement I detected.

'Please, not now...' Maddy said, her voice barely a whisper.

Alan sat down on the very edge of the sofa, and motioned for her to step towards him. I watched, fascinated by what was unfolding between them. She stopped in front of him, her head bowed and her hands at her sides. She looked like a recalcitrant child, bowed with guilt for all her misdemeanours, meekly waiting to be scolded.

'Across my knees,' he barked, 'I shouldn't have to tell you that.'

She glanced towards me, her face red with shame, her dark eyes unable to meet my own. My heart was pounding and the excitement in the room was electric. Very slowly she complied, moving gracefully into place across his lap. Of course her short dress revealed all, and I enjoyed everything I saw. Her tight black panties were but a sliver of darkness between her bottom cheeks, the tight material parting the round globes of flesh as Alan pulled the dress higher.

In moments I was treated to the gorgeous sight of her posterior, the dress pulled up to her waist completely by her husband. The stockings were pulled tight by lacy black suspenders, which were pressed firmly across her bottom cheeks, and which served to part them slightly. Her panties were a thin satiny thread, contrasting to the whiteness of her skin.

Alan smiled, he was showing his young wife off to me, and enjoying every second of it. She muffled her complaints, and stilled for a second, realising perhaps that the time for resistance was over. Her long legs had never looked better, I was certain of that.

'Next time,' Alan warned her, 'perhaps you'll think twice about making stupid remarks to our guests.'

He raised his hand high above his head and then brought it down swiftly. The slap of flesh on flesh filled the room, a sharp sound that brought a wail of horror to her pretty lips. He waited a moment, giving me time to admire the red imprint of his hand against her right bottom cheek, before marking her again. His hand made a graceful curve, then slapped down hard against her buttock. Again and again, such hard strokes of the hand I'd never seen. She struggled and wriggled, but to no avail, he was intent on punishing his pretty wife completely.

Her struggles succeeded only in arousing me further, each twist of her waist, each curve of her bottom only revealed more of her flesh. The panties were pulling tighter between her rear cheeks, exposing more of her reddening punishment. I noted the way her cries of horror had softened, and that she seemed to be moving into each stroke. Yes, I was certain of that. I watched her lift her posterior towards the stroke, offering her pert backside for her husband to spank.

'I see what you mean about having to warm her up,' I ventured to say at last. I was smiling, not even attempting to hide my pleasure. Her backside was tanned an even pink glow, contrasting to the darkness of her stockings and the whiteness of her upper thighs. She looked delicious, and with her punished bottom displayed so prominently I could hardly control my own feelings.

'She does need a firm hand, sometimes,' Alan admitted, slowly rubbing his palm across the reddest part of her bottom. He was savouring every second, and she in turn was reacting to it fully, her breath sharp, her eyes half closed with pain and pleasure.

'I can see that,' I agreed.

'But we're not finished yet, are we my dear?' Alan continued, a cruel, taunting twist to his voice.

'Please... Don't...' she whimpered, covering her face with her hands.

'You've been very bad these last few days, a few slaps on the backside aren't enough to pay for that,' he said, then added, 'even if it does hurt.'

He pushed her off his lap very roughly, and she fell heavily to the floor, her finger-marked backside making contact with the coldness of the floor. She winced, looked at me with nothing but shame in her eyes, and then turned back to her husband. Her lips were trembling and I feared tears. She bit her lip, trying to hold back everything she felt.

'Get that off,' he told her gruffly, pointing to the little black dress, which no longer looked as elegant as it had earlier.

'But... but...'

'Now!' he ordered, in a voice that brooked no

disagreement.

She stood up shakily, keeping her back to me, and pulled the dress off over her head. For a second no one said anything. She stood balanced on her stiletto heels, an image to enjoy. She had been topless under the dress, and from the rear I could see only the gentle curve of her breasts. Now she was clad only in stockings, panties and suspenders.

'Get those off too,' Alan decided, slapping her hard on the bottom and making her squeal.

This time there were no complaints, as if she had finally realised that resistance was pointless. She unclipped her suspender belt and pulled her panties down to her ankles. Now I could see the full roundness of her derriere, the firm globes of her shapely backside flushed pink from her spanking. She crossed her hands across her chest, covering herself while keeping her back to me.

'Well?' Alan asked, turning to me with a smile. He was justly proud of his wife's body, I could see that in his eyes.

'I'm just glad you've got her under control,' I commented, unable to keep my eyes from her backside. 'Only I wonder if she's really been taught enough of a lesson tonight.'

For a moment he seemed thrown by my remark. I don't know what he'd been expecting me to say, but it wasn't that. 'You don't think she's been spanked hard enough?' he asked. I saw her swallow hard, gulping with anticipation.

'A few slaps with the hand aren't really enough,' I explained. 'It's not exactly discipline, is it? I mean, you've tickled her, but that's hardly what I call punishment.'

Alan nodded, intrigued by what I was saying. I saw her flick her eyes towards me and then look away, still too afraid to look me in the eyes. I was no longer worried; I liked the look of her and was staring openly, enjoying the sight of her reddened posterior, and of the way she was standing there between Alan and myself, vulnerable and exposed.

'And what do you call a proper punishment?' he asked

inevitably. I liked the note of challenge in his voice; my remarks had irked him in a way he'd not counted on.

'I'll be back in a second,' I told them both, and turned to leave the room.

'Where are you going?' she asked softly, hardly daring to speak.

'Never you mind where he's going,' Alan scolded.

I was in the kitchen in an instant, knowing exactly what to look for and where. I'd been their guest many times before and knew their house as well as I did my own. In seconds I had what I wanted and marched straight back into the front room.

'May I?' I asked, pointing to the sofa.

Alan stood up to make way for me. Maddy was panicking, trying to cover her breasts and her sex with her hands, which only made Alan and myself smile.

'Across your lap, or on the floor?' Alan asked.

'My lap, I think.'

She took one long beseeching look at Alan, but there was no mercy for her. I made way for her and she slipped over across my lap, the warmth of her body and the scent of her enveloping me immediately. My hardness pressed against her side, but I made no move to hide that. Her bottom was pink and soft, her buttocks slightly parted so I could glimpse the swell of her pussy lips.

I raised my hand and then brought it down hard. She squealed, her cry filling the room, a few decibels louder than anything Alan had elicited from her. I looked down and saw the fresh, red imprint of the wooden spoon across her right buttock. I touched it with my fingers, pressing hard against the redness, feeling the contours of the raised flesh. Alan peered across and nodded appreciatively.

Maddy seemed to be having hysterics, but I didn't let that interfere at all. The spoon smashed down hard again and again, the sharp slaps of wood on her firm flesh a delightful sound to my ears. I patterned her body with red marks, each as sharp and well defined as the last, across her buttocks, at the top of her legs, between her thighs. She squirmed and struggled, and I was in torment as my hardness pressed her soft body.

She cried out once, louder and more intense, and I realised that the pain had become pleasure for her. Her sex was moist, and I saw the sinuous way she moved and offered herself to the strict punishment I was giving her.

'Well?' I asked, a note of triumph in my voice.

'I see what you mean,' Alan replied thoughtfully.

'Stand in the corner,' I told her dismissively. Meekly she did as she was told, easing herself off my lap and limping to the corner. She understood what I was after, and turned her back to us so we could admire her punished backside from a distance.

Alan passed me my drink, and we stood in silence contemplating his wife's chastised body.

'Do you use a strap?' I asked, enjoying the warmth of the drink.

He nodded. 'Occasionally, though I prefer to use my hand. I've thought about getting a cane sometimes, like those old fashioned ones you see in documentaries about Victorian times. What do you think?'

'You have to be careful with a cane,' I explained, 'but if used properly they're an excellent instrument of correction.'

He laughed. 'You know,' he said, 'if I'd known you were such an expert I'd have called you in sooner.'

'She's slacking over there,' I pointed out. Maddy was no longer standing as straight as she had been, and she was touching herself surreptitiously, tracing the marks on her backside with her fingers.

'You'll stay the night?' Alan asked me quietly.

I gestured with my empty glass. 'I can hardly drive after what we've had in the restaurant and this.'

'Good, the spare room's all made up for you. Now to put things right.'

I gave him the wooden spoon and watched him cross the room. Maddy was taken by surprise when he grabbed her by the arm and pulled her to the armchair.

'Sometimes you just don't learn,' he snapped. He pushed her over the padded arm of the chair, pushing her legs apart with his foot. She was bent over, her beautiful breasts hanging free, the ripe nipples exposed completely. There was a dazed look in her eye, as though she had no idea what was going on.

'How many?' he asked.

'Six, and make them count,' I told him.

She cried out before the first stroke had even touched her. It snapped hard on her thigh, and then again, but higher up. He had taken my example to heart, and each stroke counted, each touch of the rough wooden spoon left it's mark on her quivering body. She sobbed and moaned, and I couldn't tell what was pain and what was pleasure for her.

She climaxed again, clawing at the armchair as her body spasmed from the intense sensation of being punished. When he released her I knew she had enjoyed an experience more intense than anything she had ever felt before. Not only had she been cruelly chastised by her husband, but her punishment had been witnessed by me, and I had punished her as well.

'Now it's time for you to get to bed,' Alan told her, his voice a whisper of excitement.

Hesitantly, as if afraid that she'd collapse, Maddy pushed herself from the armchair. She turned and kissed Alan on the mouth, a hot, passionate kiss that had her melting. I saw his hands reach down to explore the smarting cheeks of her behind.

At last he released her and she turned to me. Her chest was patterned red too, as though her pleasure had exploded all over her. She walked towards me and I took her in my arms. We kissed, our mouths joining, her body pressed onto mine. I could not stop myself, my arms traced the curve of her back and found the firm roundness of her bottom, her flesh giving over a raw heat that was completely sexual.

'Thank you,' she whispered, her eyes ablaze with gratitude and excitement. 'This has been the best birthday present I've ever had. I'm so happy, so very happy.'

'It's okay,' I told her, 'I'll be here tomorrow morning too. If thing's aren't right I'm sure Alan won't mind if I put you across my knee.'

She turned to him excitedly, and he nodded his assent. 'It seems to me that I've got a lot to learn too,' he admitted. 'Anytime you think Maddy needs warming up, then be my guest.'

'And this,' I said quietly, 'is the best birthday present I've ever had.'

Promotion

'You're not nervous, are you?' Todd asked me as we pulled up to the massive wrought iron gates that guarded the entrance to the estate.

'A bit,' I lied, smiling because I could tell he was as nervous as I was. He'd been nervous about it all week, ever since he'd got the phone call from Jack Salter.

Todd smiled back, and was about to say something when the gates began to creak open. 'Don't worry,' he said, looking away from me and towards the estate, 'Jack's a nice guy, I'm sure you two will get on.'

He steered the car carefully between the black gates and on to the gravel drive that curved ahead of us into a dense copse that almost obscured the view of the grand house in the distance. Of course I was nervous, why shouldn't I be? Not only was Jack Salter extremely rich, powerful and well known, he was also Todd's boss. Now, out of nowhere, the two of us had been summoned to his estate to meet him. It was routine, Jack liked to get to know all of his employees, but it still made us nervous. What if I said something stupid? What if I embarrassed Todd? What if… All week I'd been going over the possibilities and all week I'd been hoping that something would crop up and we'd have an excuse not to go.

Todd drove slowly, the tyres crunching up the gravel, until we were through the trees and in clear view of the house. I'd seen it once on TV, but now, in the glorious summer sunshine and under a clear blue sky, it looked like a palace. Which it had been, once, before Jack had taken it off some down-at-heel aristocrat and restored it to its full, majestic brilliance. The acres of land around went with the house, a vast expanse of rolling green, woods, and stretches of water glistening in the sun.

'It's like something from a film,' I said, my voice almost a whisper despite the fact that we were alone and in the car.

'They say this place put him back a few million,' Todd said, a note of pride in his voice. That was the thing about Jack Salter, he seemed to inspire loyalty in everyone who came into contact with him. I knew Todd was the only one who felt a sense of admiration for a man who'd made millions from nothing and yet still came across as a normal sort of man rather than an accounting machine with a computer instead of a brain.

'I wish we didn't have to do this,' I said quietly as Todd steered the car into a space near the entrance. Ours was the only car there, alone in the shadow of the great mansion, which only added to my nervousness.

'Don't worry,' Todd insisted, trying to inject a relaxed note into his voice. He was tense, but I knew he couldn't admit that to me.

'What if I say the wrong thing?' I asked.

Todd took my hands in his and looked at me. 'Don't worry,' he repeated, 'he doesn't bite. Look, forget everything you've heard about him, treat him as though he's just some other bloke.'

I shook my head. 'But he's not, is he? I mean, he's your boss for a start. Our whole future depends on him, doesn't it? I mean, if he likes you then you'll do well, and if he takes a dislike to you then…'

Todd cut me off right there. 'Don't think about it like that,' he insisted. 'Just relax, okay?'

I nodded, though there was no way I could relax. 'I'll do my best,' I promised, feeling once more out of my depth. God, here I was only just gone eighteen, and I was going in to meet one of the most powerful men in the country. What could I possibly have to say to him? I knew I was going to come across as some tongue-tied silly girl…

Todd was out of the car first, and he came round and opened my door. I stepped out and felt the cool breeze touch my thighs. I was wearing a summer dress, short, loose, cotton, and way too simple for the occasion. It was Todd's idea, and now I wished I'd dressed up a bit more.

'You look fine,' Todd remarked, as though reading my mind.

He took my hand and we began to walk towards the house. In the distance I could see a group of men working in the fields, putting up fences, and beyond them a lake sparkling with jewels of light. It was so peaceful, a perfect summer's day, the sort that only the very rich can afford.

There was someone at the door to greet us, a ready smile to hand. She was tall, elegant and tanned, with long blonde hair and deep blue eyes. Todd had obviously met her before, they shook hands and said hello and then she turned to me.

'You must be Elaine,' she said simply, speaking with the effortless diction that only those born to wealth can acquire.

'Hello,' I replied, nervously returning her smile. She seemed friendly enough and I longed to know who she was. Jack wasn't married, we all knew that, but was this woman his girlfriend? Whoever she was she was dressed immaculately in long wrap-around skirt and a simple silk blouse. Simple but expensive, that was obvious.

'I'm Amanda,' she said, 'I work here at the house. Come on, Jack's out by the pool.'

We entered the house and followed her through a hall that could easily take our flat and still leave room for a party. The walls were lined with ancient portraits, coats of arms and the like. A wide oak staircase curved upwards to our right and left, heading up to a first floor landing that looked down over the hall. There were doors to left and right, and corridors leading off all over the place. I felt dwarfed by it all.

'This place is amazing,' Todd remarked, probably impressed by the vast scale of things. He always seemed to take pride in Jack Salter's success; there was never any hint of envy in his voice.

Amanda laughed softly. 'I don't know,' she said, looking over at us and smiling broadly, 'I sometimes feel like I need a road-map to find my way around.'

I smiled because she had put into words exactly what I was feeling. 'It's like visiting a stately home,' I said.

She laughed again. 'I know,' she agreed, 'but at least there are no crowds here.'

Although outside it was hot and sticky, inside the air was cool and still, as though the house was untouched by what went on around it. We walked in silence until we came to a door which lead out to the back. Amanda opened it and the bright light spilled inwards, offering us a view of the back of the house and the rest of the estate. The light dancing on the pool was dazzling, a shimmering gold vision that drew the attention instantly.

'Go on through,' Amanda told us, perhaps sensing our nerves.

I followed Todd, stepping on to the paved path that cleaved a pure green lawn in two and which led directly to the pool-side. Jack was there, on his feet and waiting for us. He looked relaxed in pale cotton trousers, a short-sleeved shirt and deck shoes, the only sign of ostentation the gold ring that flashed in the light as he held his drink.

He walked over to meet us, flashing a smile that seemed like the real thing rather than a mask of politeness. He shook Todd's hand vigorously and then turned to me, fixing me with his grey-green eyes. My stomach did a somersault as I shook his hand and mumbled a hello to his greeting. I'd seen him on TV and in the newspapers, but in the flesh he was different. His dark brown hair was streaked with silver, his face slightly lined, and the expression in his eyes both intense and detached. I was blushing, I realised, and that made my face burn even more.

'Looks like we've picked a good day for this,' Jack said, his gravely voice filled with good humour. He indicated that we should take a seat, and there were several arranged in a semi-circle facing the cool blue water of the pool.

'You must be parched,' Amanda said, smiling at me in particular, 'what would you like to drink?'

I hesitated, wanting Todd to sit down first so that I would know where to sit too. 'I'll have anything cold,' I said, slightly flustered.

'Mineral water for me,' Todd said, speaking confidently.

Amanda was still waiting for me. 'Elaine?' she asked. 'Would that be okay for you too?'

'Yes, please,' I agreed.

Todd finally took a seat next to where Jack had been sitting and I sat next to him, reaching out so we could hold hands. I was trembling slightly and my nerves showed no sign of abating. I glanced at Jack and saw that he was looking at me. I lowered my eyes instantly and blushed again. For some reason I hadn't expected to find Jack such an attractive man, perhaps because in my mind I'd never seen him as anything but Todd's boss, some absent figure who had so much power over our lives but who hardly knew we existed.

'This is great,' Todd said eagerly, looking across the cool expanse of the pool to the rolling lawn that stretched out into the distance.

'On a day like this who could ask for more?' Jack asked.

'That's right,' Todd agreed. I could sense his excitement, he was so pleased that we had been asked, and was dying to make a good impression.

'What do you think, Elaine?' Jack asked.

I smiled shyly at him. 'I think this is just so… Just such a perfect day…'

'It is,' Jack agreed, flashing me another smile.

I returned the smile, our eyes meeting for a second, and

then I glanced back at Todd. He was sitting on the edge of the seat, hunched forward slightly, still tense. He was all edgy, he had things to say and was just dying for the chance to get it all off his chest. For a moment we were quiet and all I could hear was the gentle lapping of the water in the pool, a sound so seductive in the summer heat. The deep blue water rippled gently, touched by the barest whisper of a breeze.

'Here comes Amanda,' Todd said, breaking the silence.

I looked up to see her coming up the path, relaxed and beautiful, her hair catching the light, her long limbs outlined by the long, wispy skirt. She came over with a tray and we took out drinks, the glasses icy cool to the touch and filled to the brim with sparkling water and slices of lemon.

'Would there be anything else?' she asked, turning to face Jack.

'No, that'll be all, thanks,' he told her.

She smiled at me once more and headed back to the house. For a moment I had wondered whether she might have been Jack's girlfriend or something, but now it was clear that she worked for him.

'Well, I suppose you're wondering why I've invited you out here,' Jack remarked.

Todd and I both smiled.

'I've a lot of people working for me,' Jack continued, 'and it's easy to lose track of who's who and who's doing what. That's why I like to take an interest in people, especially those people who look like they're doing well,' and then, after a slight pause he added, 'and I've heard nothing but good things about you, Todd.'

Todd looked like he'd just won the lottery. He looked both shy, embarrassed and extremely happy all at the same time. 'I just do my best,' he mumbled awkwardly. I was pleased too. I was glad that all those long hours at work, all that extra effort, had been noticed.

'I know you do,' Jack said, 'and I want you to know that

it's not taken for granted.'

'I didn't think it was,' Todd said hurriedly. 'Actually, I've been thinking about the Anderson contract…'

Jack laughed and shook his head. 'Let's just stop there,' he said gently. 'No shop talk, remember Elaine's here.'

'No, it's okay,' I protested, 'you carry on, I don't mind.'

Todd squeezed my hand; I'd said the right thing of course. 'It's just that I've had this idea…'

'No,' Jack insisted. 'This is a social occasion, no business talk, okay?'

Todd was reluctant to let it go but he nodded his assent. I felt a twinge of regret, because I knew that Todd had been building up for the chance to expound his idea for days. At work he was never allowed direct access to Jack, there were always layers of management in the way, and on the rare occasions he did meet Jack there was always something else to discuss.

'So, Elaine, tell me about yourself,' Jack suggested.

I swallowed hard. What was there to say? Again I glanced into Jack's eyes and was surprised by what I saw there. 'I… I'm going to college,' I mumbled hesitantly. My heart was beating so hard that I was certain that they could both hear it.

'Studying what?'

'Computers,' Todd replied for me.

Jack ignored him. 'What exactly?' he asked me.

I shifted uncomfortably in my seat and then became aware that my short dress had ridden up and that my long tanned thighs were almost completely on display. I looked up and realised that Jack was looking directly at me. I felt too embarrassed to move, as though smoothing down my dress would bring even more attention to the fact that he was looking at my legs.

If Todd registered my discomfort he showed no signs of it. 'Tell Jack what you're doing at college,' he urged.

'I'm doing a course in computers in business

administration,' I said, speaking quickly and keeping my eyes fixed on the swimming pool.

'Is that a degree course?' Jack asked.

'A diploma course,' Todd answered. This time I was annoyed, Todd was beginning to answer for me all the time.

'Todd, come on,' Jack said quietly, 'why don't you give Elaine a chance to speak? It's okay,' he said, turning to face me again, 'there's really no need to be nervous.'

'I'm sorry,' I said, finally plucking up the courage to smooth my dress down and to get more comfortable.

'That's okay,' he told me reassuringly. 'It's one of the by-products of being famous, it makes people nervous, I know. But there's no need to be, really there isn't.'

His expression was so charming that it made me feel much better. At least he knew how I felt, I imagined that it would have been so easy to be oblivious to such things. I glanced round at Todd, but his expression was anything but charming. I saw the darkness in his eyes and realised he was feeling bad. Jack's tone had been friendly enough, but he'd definitely put Todd in his place when he'd told him to give me a chance to speak.

'So,' Jack continued, 'tell me what you plan on doing when your course is finished?'

I was just about to answer when Amanda arrived.

She looked apologetic. 'I'm sorry about this, Jack,' she sighed.

Jack stood up wearily. 'I'll be as quick as I can,' he promised.

Amanda shook her head. 'Actually, Jack, it's not for you. It's for Todd.'

We all looked surprised, none more so then Todd. He stood up instantly. 'What is it?'

Jack walked over to Amanda and slipped his arm around her waist as she showed him the fax she was holding. 'It's your office,' he told Todd, 'it looks like they can't do without you.'

Todd read the fax quickly, his face betraying signs of nervousness again. 'Is there a phone I could use?'

Amanda and Jack turned towards the house, and as they did so I saw that his hand was resting on her bottom. They both seemed very relaxed still, but his hold was somehow more than just innocent or accidental. His hand was moulded around her bottom, squeezing gently, holding her quite possessively. I was so transfixed by it that I hardly noticed what was going on. Amanda started to walk back to the house with Todd, and Jack stroked her backside fully as she went off.

'Don't look so worried,' Jack said, turning to face me.

I swallowed hard. The sight of him touching Amanda had made my heart race once more. It stirred something within me. Although Jack was old enough to be my father, I felt drawn to him. He was an attractive man and the fact that he had touched Amanda so intimately only served to make him more attractive and more powerful.

'Is it something urgent?' I asked, at a loss for anything more to say.

'Quite likely,' he said, smiling. He walked over and sat down beside me, in the seat that Todd had just vacated. 'I'm sure Todd will have it sorted out in a few minutes.'

I smiled and nodded, nervous once more because of Jack's sudden proximity and the fact that I was finding him more and more attractive in spite of it. There was a confidence about him that I had never experienced before. He was a man totally at ease with himself and totally in control of the situation.

'I notice you keep looking at the pool,' he said, stretching his legs. 'On a day like this a good swim's like heaven on earth.'

I was grateful for a neutral topic to talk about. 'I can imagine,' I agreed, turning to face the expanse of shimmering water.

He laughed softly. 'You don't have to imagine,' he said,

'I've no objection to you taking a swim if you like.'

'But I haven't brought anything with me.'

He shrugged. 'That's not such a big deal, I'm sure Amanda's got something you could wear back in the house.'

The idea was appealing, but without Todd there I didn't know what to do. 'No, it's okay,' I said, 'I'm sure you didn't invite us round so we could use your pool.'

'What did I invite you round for?' he asked.

His voice was low, quiet, almost a whisper. I glanced over at the house, but there was no sign either of Amanda or of Todd. 'You invited us round to get to know us a bit,' I ventured nervously.

'Almost right,' he said, smiling.

I avoided his eyes. 'What did you invite us for?'

'So I could meet you,' he replied.

For a moment I expected him to laugh, but he wasn't joking. I blushed furiously, unable to react any other way. 'Why?' I asked, finally.

'Because Todd is likely to go far in my organisation, so I need to know as much about him as I can, and that includes finding out about his partner.'

Any further conversation was cut off when we spied Amanda and Todd coming back. Even from a distance I could see that Todd was flustered. As he drew closer I could see that beads of sweat had formed on his face, making him appear even more agitated.

'I'm sorry about this,' he said, directing himself to Jack and not to me.

'A major disaster?' Jack responded calmly.

Todd smiled, but it was more nerves than anything else. 'No, it's not a disaster, but I do need to go in to work I'm afraid.'

I stood up, and it was only then that Todd seemed to remember who I was. 'Never mind,' I said quietly, 'I'm sure it won't take you long to clear it up.'

Jack looked at Todd and then at me. 'If they need you

then they need you,' he told Todd, 'but does this really have to spoil Elaine's day?'

'No, it's okay,' I insisted quickly, attaching myself to Todd's arm, 'I can wait while Todd sorts this thing out.'

Jack shook his head. 'Nonsense,' he declared, 'on a hot day like this the last thing you need is to sit in a car and swelter or to hang around an office while Todd's rushing around sorting things out. Why don't you stay here? Todd, what do you say?'

I squeezed Todd's arm, desperately hoping he'd take me with him. 'If you really don't mind,' he told Jack.

Jack laughed. 'Why should I mind? In fact Elaine was just saying how she'd like to go for a swim. Amanda, can you fix her up?'

Amanda smiled graciously. 'Of course, Elaine, it'd be a pleasure.'

I was frozen into place. I didn't want to stay. 'But…'

'There's no buts about it,' Jack said, standing up. 'Todd, how long do you think you'll be?'

Todd shrugged. 'Most of the afternoon,' he guessed.

'In that case we'll expect you back at around six,' Jack said.

Todd looked relieved. 'I really am sorry about this,' he said, but again he was speaking to everyone but me.

'Let me see you out,' Amanda said, taking a step towards the house.

Before I knew what was happening Todd had pecked me on the cheek, whispered a hurried goodbye, and was on his way. Instinct told me to chase after him, but I knew if I did that I would ruin things for him. I watched him go, suddenly afraid that I was going to be left alone with Jack for the rest of the afternoon.

'That's a smart young man you've got yourself,' Jack said, turning to face me. It wasn't idle chatter, I could tell he meant it and that he took such things extremely seriously.

'Thank you,' I said, sitting down again. The sun sparkled

on the water and the rolling lawn looked lush and verdant as it stretched out ahead of us.

Jack walked to the water's edge and then turned to me. 'He's also a very accommodating young man,' he continued. 'What about you?'

'Me?'

He looked at me earnestly, his eyes boring into me, as though he could see through me and into what was in my head. 'Yes you,' he said, his voice assuming that low tone that touched something deep inside me. 'Are you accommodating?'

My face was red again, but this time I did not look away. 'I don't know what you mean,' I told him, doing my best to meet his steady gaze.

He smiled. 'I'm sure you do,' he said. 'I like you, I think you'll be good for Todd. You're a smart girl, ambitious too, I imagine.'

I should have been flattered by what he was saying, but instead I felt as though a trap were being laid for me. Jack's charming smile did nothing to hide the dark undercurrent in his voice. I swallowed hard and turned away, unable to face him any longer.

'Elaine?'

I turned with relief to face Amanda, who had returned after seeing Todd out. Her smile was warm and friendly, and I breathed a sigh of relief for her presence. 'Come on,' she suggested, 'come back to the house and I'll see what we've got for you.'

Jack nodded approvingly. 'Yes,' he said, 'the water's at its best on a day like this.'

'Poor Todd,' Amanda said as we walked back into the cool interior of the house, 'fancy having to drive back in all this heat.'

'I would have gone with him,' I told her quietly, wondering if she had picked up on my disquiet.

'Why?' she laughed. 'You couldn't have helped, could

you?'

'It's not that,' I admitted.

We walked into one of the rooms at the top of the stairs. The window was open and the sun was streaming through, making the room appear light and airy despite the heat. A large double bed sat under one wall, flanked on either side by dark wood cabinets, and a half open door led to an *en suite* bathroom in the other corner.

Amanda sat on the edge of the bed and crossed her legs, causing her long skirt to fall open almost to the top of her thighs. Her skin was tanned a golden brown, her long, smooth thighs perfectly proportioned. She was beautiful. I had seen models on the catwalk who would have given anything to have her style, elegance and good looks.

She smiled. 'What is it then?'

I looked at her and remembered the way Jack had stroked her backside. 'Nothing,' I said, realising that what I had to say sounded silly.

'Is it Jack?' she guessed, not losing her smile.

I nodded reluctantly. 'He scares me,' I confessed, barely whispering the words.

'He's a very powerful man,' she said simply. 'Of course that scares you. What are you? Nineteen? Twenty?'

'Eighteen,' I said.

'Then that's no surprise. Jack's an attractive man, he has money, power, intelligence. Of course that's going to scare you.'

'What about you?' I asked, too shy to make my question more explicit.

She touched her tongue to her glossy lips before replying. 'I work for Jack,' she explained, 'and when he wants me then I'm there for him, in every sense of the word.'

My face coloured again. 'And does he…?'

Her smile broadened. 'Often,' she said. 'Come on, we're not here to talk about my sex life. Let's get you changed for the pool.'

She stood up and walked to one of the wardrobes. A few seconds later she turned round and offered me a one-piece black lycra swimsuit. 'There, this should fit,' she said, handing it over.

The fact that I now knew that she and Jack were lovers meant I was a little more relaxed. After all, with her around why should he be interested in me? 'Where shall I change?' I asked her.

'Here,' she replied, as though it were obvious.

I smiled shyly. I would have preferred some privacy, but Amanda made me feel safe. I turned my back to her and slipped out of my little dress, letting it fall in a bundle around my ankles. I caught sight of myself in the mirror on the wardrobe, my pale skin matched by ivory coloured bra and lacy panties. I unclasped my bra and let that fall too, and then wriggled out of my panties.

'You're very beautiful,' Amanda murmured softly.

I turned and saw that she was watching me intently, her brilliant blue eyes fixed on me. I half smiled and hurried to put the swimsuit on, but she stood up and came over to me. She put her hands on my shoulders and turned me so that she could look at my reflection in the mirror. 'Look at yourself,' she said softly, her breath warm and inviting on the back of my neck.

I looked, but my attention was on her. She was so close to me that I could feel her heat on my naked back. 'But you're the one who's beautiful,' I said softly, unable to look her in the eye.

She kissed me softly on the shoulder. 'No,' she demurred, 'I think you underestimate yourself.' The feel of her lips on my skin was an unexpected pleasure, the soft coolness of her mouth like a whisper on the breeze. Her hands moved down and round, coming unexpectedly to cup my breasts. My nipples were already beginning to harden in response, even though I felt as much fear as I did arousal.

She held me for a moment, her hands holding my breasts,

my nipples pressing against her fingers, and all the while her eyes were on mine. My face was flushed red, but there could be no denying the sudden excitement that flared in my tummy. She kissed me again, and this time I turned towards her. I didn't know if it was what I wanted, but her lips seized mine suddenly and her tongue slipped into my mouth. I returned the kiss, my head swimming with conflicting feelings, even though I could feel the fire between my thighs.

She turned me towards her fully and we kissed again, a long, slow kiss that made me feel dizzy. Her hands stroked my breasts again, pressing hard, holding me possessively in the way that Jack had held her.

'You see,' she said, her mouth still close to mine, 'you are beautiful.'

'I…'

She kissed me again, pressing her mouth to mine and pushing her tongue deep between my lips. Her hand slid smoothly down my back and she held my bottom, pressing me against her body. I was naked and felt defenceless, powerless to resist her. My arms went around her neck instinctively, and my kisses assumed an urgency driven by this unexpected desire.

'Jack's waiting…' she whispered, moving back a little. Her eyes glowed with desire, a desire that I felt too.

The sudden loss of contact gave me a chance to react. I stepped away from her, frightened to go any further. 'Please,' I said, 'let's stop this now.'

She half smiled and then stepped back to sit on the bed. Her skirt fell open once more and I had to tear my eyes away from her long, lithe thighs. What was happening to me? I'd never kissed another woman in my life, and yet I had accepted her caress as naturally as I would have Todd's. Except Todd had never made me feel so sexy or so desirable.

I put the thought out of my mind and pulled the swimsuit on quickly.

'There, I told you that would suit you,' Amanda commented happily.

I looked in the mirror and realised she was right. The dark black material contrasted with the slight pink flush of my skin. The fact that it was not too revealing only served to make it look even sexier.

'It does look good,' I said, unable to hide the fact that I was surprised as well as pleased.

'Come on, the pool's waiting,' she said.

I slipped my sandals back on and we walked back through the house. I was nervous again, suddenly afraid that Jack would sense what had passed between Amanda and myself. Did Jack know that Amanda like to kiss and touch other women?

Jack stood up as we approached. 'There, isn't this better than going back with Todd?'

The truth was that I wasn't sure. Amanda's behaviour – and my response – only seemed to complicate things even more. The only thing I was sure of was that the water looked incredibly inviting.

'Can I go in?'

Amanda stood by Jack and he slipped his arm around her again. 'Of course,' he said, gesturing at the pool, 'just enjoy yourself.'

I smiled and stepped into the water. It was colder than I had anticipated, but once I launched myself into it all my misgivings were swept away. The water was perfect. I swam to the other edge of the pool and turned back to see Amanda and Jack both looking at me, smiling. His arm was around her waist and I knew that he was probably stroking her backside again. The thought excited me once more, and I was glad of the water to hide the fact that my nipples were erect again.

I swam for a while, giving myself a chance to relax. Jack and Amanda were sitting down, talking quietly and ignoring me, which was just what I needed. The atmosphere was dreamy; it felt as though nothing in the world could destroy it. Occasionally I'd rest, holding onto the pool-side to enjoy the view of the distant trees, or to admire the grand old house, touched by the light of the sun.

'Do you want another drink?' Amanda called to me later.

I shook my head. 'No, I haven't finished my last one yet,' I replied.

She walked over to my seat and picked up my glass, still half full. She walked over to the edge of the pool and knelt down to offer it to me. I swam back, using long, deep strokes to propel myself through the cool water. As I drew closer I had to stifle a cry of shock. Amanda's split skirt was open and this time I could see that she was wearing nothing under it. Her sex was revealed, shaved, completely naked. She smiled to me, making no move to cover herself, as though she were enjoying my shock.

'Don't you like it?' she asked quietly.

Jack was sitting back, reading a book, his feet up. I glanced at him but he showed no sign of knowing what was going on. My hand was shaking as I took the proffered glass. I looked into Amanda's eyes and saw the desire there, still aflame. My heart was pounding as I looked between her thighs again and realised that I felt attracted to her.

'It's okay,' she whispered, 'you don't have to say anything. I can see it in your eyes.'

I coloured instantly. It seemed that I could not deny myself. I felt completely defenceless, unprepared to deal with the strange yearning she had created within me. I had never imagined myself capable of feeling desire for another woman, but then I'd never met a woman like Amanda before.

'Had enough already?' Jack called.

'Yes,' Amanda replied for me, 'she was just getting out.'

She stood up and let her skirt fall chastely around her once more. I looked at her, so effortlessly cool and yet so incredibly sexy at the same time. And what about Todd? I had never been unfaithful in the two years we'd been together, not once had I felt attracted to anyone else. But in the course of a single day I had found myself drawn first to Jack and now I felt something even stronger towards Amanda.

'Come on,' Amanda urged me, 'I'll show you where the showers are.'

I climbed out of the pool and stood there for a minute, rivulets of water coursing down my body and forming a puddle around my feet.

'I told you that'd be good,' Jack remarked, smiling.

'It was, thank you,' I said, trying to avoid his eyes.

'Good, now we need to talk,' he added, his tone quite insistent.

I nodded. 'Of course,' I agreed.

'Come on,' Amanda said, 'I'll show you where you can get changed.'

I followed her round the paving alongside the pool and then to a small chalet hidden behind dense bushes and shrubs. There was a shower block there, on one side, and a couple of changing rooms next to a larger games room and bar.

'Amanda… Please, we mustn't…' I said as she took me by the arm and drew me closer to her.

'It's okay,' she said softly, 'just trust your own instincts.'

That was the problem, I could no longer trust those instincts. 'I don't want to do this,' I whispered as she kissed me lightly on the cheek.

'Is that the truth?' she asked, kissing me once more. She was so close I could breathe her scent and feel her warmth against the coolness of my wet skin.

I looked away. 'This isn't fair on Todd,' I told her.

She took my face in her hands and made me look directly at her. Our eyes met and I melted inside. She kissed me on the lips, softly at first, but I opened my mouth to her, unable to hold back. We kissed for a long while, mouth to mouth, our bodies close but not quite touching.

I allowed her to slip the swimsuit from my body so that I stood wet and naked in the bright summer light. The fullness of my breasts was emphasised by the hardness of my nipples, and I could feel the wet heat between my thighs. She found a towel and rubbed me down quickly, her hands brushing against my breasts, thighs, bottom and tummy. When she finished I fell into her arms and we kissed again, a harder, deeper, more sexual embrace. Her fingers stroked pleasure across my breasts, making me moan softly.

'In here,' she suggested, taking me by the hand and leading me into one of the changing rooms. I barely had time to register how spacious it was before I had my arms around her and we were kissing once more.

She took my hand and pressed it against her breast. I touched her gently, half afraid of myself for doing so. She used her fingers on my nipples, and then she bent low to take one into her mouth. I staggered back against the wall as the waves of pleasure rocked through my body. She teased each nipple in turn with her mouth, making me close my eyes and cry out with pleasure. I had not known that such pleasure existed, she suckled lovingly, her tongue lapping across my nipples of such blissful sensation that I knew I would soon climax if she didn't stop.

I parted my thighs and felt her fingers stroke me there softly, barely caressing my pussy lips yet sending tendrils of pleasure snaking through me. The pleasure in my sex and the pleasure in my nipples was the same thing, a single interconnected sensation that made me sigh and whisper as she touched me.

Her fingers found my moisture, seeping like honey from my sex. She teased my pussy lips apart, opening me to even greater pleasure. I rocked against her fingers, grinding myself down, rubbing my clitoris against her hand as her fingers penetrated my pussy. I felt engulfed by waves of pleasure that left me gasping for more.

She knelt down in front of me and looked up, a wry smile on her lips. 'Do you really want this?' she asked.

'Yes… yes…' I whispered deliriously.

She kissed my pussy gently at first, the cool lips of her mouth touching the moist lips of my cunt. I was wet with desire and she licked it up with the very tip of her tongue. She smiled and then began to suck me there, using her lips and tongue to taste me, to push into my sex, to lap against the swollen bud of my sex. I arched my back as she swirled her tongue over my clit and used her fingers to go inside me. I shuddered and moaned as another finger pressed against my anus and then, wet with my pussy juices, she penetrated me there too.

My cry of orgasm reverberated around the room as I climaxed over her mouth. Her fingers were inside me and my body flexed and convulsed as the pleasure took me. I slumped down into her waiting arms, my strength taken from me by the power of the most intense orgasm I had ever experienced.

She held me tightly for a while, kissing me softly so that I could taste myself on her mouth. I opened my eyes and gazed at her dreamily.

'So beautiful,' she whispered, and kissed me once more.

'I've never…'

'Don't talk,' she told me, putting her fingers over my lips. I could breathe the scent of my sex on them and the thought excited me again. My body was tingling all over. No man had ever made me feel so alive.

She took my hand and kissed my fingers lovingly. 'And now it's my turn,' she said quietly.

I lay down on the floor and she squatted over me. I looked up and could see the pert curves of her bottom, the dark button of her anus, and the puffy lips of her pussy. She lowered herself over me and I reached up to hold her bottom, gently pulling her pussy lips apart. I pressed out my tongue and touched it gingerly between her thighs. I had never tasted another woman before but she tasted good, and soon I was lapping greedily at her sex.

She moaned softly as I licked and sucked and my fingers explored her body. As she moved I pushed my tongue against her anus and she murmured her approval. I licked her long and slow, caressing every inch of her pussy and anus before searching for her clitoris. Her own fingers sought my pussy once more and she soon fell across my body.

The pleasure of being licked again was redoubled by the pleasure of licking her. We sucked and explored, giving each other an unselfish pleasure that made me whimper and writhe. When she was close to coming she sat up again, pressing her bottom over my face so that my mouth could connect directly to her sex. I pushed my tongue into her again and again and then used my fingers on her clit. She bucked and squirmed and then her strangled cry of pleasure filled the room.

I climaxed a second time, this time I was on the floor, my tummy pressed flat and my bottom lifted high. Her fingers fucked me hard, pushing into my wetness while she licked my anal hole repeatedly until I orgasmed.

She found a robe for me and wrapped me in it, kissing me all the time, whispering endearments and promises. I felt too dazed and confused and sated to register what was going on. We emerged from the changing room into the searing light and still I did not know what was happening.

Jack was waiting for us by the pool-side.

'Well?' he asked her.

She smiled. 'She was a good girl for me,' she reported.

I turned to her and tears filled my eyes. 'But…'

She kissed me tenderly on the mouth. 'This is what you wanted,' she said, 'and it was what I wanted to.'

Jack smiled at me. 'It's good to see that you're a smart girl, too. I'm sure you and Todd can both go far in this organisation.'

'I don't understand,' I whispered.

Jack took me by the hand and pulled me down onto the seat beside him. He pulled my robe open to expose my breasts, the nipples still red and erect where Amanda had so skilfully sucked them. I reacted instantly and pulled away from him.

'Do I really need to punish you?' he snapped irritably.

Amanda took my hands and forced them away from my robe. 'Be a good girl now,' she cautioned, looking me in the eye as she spoke.

'I trusted you…' I said, my voice filled with a sudden bitterness.

She leaned forward and kissed me hard on the mouth. I tried to turn away, but then I found myself responding once more. My mouth opened to her and I tasted my juices on her lips. She kissed me hard and then pulled away from me sharply. 'Be good for Jack, now,' she told me.

I let her guide me across his lap, moving into place so I was poised over his knees. The robe was pulled away gently so I was naked again. I looked back over my shoulder and saw that he was enjoying the view of my bottom, offered up so temptingly.

'I knew you'd turn out to be an accommodating girl after all,' he informed me calmly. He stroked a hand down the length of my back and then the other up the inside of my thigh. I sighed as he rubbed and caressed my body, his powerful hands moulding my body, exploring every inch of me. When his fingers grazed against my pussy lips I felt the pleasure explode inside me. He parted my bottom cheeks gently and caressed my pussy lips from behind, taking the wetness and then touching it to my rear hole. I sighed and, almost against my will, I lifted myself higher, opening myself completely to his explorations.

'This is to remind you to always be good,' he warned.

I screamed with the sudden impact of pain. I turned and looked back over my shoulder and saw him raise his hand again. He swept it down in a wide arc that finished explosively on my bottom. I began to struggle and Amanda held me in place, pressing down on my shoulders as he beat me again and again. Soon I was lost in the rhythm of the punishment, the heat of correction mingling with the heat of my desire. My sobs of pain were sucked into Amanda's lips as she kissed me hard, pressing her mouth to mine, pushing her tongue between my lips.

Soon I could not tell where the pain ended and the pleasure began. I was lifting myself into each stroke, offering up by backside so he could punish me harder. My sobs of pain and complaint were now sighs of compliance. He spanked me across both bottom cheeks and across the top of my thighs. I knew my skin was marked a deep scarlet, that his hands were imprinted on my flesh, and yet I wanted more.

Amanda lay back on the ground and opened her thighs to me. Jack eased me from his knees and I knelt down between her long, smooth legs. I looked back at Jack, and he nodded his assent. I put my lips to Amanda's pussy and pressed my tongue into her groove, working her juices onto my tongue so I could swallow them greedily. She moaned audibly, her pleasure spurring me on.

In a moment Jack was on his knees behind me and I felt his cock press against my sex. Despite the smarting pain on my bottom and across my pussy lips I was completely wet. I moved into place and felt his cock slide deftly into me. He filled me completely with his hardness, going deep into my cunt and making me tremble with pleasure. He took me by the waist and began to fuck me hard, his long strokes filling my pussy, going back and forth and stoking up the pleasure burning inside me.

Amanda turned over onto her tummy and offered me her behind. I parted her buttocks and began to lick her dark, anal opening, delighting in the forbidden pleasure. My fingers pressed into her pussy, fucking her with the same joyous rhythm that Jack was fucking me with.

Amanda climaxed first, her cry of pleasure echoing across the pool and out into the sunshine. Moments later I cried out and fell forward as Jack thrust into me. He tensed and then spurted his come deep into my sex, making me climax at the same time. I lay there for a while, and then Amanda roused me and took me back to the house.

I dozed for a while, drifting in and out of sleep. Later Jack came into the room and sat on the bed. We spoke for a while and then, without any protest from me, he took me forcefully in the mouth. I sat on hands and knees and sucked his hard cock, eager to take every inch of it and then swallowing his seed with a thrill of pleasure.

Finally, just before Todd arrived back, Amanda and I made love again. Slowly this time, enjoying every second of it. I knew then that I was in love with her, and that I would be there for her and Jack whenever they wanted me.

When we had finished, and Amanda had made me look presentable again, we walked back downstairs to find Jack and Todd deep in conversation.

Todd was beaming, a look of pure satisfaction on his face. He walked over and kissed me on the cheek. 'I hear you've had a good day,' he reported excitedly.

'Yes,' I said, suddenly feeling sick with guilt.

'I'd say that you and Elaine have obviously got a good future with us,' Jack told him.

Amanda smiled. She put her arms on my shoulders and kissed me on the back of the neck. 'We knew you would,' she whispered.

I swallowed hard and turned to Todd. He grinned. 'It's okay,' he told me, 'Jack says you passed with flying colours.'

Amanda kissed me once more, on the lips this time, and her hand slipped under my dress to find that my pussy was still wet with desire.

Training

I had almost resigned myself to failure when I came across him sitting alone in a first class compartment. He looked up at me and smiled before I had time to fix my hair or anything, but as soon as I saw him I knew he was going to be the one. The train was rattling along, shaking from side to side as it picked up speed, making me feel a bit unsteady in my high heels. I struggled with the door to the compartment, hoping that the state of my hair and the way I was being thrown around by the train didn't give him the wrong impression. The last thing I wanted was for him to think I was drunk.

I heaved my case into the compartment and slid the door behind me, taking one last look in the corridor and glad to find it deserted. When I turned I found him with his face stuck in a book, reading it with the kind of fixed expression that you have to really try hard to achieve. He was deliberately ignoring me, doing his best to make me disappear, and the thought of it made me shiver with excitement. I got a good look at him; blond wavy hair, powerful build, clean-shaven, quite good looking behind his glasses.

I stepped into the carriage proper, pulling my case in with me. His baggage was in the rack above him, so I turned to the seat opposite and heaved my case up. I stretched, really pushing the case up, standing on tiptoe to get the extra leverage. The reflection in the window was perfect: my short skirt had risen up, revealing the marble white skin at the top of my thighs, the black band of my stockings, the lacy suspenders, my backside pressed out enticingly. The case seemed to be stuck, or rather I pretended it was stuck, so that I held the position for as long as possible, pushing up and down, my skirt riding higher and higher.

He turned to look in the window. I saw his eyes scan the crystal clear reflection, travelling from my knees, up a full length of thigh, over my tight round backside, pausing at my breasts, the nipples poking against my tight red top, and finally stopping at my face. Our eyes met, and for a moment I saw the hesitation, the sheer confusion in his baby blue eyes, then he turned away. The case slid into place and I relaxed, exhaling heavily, as if the effort had worn me out.

'It's a beautiful day,' he said conversationally, as I sat down opposite him.

'Yes, it's lovely isn't it,' I agreed, flashing him the sort of cold smile that I normally reserved for Jehovah's Witnesses or insurance salesman.

He nodded, then stuck his nose back into his book, reading my smile the way it was intended to be read. I sat back in my seat, leaned my head back against the wall and exhaled heavily once more. My knees were crossed, and from where he sat I knew he could get an eyeful of my long stockinged legs. I was balancing my foot on the high heel, surreptitiously pulling my skirt a little higher. Sure enough, I caught him glancing up from his book, his eyes feasting on my thighs then furtively returning to the book.

'You're a priest aren't you?' I said suddenly, though with a dog-collar, cassock, battered leather satchel and devotional book in hand he could hardly be anything else.

'Yes, that's right,' he smiled patronisingly, giving me a 'what do you want, bimbo', kind of look.

'You help people, don't you, Father?' I asked, making it sound as much like a demand as a question. My face was hard, my red lips glistening sexily, my eyes burning with a kind of fierce intensity. I was a lady with attitude, and I wanted him to know it.

'Yes... yes I do. Though you don't have to call me Father,' he said, taking off his glasses to get a better look at me.

'I want to call you Father,' I insisted. 'And you help anyone, right?'

He hesitated, but I wanted an answer, I was looking straight into those lovely blue eyes and I knew that he was hooked. 'If we can,' he agreed, his voice slow and soft, very thoughtful, very mature. I sighed, he sounded so strong, as if he were a million years old and not some young man of flesh and blood and still not thirty years old.

'Will you help me, Father?' I asked softly, turning round slightly, so that my skirt was pulled back several inches, the stocking top completely exposed, the breeze passing through the carriage grazing the smooth skin of my thigh.

'If I can,' he agreed, his eyes homing in on my thighs. He looked up from the bare flesh and our eyes met, his face flushed red, the colour burning on his pale skin. I felt the pleasure pulse through me, but on the surface I remained calm, pretended not to notice his embarrassment, nor the fact that he couldn't keep his eyes off my legs.

'This is a sort of confession, Father,' I started, putting my face in my hands, guiltily.

'But this isn't a confessional...' he interrupted.

'But I need this!' I cried, looking up at him with an expression of purest pain and anguish. My eyes were already wet with tears, I saw him through a blur, looking quite alarmed.

'As you wish... my child,' he stuttered.

Again I sighed, the excitement growing inside me, making my pussy begin to throb deliciously. 'There's something inside me, Father. Something that makes me think evil thoughts and do sinful things. It's inside me Father, and I can't help myself... Something shameless...'

'I see, my child,' he whispered, raising his eyebrows and fixing me with a look that had me squirming. 'What sort of sinful thoughts and deeds?'

I hid my smile by taking my head in my hands, bending low to hide my pretend shame. He was hooked, and now came the interesting bit. I uncrossed my legs, put them down straight, very modestly, side by side, but with my skirt pulled right back. He could see nearly all of my legs, he could see the white flesh of my thighs on both sides, and he was certainly enjoying the view.

'Everything you can think of, Father. Not just sinful thoughts about having sex with men I know. I'm ashamed to say it, Father, but I fantasise about making love to complete strangers, to men I have never met before and will never meet again.'

'I see,' he nodded. 'And do you act upon these sinful impulses?'

'Yes, Father,' I whispered, turning away from him. I caught sight of him in the window, the dirty glass acting as a perfect mirror. He was leaning forward, listening intently, but not intently enough. 'There are other things too, Father,' I added, realising that boring old promiscuity was not going to do it for him.

'Other things? Other sins of the flesh?'

'Yes, Father,' I half sobbed. 'Other sins of the flesh. In my mind I dream of other women, Father. I desire sexual contact with other women. I dream of lying naked in their arms, of being touched by feminine fingers, of being kissed by feminine lips. I dream these things and my body grows hot, I grow restless, unable to cope unless I touch myself. Is it wrong, Father?'

'It is very wrong,' he decided, and that made me feel even more excited. I loved being told I was doing wrong, it seemed to trigger a signal deep in my sex. I was wet, I could feel my pussy growing deliciously moist. 'Do you act on these desires?'

Was that it? Did the idea of two women getting off on each other ring any bells for him? 'Yes, Father... I have made love to other women too. I know it's wrong, I tell myself I shouldn't but then the desire is too strong. I let myself be seduced. I enjoy the feel of another women putting her hand under my skirt. I enjoy her fingers stroking my thighs, of touching me *everywhere*. And Father, I have allowed myself to be seduced by two women together. They made love to me, sharing me... I'm so ashamed...'

'Two women together?' he repeated, his face growing red. The idea seemed to appeal to him. He was leaning closer to me, his eyes fixed on my body, hands together under his chin. He looked good enough to eat.

'Yes, Father, on a number of occasions. I couldn't help myself. I met one of them at a health club. She came up to me in the showers and began to soap my naked body. The feel of the hot water coursing down my skin and the feel of her fingers on my back soon had me aching with desire. Her fingers touched my breasts as if by accident, but then I responded, I touched her back. Soon we were making love under the jets of water, kissing, sucking, touching each other. I wanted to resist but couldn't.'

'And the other woman?' he asked hotly, sounding rather strained. He crossed his legs, and I cursed the fact that he was wearing a cassock, I couldn't see the size of his erection. Almost there, I told myself.

'We made love until I'd climaxed, and then she called to her friend. I was still feeling dazed, it had been a very violent orgasm, and I hardly knew what was going on. Before I knew it I was making love with the second woman, she was exploring my naked body under the rushing water. They took it in turns, making love to me several times. After that they took me whenever they felt like it. They would call me up and tell me to be a certain place at a certain time and I would go. Sometimes they made love to me in turn, sometimes it was all three of us together.'

'I see,' he said, shifting round, trying to make himself more comfortable. 'You say they took you whenever they wanted. Surely it is correct to say whenever *you* wanted.'

'Are you blaming me, Father?' I asked, sounding appalled by the suggestion. 'I was weak, they took advantage of me. I couldn't resist, they only had to caress my body, touch me in my feminine places, and I was at their mercy.'

'So there was an element of coercion involved? They forced you?' he asked excitedly.

Bang! That was the key. 'Yes, Father,' I said, and it took all my willpower to keep that miserable tone. 'They forced me, much as I didn't want to. And sometimes if I wasn't good they would punish me.'

He coughed, his eyes bulging dangerously. 'Punish?' he managed to ask, straining to catch his breath and appear calm.

'Yes, Father. On many occasions they physically punished me. It hurts even to talk about it.'

'Then it is good that you talk about it,' he insisted. 'If you bottle it all up then it does no good.'

'They would punish me like a naughty girl, Father. One of them would pull my knickers down and bend me over her knee. I'd beg her not to chastise me, but it wouldn't do any good. She would pull up my skirt and then spank me several times on the bare bottom. It hurt me so much I'd scream and sob, but that only made her more determined.'

'How did she punish you? With her hand? A slipper?'

'It started with her hand. But then she moved on to using the flat side of a hairbrush. She would smack me until my bottom was red hot. I could see myself in the mirror. By the end of a session my bottom would be patterned red and pink, all over my buttocks and at the top of my thighs, and even on my breasts sometimes.'

'Would you have to display yourself?' he asked eagerly.

Display myself? I didn't know what that meant, but I could tell from his eager expression that it was important to him. 'I'm not sure what you mean, Father.'

'Did she make you stand in a corner, displaying your chastised posterior?'

'Yes, yes. She would make me stand in a corner, holding up my skirt so that she and her friend could admire by smarting backside. It was so humiliating, Father. But the worst of it was that I enjoyed the humiliation, I enjoyed being spanked. Afterwards they would fuck me like a whore, and I'd have the most intense orgasms of my life. I loved being degraded by those two women.'

He said nothing, his posture matched my own, he was leaning forward, face hidden in his hands. I could see his hands were shaking, and the colour had drained completely from his face. Outside it was raining, the world speeding past was a liquid blur. Had he read Freud, I wondered. Did the symbolism of speeding trains mean anything to him?

'Will you help me, Father,' I pleaded.

'What can I do, my child? Do you seek forgiveness for these wanton sins?'

'More than forgiveness, Father. I know I have sinned and I need to be punished, I need to suffer for all the wrongs I've done,' I said evenly, the excitement pulsing in my veins making it harder and harder to control myself.

'Punishment?'

Our eyes met and I saw the doubt expressed there. 'Yes, Father. Punish me.' I fell forward, to my knees, in front of him. He tried to sit back but I buried my face in his lap, pressing my tits against his thighs. My face brushed against his prick, it's divine hardness buried in the thick vestments that were a mark of his ministry.

'As you wish, my child,' he whispered, his voice quivering, ready to crack. I sat up on my knees and rolled my skirt up, revealing completely my black stockings and suspenders. He sat back and I bent over his lap, lifting my backside up as high as possible. My panties were soaked through, the dark patch between my thighs clearly visible. He pulled my knickers down and I felt the breeze brush between my thighs.

The first smack sounded so unreal, a high pitched slap of skin on skin that was almost drowned out by the rattle of the train. If the sound was unreal then the sharp dagger of pain that shot through me wasn't. It stung, but the pain was turned to pleasure, the red imprint of his hand connecting to the delicious excitement in my pussy. He spanked me several times, long hard strokes, moving from buttock to buttock, rouging my skin and building layer upon layer of exquisite pleasure.

'I've been a bad girl, so very bad,' I cried, wishing he would verbally chastise me as well as physically.

'So very bad,' he repeated breathlessly. 'And now you are being spanked for it.'

The heat on my backside was delicious in itself, but I wanted more than just a sound spanking. 'But, Father,' I cried, 'this is how those sinful women treated me. It's the same pleasure I feel, you must show me how wrong I've been...'

'How child? How?'

I passed my hand over his lap, found his prick and squeezed it lovingly. We said nothing, we understood. I slipped from his lap and knelt against the seat where I'd been sitting earlier, my backside raised, smarting painfully, the juices from my pussy running down my stockings.

It took a second, but when I turned round I saw him standing over me, his prick red and hard in his hand. I arched my back, opened my aching pussy with my fingers, then guided his cock deep inside. The pleasure pierced me. I climaxed immediately, my cry filling the compartment. He thrust forward, fucking me quickly, filling me with his lovely hardness. He was inexperienced, his rhythm rough and ready, violent, passionate. I climaxed again, enjoying the feel of his cool body against my burning backside.

His cry was muted, as if at the moment of his orgasm he remembered himself. He filled me with thick cream then withdrew quickly. I fixed my clothes slowly, slipping my panties off and stuffing them into my bag. He was already nosing through his book, his ashen face turned away from me, lips quivering tearfully.

We remained silent until the train drew slowly into the station. I reached for the bag. The skirt rose up and I knew he was looking at my uncovered backside, still stinging red.

'You know, Father,' I said, smiling guiltily. 'I tell a lot of lies.'

'I'm sorry?'

'All that stuff about the other women, it wasn't true,' I admitted.

'But why... for what reason?' he mumbled, looking askance.

'My real sin is seducing men of the cloth. Nothing turns me on more than sex with a young priest.'

The look of pain and confusion on his young face was pitiful. I sort of shrugged, grabbed my bag, and went to the door. I turned, saw him still looking lost. I stepped out onto the platform then turned back.

'It's all right, Father,' I assured him, putting my head back into the train. 'You're the sixth priest I've seduced this way. The others enjoyed it as much as you did.'

I watched him fall back into his seat, burying his head in his hands. He looked so sexy then, I almost climbed back into the train.

Assignment

Felicity arrived promptly at three that afternoon, just as had been agreed previously. She was good like that, Clive could not fault her there. In many ways she had been the perfect secretary: attentive, hard working, punctual, very good at her job in every conceivable way. Damn it, she'd even had the right degree of sexiness, and she knew how to charm clients, that too could not be denied. Perhaps that should have been a clue, the fact that she was so perfect in every respect...

'I hope I'm not late,' she remarked with a smile when he opened the door to her. She knew she wasn't late and was making a point of it, but he could forgive her the small conceits.

'No, you're right on time, as usual,' he said, making way for her. She was wearing a smart business suit of short skirt, white blouse and matching jacket. The eye was drawn naturally towards her, to her long silky smooth legs, the pale tan of her flesh contrasting to the darkness of her clothes. She liked to look good, that was obvious, and as always she had done a perfect job.

He showed her the way through the house and up the stairs to his office, aware of the way she was looking around with unconcealed interest. It was the first time she'd been to the house, and of course she was curious to see her employer's house. The office was the largest room in the house, on the first floor overlooking the garden, and beyond that the woods. Though functional it was a bit more relaxed than his other office, though it was still a working office and not a den for him to hide away in.

'There's lots of room,' she said, going straight over to

the window to look out across the way.

'I get a lot done here,' he explained, trying to carry on a conversation he hadn't planned on.

'There are less distractions here, I suppose,' she said, turning from the window and flashing him a smile. Her long blonde hair caught the light, golden curls cascading over her shoulders, lighting up her eyes and face.

'Yes, very few interruptions,' he agreed woodenly. 'Would you like a coffee before we start?'

'Love one, thanks,' she agreed.

'Make yourself comfortable then,' he suggested, pointing to the computer at his desk.

'Do you want me to make it?' she offered helpfully. 'If you let me know where the kitchen is I can do it.'

'No, it's okay. Why don't you get ready, I'll only be a few minutes.'

He left her at the desk, leaning over to switch the computer on. Her short skirt revealed much of her long thighs, and the way she moved, slow and sinuous, only accentuated the fact. She had never looked so beautiful, the streaming sunlight heightened it, and the severe cut of her suit added to it too.

There was no point rushing, and he settled back against the counter as the aroma of fresh coffee wafted around him. It gave him time to think, to ponder on what to do next. He was attracted to her of course, what man wouldn't be? And her choice of outfit was designed to allure, she was sending all the right signals. Not that he needed such signals, he'd long understood what the message was. In the past she had worn skirts inches shorter than the one she was wearing now, and worn blouses that exposed the firm bulge of her breasts. Her eyes sparkled when they spoke, and she liked to lean across his desk in a manner that was painfully arousing. It was even Felicity who had suggested working together during the one weekend when his wife was away.

Carefully carrying two mugs of coffee on a tray he made

his way back up the stairs, heavy footfalls and the heavenly smell of fresh coffee signalling his arrival. She was at the desk, busy tapping at the keyboard. She turned and smiled to him. Her jacket was draped neatly over the back of the chair, and she was perched on the very edge of the seat. Her legs were crossed, sharp high heels glossy black in the sunlight, skirt pulled back an inch more to reveal long, lithe thighs that were all the more attractive because they were bare. Her white blouse was unbuttoned, the lacy whiteness of her bra almost visible.

'That smells good,' she exclaimed, reaching out to take the cup that was offered.

'Started already?' he asked, gesturing at the computer screen.

'Yes, I was just reviewing what you'd already done,' she explained quickly.

'How did you know the password?' he asked casually.

'I guessed... I just tried Cleo and it let me in,' she said, with a slightly apologetic shrug.

'Too obvious really,' he mumbled to himself. Having his wife's name as his password had been too painfully obvious, and now that he thought about it he could have kicked himself.

'Oh damn!' she shrieked suddenly, pushing herself back from the desk as the coffee splashed down all over her.

'Are you okay?'

'Oh, I'm so sorry!' she wailed, standing up and trying to brush the wetness from her clothes. Somehow she had spilt waves of coffee all down her blouse and over her skirt, making a real mess of things. The desk was splashed with coffee too, as was the screen and keyboard.

'It's not your fault,' he said, though his voice indicated otherwise. While she was more concerned with her clothes his first concern was the computer, and the few tissues to hand were used to wipe the coffee from that.

'What do I do now?' she complained, looking down at

herself pityingly. Her clothes were ruined, the snow-white blouse would never be the same again, and the skirt sported a sharp jag of darker colour where the drink had soaked through.

'You'll have to change,' he told her, realising that there was no alternative.

'But Mr Sheppard, I haven't got anything else...' she said, looking at him with widening eyes. Was she really that shocked? Or was it a game she was playing?

'I'm sure Cleo's got something that fits,' he suggested, smiling for the first time.

'Won't she mind?' Felicity asked, also breaking into a smile of complicity.

Clive shrugged. 'She's not here to mind,' he said. 'And besides, this is quite innocent, isn't it?'

'That's right,' she agreed, happily, 'it was an accident.'

The master bedroom was on the other side of the landing, just a few steps from the office. 'This is a lovely room,' she commented admiringly, taking in the bedroom which had been interior designed by Cleo herself.

'My wife designed it,' he explained proudly.

'She's very good.'

'Now,' he said, crossing over to the wardrobe, 'let's find something for you to wear.'

'You choose,' she suggested, 'dress me the way you'd like me.'

'Flirting again,' he laughed, then turned to look at the neatly arranged outfits hanging in the wardrobe. Cleo liked to dress up, and her range of outfits was more than a match for anything that Felicity had worn to the office. He flicked through quickly and selected a loose fitting dress, long enough to cover everything and so remove temptation completely.

'Well?' Felicity asked, her voice a low whisper. She had slipped off her top and her skirt and was now standing in the centre of the room clad only in bra and knickers. Her hands were crossed coyly over her chest, a gesture of modesty that did nothing to dispel her seductive smile. Her legs were slightly crossed, one in front of the other, skimpy white panties barely concealing the bulge of her sex. As he stared she shook her head, letting the long golden tresses fall over her shoulders.

'You look stunning,' he said finally.

'Do you really think so?' she asked, turning to one side, adopting a pose.

'You know you do,' he told her.

She turned her back to him, showing him her behind, the skimpy pants pulled tight against her bottom cheeks. The supple curve of her back unblemished, the tone of her skin perfect. 'Do you really want me to wear that?' she asked, pointing to the long straight dress he was holding. 'I could work like this if you like. Until my clothes dry.'

'And we'd work, would we?'

She smiled coyly. 'We could do lots of things...'

'It was a happy accident then, the coffee?'

'What do you think?' she asked, lowering her eyes coquettishly.

'I think you have a great deal of explaining to do.'

'Oh my God...' Felicity gasped, stepping back, her face a picture of dismay as she looked up to see Cleo standing in the doorway.

'You look surprised to see me,' Cleo said, a smile forming. She raised her eyebrows expectantly, waiting for Felicity to get over the initial shock and to try to explain what she was doing.

'But... but you were supposed to be away...' Felicity mumbled, looking beseechingly at Clive for support.

'And that gave you free reign,' he remarked, walking across the room to join his wife. 'That's why you were so keen to join me this weekend.'

Felicity grabbed her wet clothes and held them tightly against her chest, trying to cover herself only moments after flaunting her desirable body. Her face blazed red with embarrassment, and her eyes were filled with nothing but confusion.

'Perhaps you'd like to explain this?' Cleo suggested, holding up Felicity's black handbag and taking a blue diskette from it.

Felicity looked dumb, her eyes fixing on the small square of plastic that Cleo held up, the silver cover catching the light from the bedroom window. 'I just wanted to make a safe copy of our work,' she whispered feebly.

'Is everything on there?' Clive asked.

Cleo nodded. 'All the files that you'd been working on at home, including the tenders for jobs that we'd only just started working on,' she explained.

'I'm sorry... I didn't want to do this,' Felicity admitted, bowing her head contritely.

'You've been breaking the law,' he explained coldly, 'you do realise that. Why did you do it, Felicity? You've been treated well, your salary's more than fair. Why did you betray us like this?'

'I didn't want to...' she wailed, collapsing onto the bed, throwing herself face down and burying her head in the pillows. 'Nick made me do it, he said it wouldn't do any harm... He said it would help us...'

'Enough of that, girl!' Cleo snapped angrily.

'It wasn't my fault... I didn't want to do it... Nick forced me...' Felicity sobbed.

'You won't get any sympathy from us,' Cleo told her. She unclipped the handle from the patent leather handbag and strode decisively over to the bed. Without hesitating she swung the looped strand of shiny black leather down onto Felicity's pert backside.

There was a sudden silence, and Clive could not help but stare at the thin red stripe his wife had smacked down onto Felicity's curved backside. A moment later Felicity dared to look up, lifting her head from the furrowed pillows to meet Cleo's steel-grey eyes. 'I've been so stupid,' she mumbled, 'that's probably the most I deserve.'

'What you deserve,' Cleo decided, 'is a sound spanking, young woman. If I were in your position that's what I would hope for, unless you'd prefer to tell your story to the police.'

'This Nick, is he your boyfriend?' Clive asked soberly.

'No, not exactly. He's a friend of a friend, but I owed him some money and he said I could pay it off by getting a few files from your computer,' Felicity confessed. Her bottom was prominently displayed, and across it the red stripe was like a beacon that attracted the eye.

'We'll deal with him later,' Cleo said. 'Now, young woman, I think it's time you accepted your punishment.'

There seemed no hesitation in Felicity's eyes, only a sparkle of excitement that she could not quite hide. There was relief also, as if a great weight had been removed from her shoulders. 'Which one of you is it going to be?' she asked softly.

'I want you across my lap,' Clive told her, pointing to the end of the bed.

'I am ever so sorry, Mr Sheppard,' she apologised, crawling across the bed to where he had pointed. She moved sinuously, her graceful body toned and tanned, a sleek creature captivatingly attractive.

He exchanged a sly smile with his wife and then proceeded to the bed. He sat comfortably and then made way for Felicity to crawl over his lap. She moved into position without question, as though it was something she was used to.

'You've been punished before?' Cleo asked, voicing the question for both herself and her husband.

Felicity's face coloured red as she nodded. 'Yes,' she admitted, her voice barely audible, 'I've been smacked before...'

Clive raised his hand and brought it down, silencing Felicity and Cleo at once. Felicity winced, held her cry, and dug her long painted nails into the bed. Her body was warm and sensual across his lap, and when he breathed her scent filled his lungs. Her lacy white panties could not hide the blush of her flesh, reddening quickly where his heavy slap had landed. A second smack, focused on her other bottom cheek, was followed by a third and a fourth. He smacked her hard, rhythmically, the flat of his hand tingling as he beat out her punishment. She was moving against him, unable to stop herself as the chastisement proceeded.

Five, six, seven. Each slap sounded through the room, and her body responded as she accepted the pain. At last she could hold back no longer. She squealed and buried her face in her hands, her long legs kicking as the strokes became harder and more deliberate.

'Stop that, girl,' Cleo commanded, annoyed by the kicking and struggling. She moved forward decisively and grabbed hold of Felicity's knickers and pulled them down sharply, exposing the punished curves tanned a deep red by the volley of hard smacks.

'Please... I'm sorry...' Felicity whimpered miserably.

'You need to be taught a lesson,' Clive hissed.

Again he began to smack her, his hand moulding to the globes of her behind, each stinging impact making her gasp audibly. At the top of the thighs her skin had reddened, and her strength was going, she could no longer hold her composure. As her flesh burned he could see the moisture pour from her sex, the redness of her bottom spreading through to arouse her sexually.

At last the spanking stopped, and Felicity almost fell to the floor. She stood up shakily, her hands moving naturally to her behind. Her face was still red, but now the flush was of excitement and not shame. All thoughts of modesty had disappeared, she no longer tried to coyly conceal her sex, all she wanted to do was to rub away the smarting pain from her behind.

'Stop that,' Clive snapped, grabbing Felicity's wrists and pulling her hands away from her bottom.

'I'm sorry, Mr Sheppard, but it does sting so terribly,' she complained with a pout. Her panties slipped down from between her thighs and down to her ankles, a frilly white bundle between her feet.

'How often have you been spanked before?' Cleo demanded, exchanging a significant glance with Clive.

'Not often,' Felicity mumbled, looking away from Cleo's piercing stare.

'Obviously,' Clive remarked. He could see the finger marks on her backside reflected in the mirror by the bed, the outline of his hand over her bottom cheeks and upper thighs.

'Why were you here today?' Cleo asked, taking a step behind Felicity. She reached down and ran her hand over the reddest parts of Felicity's behind, her fingers lightly stroking the heat away.

'To get the files,' Felicity confessed sullenly.

'Then why did you try to seduce me?' Clive asked, tightening his grip on her wrists.

'I... I didn't...' Felicity whispered, swallowing hard as she realised she was caught in his iron grip.

'But you did, my dear,' Cleo whispered softly, her voice filled with menace.

'No, the coffee was just an unfortunate accident.'

'You'll be punished again for the lies,' Clive warned. 'Now, the truth if you don't mind.'

'It was Nick,' Felicity wailed, 'he said that if we had sex you'd want to keep quiet if you discovered that the files had been copied.'

'He sounds like an excellent character,' Cleo sighed. 'Is he the one that punished you before?'

Felicity seemed to lose the power of speech. She shook her head slowly, cascading golden tresses that caught the sun, her mouth forming words that did not come out.

'Did he threaten you with punishment if you didn't cooperate?' Clive suggested. He didn't relax his grip on her wrists. Instead her pulled her arms lower, forcing her to bend at the waist, giving Cleo a better rear view.

'Or did he spank you as a reward?' Cleo suggested, smiling broadly.

'How did you guess?' Felicity asked, her voice filled with surprise, her eyes wide with shock.

'I understand,' Cleo assured her sympathetically. 'You did wrong though, and you've been punished for it. Now it's my turn to punish you, for trying to seduce my husband.'

Felicity cried out as the leather strap landed suddenly on her already punished bottom cheeks. She tried to escape but Clive held her fast, pulling her arms lower and forcing her to bend over to receive her second dose of correction. The strap swished through the air and landed with a crack of sound, each stroke succeeded by a gasp of breath from her pretty lips.

Cleo showed no mercy. She was as ruthless as Clive had been, marking Felicity's behind with line after line of redness. She understood the feelings running through the punished girl's mind, she understood also the way the pain had become pleasure through some mysterious process.

'We'll deal with Nick ourselves,' Clive was saying. 'You'll deliver the diskettes but the data will be meaningless and it'll ruin whatever scheme he's cooking up.'

'In the meantime,' Cleo added, wielding the strap with just that extra bit of severity, 'we will have to continue to look after you in case you get into more trouble.'

'If you're to remain as my employee then you have to accept your punishment regularly, both from myself and from Cleo,' Clive added.

'Yes... sir...' Felicity sighed, lifting her pert backside higher as the strap came down hard against her naked flesh.

Beauty and the Beast

Belle lived on the edge of the village, in a tumbledown house with her father and two sisters. It was a poor house in a poor village, and every evening, when the sun fell behind the distant mountains, the house was shrouded in the dark cold shadow cast by the castle high on the mountain peak to the south.

Once, when Belle was a child and her mother still lived, she asked her who inhabited the castle. The woman had looked at Belle with tired eyes and whispered, 'The Beast lives there. Alone with the base desires that no man should have. Beware my darling, always fear the Beast.' Belle had shuddered, and though her mother had long since passed away the words had remained fresh in her mind, a powerful and frightening warning.

Belle's father was a good man but weak, and the men of the village would take him for a fool. Often they would invite him to the tavern, and once there make him drink ale until he was roaring drunk. And when he was drunk he forgot all about his daughters, he forgot about their poverty, and about their humble existence in the shadow of the mountains. When he was drunk he was a man again, a hero, a lord, ready to prove his worth to all the world.

On such occasions the innkeeper would send a boy round to Belle's house, summoning her to retrieve her father. It always filled Belle with such shame to see him so drunk, his voice raised in imaginary triumph, to the raucous and cruel laughter of the men from the village. And then they would tease her too, pulling up her skirts to expose her long shapely thighs, pinching her nipples shamelessly, rubbing themselves against her body as she struggled with her father. They teased her too because she was still a child at the age of eighteen, her body still chaste and untouched by any man. The teasing made her so ashamed, her pretty little face would flame red and her clear blue eyes would fill with tears.

One evening, when the summer had already given way to autumn, the young innkeeper's son came knocking on the door of the small cottage. Belle rushed to the door, her long blonde hair flowing like gold about her pretty shoulders.

'Belle, Belle,' the young man said breathlessly, looking at her with sadness in his sharp brown eyes.

'What is it Pierre? Is it father?' Belle asked, her heart sinking at the thought that she would have to rescue him once more from the circle of sneering men in the inn.

'Yes Belle,' Pierre said softly, and something in his manner made Belle fear the worse.

'What's happened? What is it Pierre?' she asked urgently.

'It's the hunters from the village, they were just joking with him Belle, but he took it so seriously...'

'Took what seriously?'

'You know what he's like when he's had his fill of ale. He's a lion, a champion. We couldn't stop him Belle...'

'Please Pierre,' Belle implored him, her blue eyes open wide with mounting fear, 'tell me what has happened.'

'He's gone to the castle, Belle, to kill the Beast.'

Belle fell backwards, fainting away with fear and horror. Pierre reached forward and took her by the waist. He held her close, his hot breath on her fair skin. She opened her eyes and gazed into his, searching for the sign that Pierre would help her.

'We must stop him,' she whispered, holding on to his strong muscular arms for support.

'No Belle,' Pierre said softly. He kissed her gently, his lips pressing hers, his hands brushing her breasts like whispers. 'Your father has taken the fastest steed in the village, Belle. All is lost. The Beast will have devoured him already. Forget him, Belle, forget him completely.'

Belle's eyes fluttered, the feel of Pierre's fingers playing softly with her nipples took her breath away. She felt a fire igniting in her belly, making her feel hot and languid. But the delicious feeling could not mask out the full horror of the situation. With an effort she pushed Pierre away, kissing him softly on the lips as she did so, as if the desire he had awakened in her was fighting back against the urge to save her father.

'What can you do, Belle?' Pierre demanded angrily, releasing her from his manly grasp.

'I can go to him, save him. Perhaps he has fallen, perhaps he has become lost in the great forest, perhaps...'

'Stop it, Belle,' Pierre snapped irritably. 'Your father was a drunkard, a good for nothing, and it is better that he's gone.'

'No!' Belle sprang forward furiously, the anger pulsing in her veins. She pushed Pierre away forcibly, and ran past him to the horse tethered at the front gate. In a moment she was riding away through the darkness and towards the forest, Pierre's angry shouts lost in the wind rushing through her hair.

Belle rode hard and fast, not wanting to stop, not wanting to think of all that Pierre had said. The galloping of hooves, the feel of the strong animal between her thighs, the exhilarating feel of the night air rushing past, soothed her anger. In a while she was riding through the forest, the darkness closing in on her, the thick trees crowding round her as she rode.

A path through the forest seemed to open up and when she looked back it was gone, as if the forest were opening itself for her, sucking her into the darkness that led to the castle. The canopy of trees obscured the moon and the stars, and when at last Belle was at the castle gate she suddenly felt nervous, realising that she had no way back, no way to navigate through the darkness.

Belle dismounted. She held the reins tightly and pulled the horse towards the gate, glad to have the hot sweating animal beside her, it's breath misting in the cold night air. The drawbridge fell suddenly, the rattling chains and booming wooden track frightening the horse. It reared up, knocking Belle to the ground, then bolted away into the forest that swallowed it up, leaving her alone and afraid.

She walked hesitantly across the drawbridge, following the candlelight that flickered before her, floating like magic on the air. She walked through long corridors of stone, the light leading the way, cutting a path through the darkness just as the forest had opened for her. She was led into a great dining hall, the table set for two, flickering candles throwing a soft orange light.

'Hello? Is anyone there?' Belle asked, her sweet voice carrying like music into the thick black darkness.

'You have come,' a voice boomed from the darkness, a deep voice, rich and powerful.

'I've come for my father, is he here?' Belle asked, spinning round slowly, searching for the source of the great voice, a voice that effected her strangely, making her nipples pulse as they had done under Pierre's fingers.

'Yes child,' the voice boomed, 'he is here. Locked in a dungeon where the light never shines.'

'Please sir, he meant no harm,' Belle pleaded, her voice full of the sound of tears.

'Nonsense!' the mighty voice cried angrily, the echoes bouncing from wall to wall until it faded to silence.

'Please sir, let him go. He is a good man, foolish at times but good at heart. Please sir, I have two sisters. Without him they are lost...'

'I care nothing about your sisters! I care nothing for him. He came here to destroy me, do you wish that I allow him that pleasure?'

'No, sir, no. You are kind, I can feel it in your voice.

Please spare him, great sir, take me in his place.'

There was a pause and Belle breathed hard, her heart pounding while she waited for the Beast to decide. She had not lied, there was indeed something in his voice, some undercurrent that she hardly understood but which she was certain carried with it the seed of good.

'There is a steed that awaits him at the gate. It is your choice, child. I give you the key to his cell, you may decide which of you is to stay.'

From the darkness the key floated forth, hanging in the air before Belle's disbelieving eyes. She reached out tentatively, sure the ghostly key was an image borne of her fear. She touched it and it was cold and real, an iron key that weighed heavy in her hand. The light floated before her again, ready to lead her to the dreaded dungeon under the castle.

'Thank you good sir,' she cried happily, her great joy filling her with optimism. She ran, bare feet padding on the stone floor of the castle. The dungeon was deep underground, and Belle let herself be guided by the strange light. The dark caverns echoed with the cries of lost souls wailing in the night, evil spirits cackling and baying for blood. Belle ignored everything, carried along by her certainty that the Beast was good at heart, just as her father was.

'Belle, is that you?' a tired voice asked, peering from the jet-black cell at the beauty cast in gold by the flickering light.

'Yes father,' she sighed, pushing the key into the rusty old lock and turning it with all her might.

'No, Belle, you must leave. You must leave.'

The door creaked open and the old man fell forward, clasping his beloved daughter in his tired old arms. 'No father, you must leave now. There is a mount waiting for you, to carry you through the forest back to my poor sisters.'

'But the Beast?'

'I will stay in your place father. Now, you must leave before he changes his mind.'

'But he is a Beast... You are so innocent, child, you do not understand what cruel and base desires lurk inside his soul.'

'Surely they are stories to frighten children,' Belle said bravely, managing a half smile to hide the fear deep in her heart.

'No Belle,' the old man whispered, 'I have already experienced the evil at his heart.'

Belle cried out, putting her hand to her mouth and staring wide-eyed at her father. He had staggered out into the light and Belle saw that his hair had turned from jet-black to snow-white, and his tired eyes were full of the horrors of which he spoke.

'I must stay father,' she said weakly. 'I have promised the Beast and cannot break my word. Please father, leave now and forget that you ever had me as a daughter.'

The old man kissed Belle on the forehead, his eyes filled with tears, and then he followed the light that was for him. In a moment he was gone and Belle was trembling, more alone than she had ever been in her life.

'You stayed,' the Beast said simply when Belle returned to the dining room.

'As I said I would,' Belle replied, holding her head up defiantly, willing herself not to be afraid of the thing that spoke from the shadows.

'You are foolish, more foolish than I ever imagined possible. Did you not see the fear in his eyes? Did you not comprehend the terror that he has suffered?'

'But there is something noble in you, sir. I can sense it. Am I not right, sir?'

The laughter filled the great room, reverberating and resounding until it filled Belle's ears with its harsh evil sound. She fell to the ground, covering her eyes as the thing emerged from the shadows.

'Do not speak of nobility to me!' the Beast roared. 'Look at me child! Am I noble? Am I?'

Belle looked up, her face as white as a sheet. The beast towered above her, a foot taller than any man she had ever seen, it's body swathed in bands of leather and thick animal hides, great thighs like an animal, arms bulging with hard muscle. It's face was obscured by a mask, but it's eyes shone through two slits, dark eyes that burned with a radiance that could have been good, evil, or something beyond that.

'Please, sir...' Belle whimpered, turning away from the vision before her, half man and half animal.

It bounded forward, and with one swipe of its hand it had torn Belle's dress to shreds. She flinched, tried to crawl away, but it held her fast. Her nakedness was before the Beast, her long thighs of alabaster, round breasts with red-tipped nipples like ripe berries, a tight triangle of hair to obscure the fleshy pink between her thighs. She was afraid, but excited too. The Beast's hot breath caressed her nipples, kissed her lips with a whisper.

'Such purity... such purity...' the Beast whispered to himself, his voice lost in wonderment. 'Such purity needs to be defiled!'

The Beast seized her in his hairy arms and turned her over, letting her fall to the floor once more, her full round bottom sticking up in the air. He touched her vilely, parting her bottom cheeks, stroking her between the thighs, rubbing his hands up and down her long thighs. Belle cried out, too afraid of him to enjoy the sensual feel of his body against hers.

'To be defiled!' the Beast repeated, his voice low and guttural. He pulled Belle closer and kissed her on the neck. His mouth was hot and sensuous, his lips skating over her soft skin. He moved down and kissed her between the bottom, his tongue snaking gently into her tightly puckered rear hole. Belle struggled, but the feel of his hot wet tongue entering her from behind made her feel faint with a sudden passion.

Belle struggled, trying to fight the strange passions bubbling inside her. She pushed and kicked, her tiny fists nothing against the Beast's great body. This futile resistance inflamed the Beast's anger. He pulled away from her, his long sinewy tongue still tingling with the forbidden taste of her rear hole. He pressed her down with one heavy hand and then began to beat her mercilessly, spanking her naked bottom with slow deliberate strokes.

Belle screamed. She could feel the soft skin of her tight round bottom flaring red. But her cries were to no avail, the Beast knew no mercy, the chastisement continuing until Belle's cries had become soft whispering sighs. Belle ceased squirming. The stinging fire on her red bottom cheeks was transformed into a delicious sensation pulsing through her body, making her nipples tingle with pleasure.

The Beast moved round, his hands seeking Belle's breasts and then pulling at the nipples, his claws squeezing tightly so that the pain danced through her. Belle felt lost, his strong arms were everywhere, touching, teasing, hurting, soothing. His tongue was now lapping at Belle's sex, the treasure that she had so jealously guarded from the louts in the village. She sighed, opening her thighs to his tongue which was alternately soft and smooth or hard and violent, going into her far deeper than any man could with any part of his body.

'And now to take you!' the Beast roared, licking his lips like an animal about to devour it's prey. 'I'll take you just as I took your father!'

Belle screamed. The Beast drew back and pulled the hides from its body. Her eyes were fixed on the monstrous organ that jutted from between its thighs. She wanted to scream again but held back, her voice lost in amazement. The Beast's stiff organ rose violently, many inches long, many inches round, the purple tip as long as her fingers.

'Please don't hurt me,' Belle whispered. She drew back instinctively, suddenly realising that her sex was aching, pouring forth a thickness that was white and creamy.

'Do you desire me, Belle?' he asked, his voice losing the cold harsh edge.

'Yes... yes...' Belle cried joyously, tasting the sweetness pouring from her sex, putting her fingers between her thighs and then sucking them clean.

'Do you desire the Beast? The thing that will take a woman and use her like a whore? The thing that will mark you with its scent the way an animal will mark its mate? Do you desire the animal that is man and the man that is animal?'

'Yes! Yes!' Belle cried.

The Beast rose silently, its cry of triumph shaking the very foundations of the castle. It stood over Belle and marked her as its own, a pure silver liquid gushing from it's hardness, spraying over Belle's nakedness, making her body shimmer and sparkle under the candlelight. Belle lay back, letting the hot liquid bathe her body, splashing onto her reddened nipples, onto her belly, into her sex, sighing with a secret pleasure as she did so. The Beast anointed her with the silver rain that jetted from his hard animal maleness, directing it from head to toe, to cover Belle in his essence.

Then Beast fell upon her, turned her over once more and pressed his hardness deep into Belle's aching sex. Belle cried out, mewing like an animal, letting the pleasure pierce the shell of humanity. She was part beast too now, part animal and part woman. The stiff tool filled her, pressed the damp walls of her sex, going deep to the heart of her pulsing cunt bud.

'Harder! Harder!' she cried, the eruption building inside her as the Beast covered her body. She screamed, her body froze, her back arched and her reddened buttocks pressing hard against the mat of hair that covered the Beast's body.

She had crossed over, she was part of him now, no longer Belle, but the Beauty that Beast had desired.

Exchange

Edward had expected to find Mercedes curled up in front of the TV when he returned home early from work. The world of afternoon television seemed to be endlessly fascinating to her, a world peopled by bronzed Australians facing moral dilemmas which were tackled with a cup of tea and lots of hugs. There was nothing like it on French television, and it had seemed to Edward that Australian soaps were the highlight of Mercedes' visit to England.

He slipped off his coat and stashed the briefcase in the study on the ground floor. The house was silent and he savoured the peace and quiet, a haven compared to the hustle and bustle of his office, or the organised madness of the motorway. Perhaps Mercedes had gone out for the day, she had spoken a number of times of visiting central London and he had supplied her with travel details and timetables. He hoped she had in fact gone out, it would leave him an afternoon of peace and quiet to enjoy.

Back in the sitting room he poured himself a scotch and looked around. As usual the evidence of Mercedes' presence was all around: the shoes she had kicked off casually and left in the middle of the room, a Parisian magazine left lying on the sofa, an empty coffee cup on the floor, waiting to be accidentally kicked over. It was annoying that she was so untidy because Jennifer had left strict instructions about it before she had departed. At the time Mercedes had listened gravely and assured Jennifer that all her instructions were to be followed to the letter.

The drink felt good, the warmth oozing down Edward's throat and spreading through his body. The strains of the day were beginning to fall away, and again he closed his eyes to appreciate the heavy silence of the house. The exchange visit had been Jennifer's idea, and though reluctant at first, he had finally agreed to it. His wife had decided to pick up on her French again, and had enrolled for classes at the local college. It had been a good idea; Edward often travelled to France on business and though he could order a meal and make himself understood to taxi drivers he could not hold a conversation with his French associates. There was no time for him to take classes, but Jennifer was a good teacher and she was soon helping him with the language too.

The exchange visit was the perfect opportunity for her to take a break in Paris and to practice the language with the natives. However, they had both imagined that the student she would exchange with would be of a similar age to Jennifer, in the late twenties. Mercedes had turned out to be not yet twenty and able to speak perfect English. Still, she was keen to travel to the UK and her own family just as keen to have Jennifer visit them. Perhaps, Jennifer had joked, it was the family that wanted to learn English, and not Mercedes.

It was too early for a second drink, and besides, there was probably still time for him to call Paris. He picked up the empty coffee cup from the floor and walked across to the kitchen. There again Mercedes had left her mark, a sink full of cups, sauces and plates, an open jar of coffee left on the counter, the kitchen table strewn with newspapers and breadcrumbs. Why did the girl never clean up after herself? He was certain that she was very different at home; Jennifer had described Mercedes' family as very nice, with a large house full of people that was somehow always spotlessly clean. By their own reckoning Mercedes was a bit of a tearaway, an impulsive, bright, inquisitive sort of girl who liked to do things her way.

Edward sighed. He would have to have another long talk with the girl. But he feared it would go the way of all the talks they'd had: she would listen sombrely, nod in all the right places, call him *monsieur* in a voice of utmost respect, and then carry on regardless. Still, it had to be done. The only consolation was that the first week had passed and that she would be gone in another.

He ascended the stairs wearily, wishing that the week would pass quickly and then things could return to normal. Next time, he promised himself, he and Jennifer would go away together.

The unexpected noise from his bedroom made him stop in his tracks. He pressed himself against the wall and inched towards the door. If Mercedes was out, then who was in the room? Very slowly he pushed the door open, the bright sunlight from the bedroom spilling out into the hallway.

Thankfully the door failed to creak its normal complaint, and as it opened slowly he could see clearly what was going on. The wardrobe door was open, the mirror on the inside of the door catching the light. Mercedes was standing by the wardrobe door, rifling through the hangers heavy with clothes, examining closely the contents of the shelves and the rack on the door.

'What the hell are you doing in here?' Edward demanded angrily, pushing the door open completely and bounding into his room. He was furious. Mercedes was staying in the guestroom and she had no business whatsoever going through his and Jennifer's bedroom.

Mercedes stepped back, mouth open and blue eyes wide with shock. The colour had drained from her face, and for the first time since she had arrived she was completely speechless.

'This is our room,' Edward cried, his anger undiminished, 'you have no right to be in here. What were you doing? Well, girl, what were you doing?'

Mercedes gasped for air, her full red lips opening and closing and unable to form coherent speech. She was dressed casually in loose T-shirt and a short black skirt, slit at the back. Her eyes were made-up, long fluttering lashes, eyebrows pencilled darkly to frame her pretty blue eyes. Full lips outlined in red lipstick that contrasted with the slight golden tan of her skin.

'Well? I'm waiting,' Edward continued, advancing a step towards her. His glance fell on the open wardrobe and he understood at once what it was that had drawn her attention.

'I was looking for something to wear, monsieur,' she managed to say, her voice soft and nervous.

'You have your own clothes, what did you want?'

'I wanted to travel to London, monsieur, but I did not have a summer jacket to wear with this... I thought perhaps that Madame may have had something appropriate...'

'Is that why you were looking in my wardrobe?' Edward demanded, pointing to the rack on the open door. It was lined with belts, canes, a heavy black paddle, all reflected in the bright light of the mirror.

'I... I...' she struggled for an explanation, but instead her eyes became fixed on the implements of punishment so neatly laid out.

'You were stealing,' Edward decided suddenly, his voice losing the harshest edge of anger but becoming lower and more devious.

'Non! Monsieur! You are mistaken... This is not true...'

'Perhaps, perhaps not,' Edward said. 'But how would it seem to your college if I rang them and explained these circumstances? Even the suspicion would look very bad for you.'

'Please, monsieur, I am very sorry for this. I did not come to steal. I was here to search for a jacket... in the beginning.'

Edward nodded. He could see that the truth was going to come out, she was not a thief but neither was she always truthful. If Mercedes had really been looking for a jacket she would have looked on the coat rack downstairs, or else she would have looked in Jennifer's side of the wardrobe. As if to prove the point he opened the other door of the wardrobe to reveal the closely packed hangers full of Jennifer's clothes, all of them apparently undisturbed.

'The full story, girl,' he told her firmly. He closed the second door of the wardrobe but left the first one open, noting the way the young French girl's eyes kept returning to the long leather belts and the canes hanging from the rack. How long had she been studying the various instruments of punishment in his collection?

'I was looking for a jacket but when I opened the wardrobe I saw these things... I was fascinated by it, monsieur... They are not for wearing?'

Edward smiled. 'No, they are not for wearing,' he admitted. 'They are for using, for punishing bad girls who should know better.'

'Like me?' Mercedes asked, her voice barely a whisper. She looked at Edward strangely, her eyes filled with fear and excitement in equal measure.

He nodded. 'You have taken advantage of my hospitality, young lady. This has been the last straw. I have a good mind to send you packing this instant, and to inform your family about your behaviour while you have been here. Do you think they will be pleased to hear this? Will it make them proud?'

Mercedes shook her head slowly. He could see the implications filtering through her imagination, the horror of it dawning slowly. Her eyes returned to the instruments of punishment, and the fascination she felt was self-evident. Any other woman would have ignored them, closed the door, not even noticed them, but not Mercedes. Just the look of the long bamboo cane with the curved handle seemed to attract her gaze and attention.

'I am truly sorry, monsieur,' she whispered, looking up into his eyes appealingly.

He reached out and took the cane from the rack, swished it once through the air for effect. She swallowed hard but did not try to run away, she did not even cry out in horror.

'You know what this is for,' he told her calmly.

She nodded, and then, without bidding, she turned her back to him slowly. She began to bend over at the waist, moving as though in a trance.

'No, across my knee young lady,' he commanded. 'You've acted like a silly child and that's how I'm going to punish you.'

She did not know what to do or how to react. She walked across the room towards him, stopped in front of the mirror, and waited. He sat on the bed and motioned for her to join him, pointing to a spot six inches from his feet. When she was ready he put his hands under her short skirt and pulled her knickers down, the pretty white bundle of frills sliding down her smooth thighs to her knees. Her face was bright red with embarrassment and her eyes resolutely avoided his.

Her skin was soft and warm, and he could easily guess how it would react to a few firm strokes. He bent her over his knees, positioning her so that she was well placed and balanced over his lap. She made not a murmur of protest, moving as though in a dream. Her skirt went up slowly, the strong afternoon sun warming her smooth legs as the hem was pulled over her waist. She had firm round bottom cheeks, pert and well shaped, the groove between bottom and thigh deep and attractive.

'Please, monsieur... Please...' she whimpered, finding her voice at last. It was too late. She was spread across his knees, her delicious derrière displayed completely in the clear orange light. She tried to kick out but her panties held her feet together.

'This is no time for tantrums,' he told her gruffly.

The first heavy smack of hand to bottom silenced her completely. He looked down and saw her softly tanned skin marked red with the imprint of fingers and palm. His guess had been correct; she had the sort of soft, mellow skin that would colour intensely at the softest spanking. His fingers rubbed the redness, tracing the slightly raised shape of his own hand on her hot skin.

The second hard spank matched the first on the other bottom cheek, marking her symmetrically so that the terrible smarting pain would be balanced. It was her first time, he was certain of that, and he intended to make sure it would not be an experience she would easily forget.

He began to spank her rhythmically, smacking fully with the flat of his hand, first on one cheek and then on the other. Her golden orbs clenched and unclenched as he beat her soundly, tanning her skin until it glowed red all over. He dealt swift blows at the top of the thighs also, and then aimed several between her buttocks so that she shook all over with the impact.

'Well?' he demanded, forcing her to her feet.

When she did not speak he grabbed her by the shoulder and took her to stand by the mirror. She looked over her shoulder at the punished globes of her backside, patterned a deep even red all over. Her eyes widened as she was displayed, her backside still quivering with pain.

Her nipples were hard, dark points pressed suggestively against her white cotton shirt. Her lips were slightly parted and her eyes misted over slightly. She had enjoyed her punishment, though he did not think she had ever expected to receive such chastisement.

'I'm sorry, monsieur...' she whispered, her voice hot and breathless. She parted her legs slightly and bent over, sticking her bottom out more to get a better view of it in the mirror. Her eyes had been filled with tears, but now she seemed more interested in how she looked.

'So you should be, my girl,' he said softly, almost indulgently. 'Now, what are you going to do next?'

'Next?'

The house downstairs was still a mess, and there was no way that Edward planned to clean up after her. The cane was on the bed, the object of her fascination had yet to be applied to her pert and punished behind. 'I want you to clear up the mess you've made in this house,' he told her simply. 'The kitchen, bathroom and sitting room look like they've been hit by a bomb. Clear it all up.'

'Oui, I will clear it all up, monsieur,' she promised eagerly. She looked up and caught Edward's eyes in the mirror. They looked at each for a moment and then she turned away, her face blazing red with embarrassment again.

'Good. I'll inspect it all when you've finished, and if it's not up to scratch you know what to expect,' he warned her.

'The bamboo?' she guessed hesitantly.

'That's right,' he smiled, walking across the room to pick up the thin cane. He could see that it held some symbolic power for her, that she feared it as much as she was fascinated by it.

'Shall I begin now?' she asked.

'Yes, but remove your skirt and knickers completely, I want you to remember why you've been punished.'

Mercedes smiled. 'But I do, monsieur,' she sighed, rubbing her bottom with her hands. For a second she sounded grateful, there was none of the belligerence or defiance he had expected from her.

She posed herself in the mirror, examining the marks on her body, pressing her fingers hard against the reddest parts of her bottom. She unclipped her skirt and it fell to her ankles, leaving herself naked apart from the flimsy covering of her T-shirt. As she walked out of the room Edward watched her go, her punished flanks rippling sexily as she walked. She was showing off, and the quick cut of the cane made her yelp with pain. The red stripe cut a distinct track across the curves of her derrière. She almost jumped out of the room, clutching her painful bottom tightly, her first taste of the cane making her move like lightning.

The phone call to Paris got through at once, and in

moments he heard Jennifer's cheery voice. 'How's Mercedes coming along?' she asked brightly.

'I've finally had to take her in hand,' Edward admitted, smiling to himself.

'I see,' Jennifer said, pausing for a moment. 'How did she take it?'

'She's downstairs cleaning up after herself, with her bare backside smarting from a good spanking.'

'I see,' Jennifer repeated. 'Do you think she'll be good from now on?'

Edward laughed. 'Not if the way she's been studying the cane and the belts is anything to go by. I expect that the next week's going to get very interesting.'

'I'm just sorry I'm not there to see it,' Jennifer sighed dreamily.

'Don't worry,' Edward promised her. 'This exchange trip was your idea, and it's not entirely Mercedes' fault things have turned out this way.'

There was a long pause at the other end of the phone. 'Will I get the cane or the belt?' Jennifer asked.

'Both,' he promised her.

Later, as he walked downstairs with the cane in hand, he imagined the anticipation and excitement that Jennifer would enjoy for the next week, thinking of the punishment to come as soon as she was home. Her backside would be tingling before the first touch of the belt or the cane.

In the sitting room Mercedes was sprawled out on the couch, belly down, her pert backside a bright pink and sticking up in the air, as she watched the opening credits of yet another Australian soap opera. Her long limbs were spread nonchalantly across the sofa, and he could see the tinge of dark hair between her thighs and visible from behind. Young and wilful, impetuous and individual, the bare-handed spanking had not been enough. Her pretty backside would have to take a lot more correction if things were to change. The cane almost twitched in Edward's hand, readying itself for action. It was going to be a *very* interesting week ahead.

Staying Over

I looked at Jan and smiled shyly, my face turning red when she returned my smile with one of her own. The more I blushed the more she seemed to enjoy my discomfort, until I turned away from her, certain that my face was a red blaze of colour. Jan always did that to me; she could reduce me to a mumbling, shy, adolescent embarrassment whenever she liked. She was older than me. I put her at around thirty, very attractive, funny, intelligent and more sophisticated than I could ever be. Added to which she was my husband's boss's wife and a near neighbour of ours, though her massive house was a mansion compared to our little place a few streets away.

The memory of our first visit to Jan and Peter's house was still very fresh. It was the first time I had met them and I was terrified that I'd do or say the wrong thing and land my husband, Chris, in trouble. In the event Jan was wonderful. She put me at ease at once, made me feel very welcome, and by the end of the evening we were firm friends. Except that she could turn me into a silly schoolgirl at will. All it took was a certain look, a comment or turn of phrase, and I'd be blushing furiously, much to her obvious enjoyment.

We were at her house, just the two of us, because our husbands were away, out on Territorial Army manoeuvres somewhere in Germany. Usually when Chris was away I'd stay on my own, but this time Peter had suggested that I stay the weekend at their house. It was only Jan's phone call that had persuaded me to stay with her; she seemed so bubbly and eager that I hadn't the heart to say no. Besides which, both of us liked a good natter and she had a lot more gossip to tell me, especially about business, and I was keen to hear from the horse's mouth how my Chris was really doing at his job.

'Come on, Susan, there's no need to look so embarrassed,' she laughed, waving her glass of white wine at me, 'I was only asking.'

'I know, but it's just that...' I let my voice trail to silence. She had been talking about sex again, teasing me because she knew how embarrassed I got talking about it. She was sitting on the sofa opposite, shoes off, feet up, cradling the glass of wine while we talked. Even at home she looked fabulous; very long shapely legs, lithe body, looking relaxed and comfortable. I was sitting in the armchair, dressed in long floppy skirt and loose top, and not looking half as good as she did, despite the fact that I was just out of my teens and a lot younger than her.

'I'm only teasing,' she smiled, swinging her long legs over the side of the sofa. Her skirt rode up and I was treated to a glimpse of bare thigh and a flash of black lacy panties. For some reason my heart was racing and I suddenly feared that she had seen where my eyes had been, and that she'd know I had been eyeing her long smooth thighs.

'I thought we were going to be talking about the office,' I said, changing the subject rather sharply.

'Oh that,' she sighed, walking barefoot across the room to get the bottle of wine, 'who wants to talk about that boring old thing?'

'Is it true that Peter's got a new secretary?' I asked innocently.

She laughed as she poured herself another glass of white wine. 'You mean the delectable Miss Fairfax?'

'Is that her name?' I asked, in my best butter wouldn't melt in my mouth voice. I had heard all about Miss Fairfax from Chris, who described her as a hot young thing with less skirt than brain, and who was lusted after by every man in the company. Her speciality seemed to be low-cut blouses and dresses which allowed her to show off her ample cleavage, for which most men were eternally grateful and were willing to forget her nasal twang and terminal stupidity.

'Naughty, naughty,' Jan cautioned, wagging a finger at me. She offered me the bottle but I declined, afraid that a second glass of wine would go straight to my head and loosen my tongue even more.

'I don't know what you mean,' I laughed. For the first time that evening I began to feel comfortable. We were about to have a real cat eat cat session, with Delia Fairfax as our mutual victim.

'I know all about Miss Fairfax,' she assured me, returning to her seat. 'All breasts and no brains, or at least that's what all the guys are saying. Though I don't hear them complaining when she has to bend over to pick up her work and they get an eyeful. Does your Chris complain?'

That stung, sort of. 'Well, she's not Chris's secretary, is she?' I sniffed.

For a moment I was certain I'd overstepped the mark. Jan's face seemed to darken, her eyes narrowed menacingly and I was sure that a storm of invective was on the way. I held my breath but the moment passed, her smile returned and I could breathe again.

'There's one good thing you can say about Delia,' Jan said, 'and that's that she responds well to a firm hand.'

'What do you mean?' I asked, confused by the unexpected remark.

Jan sipped from her glass, looking at me with her pretty blue eyes, which scanned my face looking for meaning in my blank expression. 'Just that she understands the need for discipline sometimes, not like a lot of young girls these days.'

I wasn't sure whether there was a barb in there directed at me. 'You mean you've met her?' I asked, deciding not to take the bait.

'Of course, Susan,' she replied blithely. 'You don't think I'd let a pretty little thing like her near Peter without first seeing what she's like?'

'No, of course,' I agreed. I wished I had as much say in things as she did, but then being the boss's wife certainly had its advantages. 'So,' I asked, 'what's she really like?'

Jan laughed again, her blue eyes sparkling, her red lips parting over even white teeth. When she laughed like that, so natural and attractive, I used to feel a sudden stab of emotion deep inside me, something that I was only vaguely aware of.

'She's as busty as the men say, and as flighty too, but she's harmless really. I'd say she's just a bit younger than you, though perhaps not as pretty, and certainly not as intelligent.'

I blushed, I couldn't help it. 'Thanks,' I mumbled. 'Chris never says those sort of things to me.'

'Do men ever?'

'No, I suppose not. Though I wished he'd stop drooling so much whenever he talks about Delia Fairfax...'

'Back to Delia again,' Jan sighed, shaking her head sadly. She lay back on the sofa again, crossing her legs and letting me look at her smooth, tanned skin.

'Well, I'm sure she doesn't *have* to dress in those skimpy outfits,' I complained, suddenly angry. I realised that my glass was empty and just then I desperately fancied another drink. I stood up and saw that Jan was glaring again, obviously annoyed with me.

'It seems to me,' she said slowly, 'that you're jealous of her, and it does you no good at all.'

'Why should I be jealous? Because I don't flash my whatsits every chance I get?' I was getting angrier and angrier, and forgetting that Jan's husband had the power to fire and hire Chris. I ignored the icy look and crossed the room to pour myself some more wine.

'That's not a very nice attitude,' Jan said coldly, dropping the temperature in the room by half a dozen degrees. She still looked beautiful though, her diamond earrings adding sparkle to her face, her prominent lips pursed and pouting. It confused me; the fact that she could look so attractive when she was angry, and the fact that I was noticing how good she looked.

I picked up the bottle shakily and began to refill my glass. The neck of the bottle was dappled with droplets of condensation, and I watched it slip from my hand, falling in slow motion with a sickening finality. The bottle smashed hard on the mahogany of the coffee table, not smashing, but bouncing on the polished surface and then falling to the floor. The deep scratch, almost a dent, in the table was a crescent that stood out a mile away. If that were not enough I stood, completely dumb, and watched the cool white wine pour into the thick pile of the carpet, waves of yellowy liquid glugging out and soaking into dark patches.

'For God's sake pick it up!' Jan cried, racing across the room.

I couldn't say a word; the sight of the bottle emptying on the floor transfixed me. My horror was absolute, the scar on the coffee table was leaping out at me and grabbing me by the throat. It wasn't wine spilling out on the floor, it was my future seeping away.

Jan grabbed the bottle, but it was almost empty. She glared at me angrily, and if looks could kill then I was a dead woman for sure. She pushed me out of the way but there was nothing she could do, the damage had been done, and done by me.

'I'm sorry,' I whispered, amazed to find that the power of speech had returned at last.

'Sorry? Sorry? Is that all you have to say?' she screamed, absolutely livid.

'I'm sorry, I'll pay for the damage of course...' I said quietly, backing away from her slowly.

'Of course you'll pay! Look at it! Look what you've

done!'

'I'm sorry...'

'And you had the gall to complain about Delia?' she continued, raising her eyes in disbelief.

'I said I'm sorry,' I said, in a voice so small it was hardly there.

'At least Delia knows when she's been a bad girl.'

That did it. My sense disappeared there and then, finished off by the mere mention of Delia Fairfax again. 'What do you mean?' I whispered.

'Delia Fairfax would not only have cleared this mess up, and offered to pay for the repairs, but she would have accepted her punishment too.'

'I will pay...' I repeated, aware that I hadn't even tried to clear the mess up.

'And the rest?'

'If I need to be punished...' I began, then stopped. It occurred to me that I had no idea what I was talking about, and rather than make an even bigger fool of myself I shut up.

'You do need to be punished, young lady,' Jan warned me. Her temper seemed to be going and I was grateful for that, and eager to seize on the chance to make things up.

'What sort of punishment?' I asked innocently. I imagined that I'd have to spend the weekend doing all the washing up, and the hoovering, and any other task deemed appropriate.

Jan went back to the sofa and sat down, placing her knees close together and sitting on the edge of the seat. 'Come here,' she ordered, pointing to a spot a few inches to her right.

I walked across the room, trying not to look at the damaged coffee table, the sheen of polished mahogany spoiled by the deep crater I had accidentally created. I stopped in front of her, ready to be lectured and strangely excited by it.

'I think a firm spanking is in order,' she explained, in a voice so clear and commanding that it went straight to the heart of me. 'You've been a bad girl, not just by making the mess, but also what you were saying about Delia, and what you were inferring about her and Peter.'

My mind had stopped at the word spanking. I looked down at her, my heart racing and my face flushing red with shame. 'A spanking?' I repeated nervously.

'Yes. I think you'll remember it well, and it'll teach you to behave yourself in future,' she explained calmly.

I could think of nothing else to say, my mind had gone completely blank. My only thought was that I shouldn't cry, that I would hold back the tears of confusion and horror that welled in my eyes. Jan patted her knees primly, and I understood that she wanted me to lie across them.

'Skirt up, girl,' she said briskly, in the no-nonsense voice which turned me into jelly.

Very slowly I hiked up my long loose skirt, lifting it higher, above the knee, over my bare thighs until it barely covered my knickers. My face had never been redder and I hardly dared to look at her, knowing that her eyes were eating me all up.

When I hesitated she grabbed my wrists and pulled me over her knee, balancing me on the end so I had to reach out to hold myself in place. She pulled my skirt up all the way, revealing my lacy white panties pulled tightly between by firm round bottom cheeks.

'Is this going to hurt?' I asked, stupidly. I had never been spanked before, not even as a child.

'It wouldn't be a punishment otherwise,' Jan told me.

If I had anything else to say it was silenced by the sudden stinging on my behind. I squealed, shocked by the hard smack that fell on my right buttock. It hurt terribly, a sharp stinging on my flesh. I looked back and saw Jan's hand raised high again. She brought it down hard on my backside. I bit my lip to hold back my cries. Again and again she raised her hand and brought it down hard, smacking with a sharp slapping noise that filled the room with its heavy rhythm.

Before very long my behind was alive with a red, smarting pain that seemed to ooze through my body. The feeling of abject shame and humiliation I felt worsened the burning sensation. I buried my face in the cushions on the sofa as Jan proceeded to give me twenty hard strokes with the flat of her hand.

'I hope that in future you'll behave yourself properly,' Jan told me. Her voice had lost none of its venom and I knew she was still angry, and that made me feel worse – much worse.

'I will, Jan, honestly I will,' I promised tearfully.

She allowed me to stand up, and unzipped my skirt so that it fell in a bundle around my ankles. I knew that the redness of my behind was matched by the redness of my face as I stood in front of her, my backside quivering and stinging with the residual pain of so many bare hand smacks.

'Turn round then, let me look at you,' she ordered.

I turned round and she touched me, stroking her hand to my punished skin, over the lacy panties which had been pulled tighter into my body as I had been bent across her knees. She hooked a finger under the panties and began to inch them down. Instinctively I grabbed my knickers and tried to pull them up, and as I did so I nicked her skin with the sharpness of my long painted fingernails.

She slapped my hand sharply and pulled my panties down to my knees, exposing the roundness of my bottom to her view. She touched me firmly, pressing her fingers into the heat of my flesh. It felt good; the raw heat cooled down by the pressure of her fingertips, sending spasms of pleasure that pierced my body.

'Look.'

She showed me her hand, a red mark across her first

finger, where I had scratched her with my nail.

'I'm ever so sorry,' I whimpered.

'Not sorry enough, obviously,' she said. 'Stay there.'

I didn't have the heart to disobey. I felt miserable, the pain in my flanks had lost the sharpness and was now an ebbing warmth that was affecting me strangely. I was miserable, but excited also, and that made me feel nervous. Jan had walked across the room and was now returning. The slipper she held in her hand made my heart sink even lower for I knew I was to be punished again.

'I said I'm sorry,' I whispered, rooted to the spot and unable to move.

'That's all you've been saying all night.'

She sat back down. This time her skirt was raised high and I couldn't help but stare at her lithe thighs, her skin as smooth as silk and tanned a pure gold. I went across her knees again, this time with my knickers around my ankles and my pink derrière completely on display. I clenched my backside, embarrassed by my nakedness, and certain that she was enjoying my shame in some way.

I turned in time to see her lift the heavy leather slipper, one of Peter's I guessed. Her hand was poised for a moment and then came down swiftly, in a graceful arc that finished with a wicked smack on my bottom. This time I did not scream. I clenched myself again as the leather slipper was applied slowly and methodically by Jan. She beat me on both bottom cheeks, at the top of my thighs, between my thighs. The pain was incandescent as each blow was stroked onto my bared backside, first on one side and then the next, a pause between each stinging stroke.

Jan's thighs beneath me were a torment; she felt warm and soft, and the rubbing of her skin on mine was driving me insane with pleasure at the same time as the pain on my sore round cheeks. The heat on my behind slowly merged with the heat in my belly until I didn't know what was what, and all the sensations merged into one powerful feeling of excitement. My strength ebbed away, my thighs had parted and I was lifting my bottom to meet every downward stroke.

'Well, well,' Jan remarked, dropping the slipper beside me on the sofa. I winced when her fingertips made contact with my raw skin.

'Don't... please don't...' I begged as she stroked over the curves of my backside, and then over the groove between my buttocks and thighs. I was still over her knees and vulnerable, and she was exploring my body completely. I didn't have the strength to stop her, no matter how much I tried to squeeze my thighs together.

Her fingers stroked between my thighs, teasing me deliciously. I caught my breath, held it and then sighed, unable to hide my pleasure. Her fingers teased into my body and touched me there, sending a million spirals of pleasure through my soul. I lifted myself, opening to her explorations.

'Look,' she said, offering me her fingers, coated with moisture from my sex.

I was overcome with shame; that which I had struggled to keep hidden was now apparent. She had spanked me and I had found pleasure in it, excited by my punishment and by the beauty of her body.

'Please... Don't tell Peter or Chris...' I begged, sighing once more as she rubbed her fingers between my thighs, caressing my tight rear hole before entering my wetness again.

'You *have* been a bad girl,' Jan said, 'and I'm sure the men are going to want to know all about it.'

'Please, I'll do anything,' I wailed. I tried to lift myself but she used her hand to spank me hard, three swift strokes at the top of the thighs. I could do nothing, except take my spanking and listen to her.

'You've always been a good girl,' Jan told me, her voice becoming tender once more. 'But today I saw a side of you

I didn't like, and I think it's going to take a few more sessions before you've really understood what it is to be truly good. Like Delia, I think you need a firm female hand to keep you in place.'

'Yes, Jan,' I submitted softly.

'Good. It's still only Friday night. We've two days before the boys get back, that's two days for me to straighten you out. Agreed?'

I nodded vigorously. My face was red again, but secretly I was thrilled. I didn't know why, but I understood then and there that Jan wanted to help me. Besides which, I was starting to enjoy the discipline she had so adroitly administered.

'Good. Now, up you get. I think it's time for us to get to bed. You can clean up tomorrow.'

'Yes, I will, I promise,' I said. I stood up and bent over to pick up my skirt and clothes and she touched me again, running her hand over the length of my thigh and stroking my sore bottom cheeks. I accepted her touch with a smile, wincing only when she touched the sorest marks left by the slipper.

'Right, I suggest you have a quick shower, and then I'd like a word with you in my room before you retire. Oh, and leave your clothes here, I think you should perhaps spend some time walking around like that, it'll remind you of why you've been spanked.'

I accepted that also, without question. The shower sounded so inviting, and I skipped up the stairs feeling elated, happier than I had done for a long time.

The hot water soothed me, and as I soaped myself my body responded naturally, my nipples puckering as the water trailed down between my breasts. My backside was a haze of feeling, very warm and exciting, and I couldn't help but touch myself where Jan had touched me. I felt deliciously sensual, and that pleasure I gave myself was complete bliss. I emerged from the shower feeling more refreshed than I had done for a long time.

Putting on a robe I went directly from the shower to Jan's room, across the hall from the spare room that I was staying in. I was naked under the robe, by body tingling all over. I knocked hesitantly and waited for Jan's answer before going in.

'I just wanted to check your bottom before you go off to sleep,' she explained, as though oblivious to my shy looks at her half naked body. She had undressed and was wearing only a lacy half-cup bra and black panties. There was no doubt that she looked after herself; her body was firm and well-proportioned, she had a firm stomach and breasts, and those incredibly long legs.

'The pain's not so bad, now,' I told her.

She motioned for me to go over to where she was standing, in front of the mirrored doors of her wardrobe. She made me turn my back to them and then let the robe fall from my body. I turned and saw my nakedness reflected back to me, and my pink skin became a glowing red on my well-marked backside. The image excited me, my nipples hardening visibly as Jan watched.

'Bend over,' she ordered.

When I looked round I could see my nether regions exposed in the mirror, the tautness of my bottom pulling the bottom cheeks slightly apart, the dark crease between my thighs displayed fully. She touched me again, intimately caressing, her fingers teasing the labia apart to seek the juices of my body.

'Tomorrow morning I shall expect breakfast from you,' she informed me. 'I'll expect you to clean up the house and to arrange the repair of the coffee table. Understood?'

'I will, I promise,' I replied contritely.

'Any infractions will be severely punished,' she added.

'I'll do my best to be a good girl,' I assured her, in deadly earnest.

'Good. Now I want to leave you with something to think

about,' she said.

The belt whistled through the air and striped my backside forcefully. I had been lulled into a false sense of security, and I couldn't help but cry out. She looked intent, and neither my cries nor my appeals for mercy were going to deflect her. Six hard strokes of the belt were applied, each biting cruelly into my already punished derrière. I could see my reflection, my bottom displayed to perfection while she chastised me expertly.

'Now you can go to your room,' she said, running a fingernail along one of the tracks raised on my skin.

I stood up shakily, my eyes filled with tears, and yet unable to hide my hardened nipples or the flush of red across my breasts. I was aroused and excited beyond endurance by this beautiful and powerful woman. She kissed me once, touching her lips to mine, sucking the breath from my body and igniting fires of desire deep in my heart. We parted and I didn't want to. She pointed to the door and I limped out of the room, disconsolate and confused, my bottom marked with thick red stripes cut by the belt. It was going to be a long night, but already I longed for the new day to begin.

Staying Over – Part Two

The long dark hours of the night had been a torment for me, and much as I had wished for a long dreamless sleep, the moment I drifted off I was sucked into a strange fantasy that had disturbed me all the more. Waking up to the brittle light of dawn I could remember nothing of that strange dream but that Jan's lips had been fire on my body, the same fire that she had inflicted earlier that evening on my backside – first with her hand, then the slipper, and finally the belt.

What was I to do? Not only had I made a fool of myself in front of Jan, I had also been punished by her. My mind still reeled at the thought – that I, a grown woman, should be put over another woman's knee and soundly spanked. What was worse, much much worse, was that she had touched her fingers to the moistness of my sex and discovered that I had been aroused by it all. It was something I did not understand, but the more she had beaten me, the more she spanked and punished, the more excited I seemed to become.

I dressed quickly after my shower, loose skirt down to my ankles and floppy sweatshirt that hid the contours of my breasts. Deliberately shapeless, I was dressing to cover myself, too afraid to think of what the new day might bring. I skipped down the stairs quietly after getting dressed, hoping that I'd be able to concentrate on breakfast and not have to think too hard about what had happened. My only desire was to please Jan, hoping that she'd forgive me for drenching the carpet with white wine and scarring the mahogany coffee table with the bottle.

Thankfully she was still asleep when I came down, and

I had the luxury of silence as I cooked up breakfast. The last thing I wanted was to end the weekend in Jan's bad books, especially as I knew that her husband Peter always took her views seriously. My husband, Chris, would have been furious if he'd seen the mess I'd made of the carpet and the damage I'd done to their furniture.

'Ah, fresh coffee,' Jan exclaimed, walking into the kitchen suddenly, startling me.

'Sorry...' I whispered apologetically, 'I hope I didn't wake you. I was doing my best to be quiet.'

She smiled at me, her lovely blue eyes filled with amusement. 'No, it's okay, you didn't wake me. Now, I'd love a cup of that coffee.'

I jumped to it, hands almost shaking as I poured her a cup. She had taken a seat at the breakfast bar, perched high on one of the stools, legs crossed casually. Her pretty red robe hardly covered her. Her long thighs were bare and my eyes were drawn to them. She had such lovely tanned skin, smooth and flawless, it was impossible not to feel a temptation to reach out and touch her. I looked up and her eyes were on me, sinking deep into my own. I blushed red, turned away from her piercing gaze.

'I'll ring up and find someone to repair the coffee table,' I told her, placing the coffee on the bar beside her.

She turned towards me, her robe slipping open at the chest to reveal the deep cleavage of her breasts, tanned the same golden colour as her thighs. 'It's a Saturday,' she pointed out coolly. 'I just hope you're lucky enough to find someone.'

'I'm ever so sorry,' I repeated, my voice trembling. Her nipples were pressing against the thin silky robe, two points that were bulging against the scarlet material. Why was I looking at her? I felt the fear and confusion deep inside me, and yet I could hardly keep my eyes from her body.

'Well,' she purred wickedly, 'I can always put you across my knees again, young lady. Don't think I've forgotten, or

158

that I'll let your bad behaviour pass.'

I swallowed hard. 'No, of course not,' I agreed, as though it were entirely natural to be hauled across the lap of another woman and to have my naked bottom tanned red. The thought meant that the red flush of shame did not leave my face. I stood awkwardly in front of her, feeling like a silly schoolgirl about to be punished. The memory of her hand coming down so hard on my quivering bottom cheeks was imprinted on my consciousness, I could see it and feel it even as I stood there.

Breakfast was an awful, tense period. I was on tenterhooks, afraid that I'd make some stupid mistake and have to pay for it. In contrast Jan was completely relaxed, and in fact she seemed to take some pleasure from my squirming, fearful condition. I noticed the way her robe kept falling open, how she crossed and uncrossed her legs, and enjoyed the way I watched her.

'I'm going to take a quick shower,' she told me. 'There's a towel in the airing cupboard, be a darling and bring it up to me in a moment.'

I nodded and watched her go, the shimmering robe cinched tight around her waist, her long thighs barely covered, her tight round behind wrapped in red silk. My hands were shaking when I turned back to the breakfast things. Quickly I cleared everything away, anxious not to displease her.

I could hear the spray of the shower as I nervously approached the bathroom. My heart was pounding as I clutched the heavy pink towel, still warm from the airing cupboard. I knocked gently on the door, waiting for her order to enter. The water was turned off and then she called for me. I pushed open the door and entered the humid atmosphere of the bathroom.

Jan was naked, her body glistening with a thousand jewels of water, rivulets of it running down her golden flesh, over her shoulders, between her thighs. She looked gorgeous, and my eyes drank in every inch of her nakedness. She was standing in the shower, arm outstretched, a wry smile on her face. Her eyes sparkled with that faint good humour, as though she enjoyed my discomfort. Shakily I reached out to give her the towel, mesmerised by her sensual smile.

How I could let it happen I don't know, but suddenly her smile was gone and I was looking at the towel around her ankles, soaking in every drop of water that fell from her body and the slowly disappearing puddle in the shower tray.

'I see you haven't completely lost your touch,' she snapped coldly.

'I... I...' I whimpered, my face draining of colour. I knelt down quickly and picked up the towel, completely soaked through and now utterly useless.

'Is there another one downstairs?' she demanded impatiently.

'I've got one,' I reported hastily, remembering that I'd packed extra in my overnight case.

'Get it quickly then,' she snapped, 'or would you rather I froze to death?'

I hated the sarcasm in her voice, and knew that the biting anger would inevitably lead to something else. I scurried to my room and returned quickly, holding the towel close to my heart, pounding loudly in my chest. I could hardly believe what had happened, especially after the effort I'd put into preparing breakfast.

She snatched the towel from me and began to dry herself, stepping out of the shower at the same time. I watched her patting herself dry, her skin suffused with excitement, her nipples puckering so that they were hard brown peaks on her full, round breasts. Her eyes were ice cold, regarding me with nothing but anger.

'Will I be punished for that?' I asked, my voice a whisper that hardly came out.

'Oh yes,' she told me, without a shadow of doubt. 'You'll be punished, and punished well.'

'But, Jan,' I said, looking at her earnestly, 'it was an accident...'

'It was carelessness,' she replied, pulling her scarlet robe tightly around her waist. 'Don't think you can talk your way out of this, young lady. Delia knows enough not to even attempt that now, and I'm sure that eventually you'll learn the lesson too.'

I had completely forgotten about Delia. She too had been chastised by Jan. Had she taken her punishment more calmly than me? I had never even set eyes on her, but knew that she was a lively young thing, and very attractive. I had a sudden vision of her bent over Jan's knees, her pretty little rump being soundly spanked. It was a strange idea, but for some reason it excited me immensely.

'Step into the shower,' Jan ordered, snapping me back to the real world.

I complied, stepping out of my slip-on shoes, the tiles wet and slippery with water. She reached down and lifted my long skirt, pulling it up and over my waist, exposing the black panties I was wearing.

'Hold this,' she told me, giving me the tight bundle she'd formed of the hem of my skirt.

I held it high, knowing I had no choice. I could feel her eyes assessing my body, travelling up over my calves, over my thighs to rest finally on my rounded posterior. Was I still red from the previous day's punishment? I didn't know, but in any case my tight panties would have kept that well hidden. The first stirrings of desire were making me wet between the thighs, making my pussy tingle deliciously.

Without warning my panties were pulled down roughly and forced between my knees. Now I was exposed completely, my bottom cheeks displayed to Jan's obvious satisfaction. She touched me, her fingers rubbing the inside of my thigh with the kind of firm, sensual caress that caused

161

an instant tremor of pleasure to pass through me.

'Bend over,' she continued, barking her order. When I obeyed she pressed a finger into my wetness, as though checking to confirm that I was aroused. I could feel the wetness coating her fingers, and my face burned with embarrassment. My sighs of pleasure were silenced by an angry slap on the thigh.

'I do think,' she explained, 'that by the end of the day you'll not even be able to sit down. I can see that I'm going to have to be very stern with you. Do you understand?'

'Yes, I think so,' I murmured, too afraid of her to disagree. Lovely Jan, whom I had always admired and liked, was turning out to be a disciplinarian far more strict than I had ever imagined possible.

'Count out the strokes,' she added.

I tensed, hoping I could absorb the pain. She raised her hand and brought it down swiftly, the crack of flesh on flesh resounding around the room like an explosion. It pained, white hot and intense, the first stroke touching me on my exposed behind. My thighs quivered as I let out a great cry of horror and complaint.

'Silence!' she demanded. 'You failed to count out the stroke. I'll start again, just as I will every time you forget.'

Stupid me! I clenched my muscles again but to no avail. She hit home with a firm handed slap at the top of my right thigh. It felt as though the world was on fire, the sudden intense sensation giving way to a terrible smarting pain. My skin was glowing, I didn't need to look to know that. This time I didn't make the same mistake; I exhaled the count of one as though it were the only thing that mattered.

Bent over at the waist, skirt in hand, backside blazing, I counted out each stroke in turn. She was cool and efficient, spanking me on each bottom cheek in turn, making sure she turned every inch of my derriere red with pain. I howled and wriggled, the heat oozing into me, tunnelling into the desire that I could not deny. At last I was crying, wet tears rolling down my face as the pain turned to pleasure and I teetered on the edge of climax. She stopped suddenly, reached down and stroked between my thighs.

'You *bad* girl,' she scolded. My bottom was ablaze with red heat, and I raised myself, waiting with delicious expectation for the blow to land.

I screamed and wailed as the jet of cold water blasted down onto me. She had turned the shower on, soaking my clothes and me. The cold water cascaded down over my spanked backside and down my thighs. It was not what I had been waiting for, and my desire seemed to expand, so that my body hungered for release, longed to feel her fingers inside me.

'I want you dressed and downstairs in five minutes flat,' Jan warned, turning off the tap.

I stood up, body weak with desire, my backside smarting horribly. The cold water did nothing for the heat inside me, which blazed like an underground fire deep in my soul.

Jan was waiting for me, sitting in the front room, arms crossed impatiently across her chest. The stern look in her eye had not softened and it filled me with trepidation. I had dried myself quickly and changed clothes, now I was wearing a summer dress a good few inches above the knee, and so thin that she could see I was without a bra.

'There's still the repair to the coffee table to arrange,' she reminded me. 'And there are lots of things to do around the house.'

'I'll get onto someone about the coffee table immediately,' I offered. My backside was burning, sending conflicting signals through my body, but I knew I had to fight the strange feelings bubbling up inside me.

'Will I have to punish you again today?' she asked, her eyes gazing directly into mine.

'I hope not,' I answered, my voice small and vulnerable.

'Turn around, let me see your bottom.'

I turned and lifted the back of my dress, letting her see the skimpy white briefs I was wearing.

'Take your knickers off,' she ordered, 'I want to see how well you've been chastised.'

I obeyed and slipped off the white panties. The cool air touched my burning backside, which was red with her finger marks, a fact I had verified with a quick look in the mirror.

'Good,' she said, smiling. 'You look like you've had a thorough spanking. Delia is going to like that.'

'Delia?'

'She's on her way,' Jan reported, a malicious grin on her face. She was enjoying herself, her blue eyes wide with delight and her smile one of pure, wicked pleasure.

My world was falling apart. Not only was I being punished, and somehow finding a perverse pleasure in it, but now my punishment was going to become common knowledge. My mind raced with all the possibilities: Delia telling everyone at the office, the story spreading like wildfire until Chris heard about it...

'Please, Jan, anything but that,' I whispered, my vision blurred by the tears welling in my eyes. How could she be so cruel?

'It's for your own good,' Jan told me, her voice suddenly losing its harsh tone, and sounding almost tender.

'Please, can you just spank me and forget about anything else?'

'No, this is for your own good, young lady,' she said.

I looked at her, breasts almost completely exposed by her thin robe, bare thighs that did strange things to my imagination. She stood up and walked towards me, her robe falling open.

Her kiss was electric, and I felt as though she were passion itself. I let her kiss me on the lips, let her stroke my stinging buttocks, let her caress my nipples through the thin cotton of my dress. I would have done anything for her, anything at all. I longed to touch her back, to feel her thighs and breasts, to taste her flesh, but I resisted the temptation and held back.

'Be a good girl now,' she whispered.

In a daze I set to work, only vaguely aware that I was naked under the thin dress. She touched and caressed me every time she passed, keeping me hot and excited.

I called and arranged for someone to repair the coffee table.

I did the household chores.

I followed her around like a puppy.

Each time I spied myself in a mirror I saw confusion mixed with sexual arousal. What was Jan doing to me?

The carpet was slightly stained after my accident with the wine the previous evening, and so I got down on hands and knees with carpet cleaner and began to scrub it. I must have been working hard, really putting all my energy and attention into it, because I didn't hear the doorbell. The first inkling I had that someone else had arrived was when I heard voices at the door of the front room. With a sickening feeling in my stomach I slowly turned and looked up. My short dress had ridden up at the back, exposing the full length of my thighs and my naked backside, the buttocks nice and round as I was on all fours.

'I see she's been a bad girl already,' the new arrival remarked, an amused smile on her face. Her eyes were focused on my behind, pretty blue eyes that looked as though they too could become stern and cruel if required. She was tall and blonde, her hair much fairer than Jan's, and dressed in a very tight, very short skirt and a tight blouse that was low-cut enough to reveal the slopes of her firm breasts.

'Delia, this is Susan, Chris's wife,' Jan explained, not batting an eyelid at my obvious embarrassment. 'And Susan, this is Delia, whom you've heard all about.'

I stood up quickly, brushing down my short dress and

wishing the world would open and swallow me whole. Her smile grew broader; she was enjoying my distress in much the same way that Jan did.

'Hi, I never expected to meet you in this sort of situation,' Delia giggled.

'No, neither did I,' I managed to say, mumbling like a naughty child caught in the act. Would she tell everyone about what she'd seen? The thought was uppermost in my mind. I was terrified Chris would find out.

'Some coffee, please, Susan,' Jan ordered, taking a seat. She had dressed for the day, a long skirt with a split at the side that fell open when she sat.

I hesitated; why was I the one to make the coffee? But I nodded mutely and made for the kitchen, feeling glad to be away from Delia and at the same time annoyed that I was being spoken to like a minion. I slammed a couple of coffee cups on a tray, milk and sugar, and waited for the coffee to filter through the machine. The laughter I heard from the other room got to me, like a stab wound in the belly.

They were chatting quietly when I came into the room, conspirators that fell silent when I entered. The tension was electric, I was certain they'd been talking about me. Delia was sitting on one of the armchairs and I walked towards her first, offering her the tray. She smiled and took one of the cups of coffee, and then added some milk. As I turned away her hand stroked up my thigh and towards my pussy, still moist with barely suppressed excitement. I had been taken by surprise, shocked that Delia should touch me in that way. I yelped and turned quickly, spilling coffee from the second cup into the tray.

'Why did you do that!' I demanded angrily. The brown lake on the tray swirled around but thankfully did not leak onto the carpet. I was livid, at that moment all I could think about was my injured pride.

'Do what, exactly?' Delia retorted, looking innocently at Jan as though she had no idea what I was talking about.

'She touched me!' I explained to Jan, my voice rising with frustration. 'She put her hand up my dress and touched me!'

'You're lying! I did no such thing!' Delia insisted, adopting an injured tone of voice.

'Enough of this, both of you!' Jan cried, her shrill voice bringing us both to silence.

I looked sulkily at Delia, my eyes narrowed accusingly. She had touched me, the bitch, and now she was trying to get me into trouble. I had imagined her to be a silly little flirt, but never such an out and out schemer. She was trying to make me look bad so that she could worm her way further into Jan's good books.

'I brought the two of you together in the hope that you'd be friends,' Jan explained. 'But it seems to me that both of you would rather be at each other's throat.'

'That's not true,' Delia interjected, pouting her rouged lips so that they were prominent and glossy. Her skin was milky white, and the red lipstick made her mouth look rosy and kissable. I could understand why the men were all in love with her.

'It's your fault,' I said quietly, looking first at her and then at Jan.

'I won't have this bickering in my house,' Jan declared. 'Do I really have to punish you both before you learn to behave?'

'But I didn't do *anything*!' I repeated, exasperated.

'Neither did I,' Delia chimed in on cue.

'That does it!' Jan decreed. She stood up, her blue eyes blazing. 'I think both of you need to be taught a lesson.'

'In front of *her*?' Delia asked, her smile disappearing at last. The horror in her eyes matched my own, her sense of superiority evaporating instantly.

'Yes, in front of her,' Jan told her. 'Now, both of you, to my room.'

I could have refused, I could have simply turned around

and walked out of the door, but I didn't. With pounding heart and excitement in my veins, I put down the coffee tray and walked to the door. Delia had fallen silent too, she was biting her lower lip nervously. She followed me up the stairs and I was aware that she could see right up my short flared dress, which flapped gently as I walked.

Jan followed the two of us into her bedroom, her silence making me feel even more nervous. I couldn't help wondering what she had planned for us. Whatever it was it had to be painful, I knew that much. She walked to her wardrobe and opened the door slowly, put her hand inside for a second, and then closed the door again. I inhaled sharply, frightened by what she had retrieved.

'Please, Jan,' Delia whispered, voicing my own feelings, 'not the cane. We'll be good, we promise.'

'You should have thought of that earlier,' was all Jan said, flexing the long yellow bamboo cane in her hands. Her eyes were cold; her anger had gone, but was now replaced with a cool determination to extract punishment.

'But it wasn't my fault...' I whispered.

'Both of you, I want you on the bed on hands and knees. Quickly now!'

We scrambled onto the bed, on all fours side by side, our bottoms raised high. My short dress did nothing to cover my behind, but Delia's was well hidden by her tight skirt.

'Skirts up, both of you, I want to see your pretty little backsides good and proper,' Jan told us.

I flipped the hem of mine over my waist, and as I did so I caught sight of Delia struggling with hers. A curt nod from Jan and I understood. I reached round and helped tug up Delia's tight black skirt. Underneath she was wearing pretty lace knickers that were pulled tightly between her round bottom cheeks. I needed no bidding. I hooked my fingers into her panties and pulled them down quickly. Her skin was hot to the touch, as though her body was responding to the anticipation of the cane.

'Good, I should think six strokes each will be enough for now,' Jan informed us.

'Please...' Delia whimpered, one last entreaty on her lips as Jan raised the cane.

I screamed, my voice filling the room and drowning out the whack of the cane which landed so forcefully on my behind. I hadn't been expecting the first stroke and the agony was unbearable. I sucked air into my lungs, hoping to breathe away the intense white heat of pain. The stripe felt like fire across my bottom cheeks. I could feel it raised against the whiteness of my flesh.

Delia cried out too, wincing and shaking as the cane swished down onto her beautifully naked behind. She arched and cried, gritting her teeth. I sneaked a look back, and saw the redness flared across her firm buttocks. Side by side, the two of us arched, naked posteriors striped red with one stroke each. I winced when Jan touched me, her long fingers exploring the single track across my behind.

The second stroke was no better then the first. I burned in agony, my bottom quivering as the redness spread across my skin. The white flash of impact turned into the intense redness that somehow seeped into the rest of my body. I cringed instinctively when the cane came down on poor Delia's backside.

A third and then a fourth stroke, Delia and me in turn. It hurt so much, more than a hand spanking, more than the slipper, even more than the belt. Yet still the fire seemed to become one with the sexual heat that ignited in my pussy. I felt excited, the pleasure incomprehensible to me, but real all the same.

'Now, girls,' Jan directed, pausing to admire our punished backsides, 'I want you to kiss and make up.'

I turned, my face next to Delia's, our eyes gazing into each other's. My mouth trembled open as the cane whistled down to strike my poor bottom. My cry was sucked into Delia's mouth, her lips crushing mine in a long, slow kiss.

Her tongue pushed into my mouth, searching, exploring, exciting. She cried as the cane fell on her too, and I felt the exhalation of her breath as I kissed the agony away.

Like lovers we kissed with passion, as the cane stroked and burned, slicing into our chastised flesh. The excitement was unbelievable; I felt myself on the edge, enjoying the pain as it broke across my skin and was expressed in Delia's sexy, welcoming lips. I climaxed suddenly, the cane striking me for the last time as Delia kissed me lovingly. A moment later Delia shivered her orgasm as I kissed her, just as she suffered the last stroke of the cane too.

'Now,' Jan informed us coolly, 'I'll expect better behaviour from the two of you for the rest of the day.'

'Yes, Jan,' the two of us mumbled, still dazed by the mutual orgasm we had enjoyed as we were being punished.

'Good. Now, I think it's time you girls showed your appreciation,' Jan said, smiling wickedly. 'I think you ought to kiss me your thanks.'

'Mmm, yes please,' Delia murmured. She sat up and turned to face Jan. From where I lay I was treated to a gorgeous view of her bottom, latticed with thin red stripes that marked her skin so deeply. As she kissed her, Jan began to fondle the cane marks, making Delia squirm excitedly. I lay back, breathing hard. My bottom ached and stung, and yet I still felt excitement and desire. Lazily I reached out and touched Delia's sex. She was wet, her body oozing the essence of her desire.

What would the rest of the day be like? And the next day, my last day with Jan before our husbands returned home? I sighed, my mind filled with images I would not even have dared to imagine only a day earlier.

Staying Over – Part Three

How could any of it make sense to me? Not only had I been spanked and seduced by Jan, the stern and beautiful wife of my husband's employer, but my punishments had been witnessed by Delia, the young and pretty secretary of whom I had been so jealous. My mind was in turmoil as I lay in bed and thought of all that had passed in the last two days...

It had begun so innocently. Our husbands were away for the weekend and I had agreed to spend the time with Jan, whom I admired so much, even though I'd secretly been slightly afraid of her. She was always so elegant, so clever and so beautiful, and yet not once did I suspect what lay beneath her stylish good manners and calm reassurance. Things had been going so well and then, in a moment I still could not comprehend, I had caused an accident and found myself across Jan's lap with my knickers around my ankles while she smacked me like a spoilt child.

The memory of that first spanking caused butterflies of excitement and desire in the pit of my belly. Why did I feel so excited by what was surely the most humiliating moment of my life? I could not explain it, but nor could I deny the fires that burned deep inside me and which caused my nipples to harden and the moisture to gather between my thighs. As I lay in bed listening to the soft ticking of the clock I couldn't help but stroke the tips of my breasts, causing pulses of pleasure to ripple through my body.

What was happening to me? I longed for Jan to walk into the room and bark an order before turning me over to punish me yet again. The memory of her mouth on mine was divine, her perfumed lips sucking the breath from my body and with it the will to resist. She had spanked me with her hand and a slipper. How good it had been. The memories added to my excitement and I felt my body responding.

The slipper had not been the worst, however; when Delia arrived, much to my shame, things had become even more difficult. I was burning with shame that silly young Delia should find me on all fours, my backside exposed as I cleaned up after the mess I had made the previous evening. I was annoyed as well as embarrassed, as it was bad enough being punished by Jan without having someone else along to enjoy it. My distress was obviously amusing to Delia, which only made me madder. It was definitely a case of hate at first sight. As soon as we set eyes on each other it was clear that Delia and I would not get along.

The end result was that both of us were soundly punished, in front of each other, by Jan. The cane was far worse than the slipper or Jan's firm hand. It had cut deep into our flesh, making us yelp and cry as she taught us the strictest lesson yet. But from that pain, that constant stroking of deep red lines across our backsides, there had come pleasure. Delia's mouth had found mine and we shared passionate kisses as we were soundly thrashed with the bamboo cane.

I turned over, unable to sleep, distracted by the constant going over of all that had happened. My body ached with excitement, my nipples pressing hard against the thin cotton T-shirt I was wearing. The clock beside the bed blinked back at me, the luminous dial telling me it was only just gone two in the morning. It was no good, I knew I wouldn't be able to sleep, no matter what. Sitting up in bed, my thin cotton panties pressed deep into the moistness of my sex, making me squirm with a momentary spasm of pleasure.

What should I do next? Jan was asleep in her own room, I was in the spare bedroom, and Delia had been consigned to sleeping on the fold-out bed in Peter's study. I had been secretly disappointed with the sleeping arrangements, after the punishments and seduction I had half hoped that Jan would let me spend the night in her arms, her naked body against my own. Making love to another woman had never even been a fantasy of mine, I was happy with my husband Chris, but now my feelings were haywire and I longed for Jan to kiss me again.

A midnight snack was not something I normally went for, but suddenly it seemed like an excellent idea. Perhaps it was the thought of getting out of my room and of having something else to think about apart from my confusing thoughts and desires. A glass of warm milk might even help me get to sleep, I reasoned, tiptoeing downstairs quietly.

The house was shrouded in darkness, the silence a blanket of serenity that I did not want to disturb. I made it down the stairs with hardly a creak of the floorboards, and then went straight into the kitchen, careful not to make any noise lest I wake Delia, asleep in the room across the hall from the kitchen.

The light from the fridge cast a diagonal of pale white across the room. Carefully I set to work, deciding that a sandwich would go well with a glass of milk. The bluish light from the cooker added a warm glow to the room as I set a small pan of cold milk to warm up. After a while I was so caught up in what I was doing that I completely forgot about the worries that had been keeping me awake.

'Have you got enough there for two?' Delia asked, startling me.

I turned quickly and clutched at my chest. 'You've frightened the life out of me,' I complained.

She giggled. 'Don't worry, Susan,' she said, 'I won't tell Jan, if that's what you're worried about.'

I studied her for a moment and realised she was genuinely trying to be friendly. She was wearing bra and panties only, pretty black lace that contrasted with the whiteness of her soft skin and the crystal blue of her eyes.

'It's only hot milk, I'm afraid,' I explained, pointing to the cooker. 'Do you want some too?'

'Okay,' she nodded. 'You couldn't sleep then?'

'No,' I sighed, 'I just couldn't.'

'This is your first time, isn't it?'

I knew what she was talking about, there was no need for her to say more. 'You won't tell anyone, will you?' I whispered, averting my eyes from hers. With what she had seen and experienced at my side, she was in a position to make my life a misery, and we both knew it. Chris would be shocked if he found out about what had happened, of that I was absolutely certain.

'But you do like it though, don't you?' Delia asked, her eyes blazing wickedly.

I said nothing, but my silence was testament enough to my confusion. She was so young, and yet it was obvious that it was not her first time. I wondered how long it had been going on, how long she had been going over Jan's knee to receive her punishments.

'Why don't you leave that,' Delia suggested, taking the milk bottle from my hands as I hurried to make her a drink too.

'What are you doing?' I asked, allowing myself to be pushed against the kitchen wall. Her face was close to mine, her eyes sparkling with delight as I struggled with my feelings. I was aware of her fragrance, her near naked body scented with perfume, her breasts pressed against mine as she held my hands at my sides.

'Isn't it obvious what I'm doing?' she whispered, her breath warm against my face. Her lips touched mine, tentative, soft, inviting.

'No! I don't want to do this!' I cried, rebelling against the desire surging through my body. I pushed her away, frightened I would succumb to her embrace and meet her kiss with an open hunger that I could not deny.

'Stop it! You know you want this!' she snapped, slapping me across the face, the sound echoing to silence as I clutched my cheek in shock. I could feel the red blush across my skin, the imprint of her fingers across my face. Tears welled in my eyes as the force of confusion and shame came over me like a tidal wave of emotion.

Delia kissed me, and this time I could not resist. My face ran with bitter tears but my mouth was open to her tongue. The ache between my thighs was unbearable, my panties were wet with honey from my pussy, and my nipples were hard points of flesh that longed for Delia's touch. I moaned softly as she slipped her hand under my long T-shirt and began to stroke the inside of my thigh, her fingers pressing forcefully against the softly sensitive flesh.

The darkness was suddenly banished and the kitchen was flooded with the harsh electric glare of the lights. I looked up, through the tears, and saw Jan standing by the door, her hand still on the light switch. I pushed Delia away and ran across the room, sobbing like a child towards Jan. The resounding slap across the face was the last thing I expected and only caused another burst of tears and more sobs from me. Why were they being so nasty? Why?

'So, this is where you've decided to play your squalid little game,' Jan stated coldly, her voice filled with anger and disgust. I shrank away from her, frightened by the hard slap and the threat in her voice. She was glaring at us, dressed in a pretty pink robe that barely covered her long thighs and which was thin enough for the dark discs of her nipples to be discernible. With both hands on hips and the austere look on her face she looked every inch the disciplinarian she had shown herself to be.

'It wasn't like that...' Delia started to explain, but I could tell that she too was afraid of Jan's temper. The self-confidence with which she had attempted to seduce me had all but evaporated. Now she slunk against the wall, her eyes averted while she waited for Jan's reaction.

'I only came down for a glass of milk...' I said, pointing to the full pan on the kitchen table.

'Is that why I found you in Delia's arms? Does that explain why Delia is half naked? Does it?' Jan demanded, advancing menacingly into the room. I cringed, my stomach turning as I realised where things were going.

'It was her idea!' Delia blurted, pointing an accusing finger in my direction. She was smirking, her pouting lips parted sexily and her eyes sparkling with anticipation.

'That's not true! You've got to believe me, Jan, that isn't true,' I cried, trying desperately to defend myself even though I was shocked by the accusation. I remembered how Delia had touched me the first time we met, and how she had taken great delight in getting me into trouble. Now she was doing it again.

'Quiet, both of you,' Jan hissed, cutting off my protestations instantly. Her heeled slippers clicked coldly on the tiles of the kitchen floor as she came towards me. My eyes were fixed on her body, focused on the tightly bound robe that showed the fullness of her breasts and the bulge of her nipples against the satin material. 'Now,' she continued, stopping in front of me, 'who was it that came down here first?'

'I did,' I admitted, not daring to explain why. My eyes were full of tears again, but now there was also a feeling of desire inside me, a feeling of desire mixed with a real fear of what Jan was going to do.

'I'm glad you admit it,' she told me. She turned on her heels and marched across the room to Delia, still leaning against the wall, her arms crossed insolently across her chest. The smile disappeared from her face and I sensed that she too feared Jan, despite the bravado with which she had flung her accusations.

'It was her idea. She said she wanted to play games...' Delia insisted, though her voice quavered as she spoke.

'I find that difficult to believe,' Jan said, 'but I suspect she was not an unwilling victim of whatever it was you had planned for her.'

'She tried to force herself on me,' I complained, my heart filled with relief that Delia's plans had been found out. The prospect of an unjust spanking suddenly receded, and I felt nothing but relief and pleasure that Delia was going to be punished for her sins.

'Susan, do you know where I keep the cooking things?' Jan asked, fixing Delia with a look that could melt an iceberg.

'In the drawer?'

'Then you know what to get me,' Jan said. I watched her grab Delia by the arm and pull her roughly across the room to the heavy mahogany table which dominated the kitchen.

Jan was right, I had guessed what it was that she wanted. Without hesitation I went to the drawer where she kept the cutlery and cooking utensils. There was quite a choice, but I selected the two items I hoped might make the most impression: a flat wooden spatula and an old fashioned wooden spoon. When I turned round Delia was bent across the edge of the table, her breasts squashed flat against the cool polished surface and her bottom offered high. Her black skimpy panties were pressed deep between her thighs, the thin black band of lace parting her bottom cheeks temptingly.

'Is this what you want?' I asked, handing Jan the spatula and the wooden spoon. She smiled slightly, her lips looking glossy and enticing, a tempting reminder of the pleasure I had experienced with her the previous day.

I stepped back a bit, anxious to enjoy every second of Delia's punishment. Her ankles were pressed together, her long legs in parallel so that her backside was nice and round and displayed perfectly, the thin wisps of lace barely covering her bottom cheeks and turning into a thin triangle of material against the bulge of her sex. Her face was pressed flat against the table, she was biting her lower lip, and her eyes looked at me appealingly. I smiled back, feeling an unfamiliar thrill of excitement at the prospect of watching another woman being spanked.

'Why is it I always have to discipline you whenever you visit?' Jan demanded coldly. 'It's not enough that you were caned earlier, now I have to punish you again. You've gone too far this time.'

'I'm sorry, it won't happen again...' Delia whimpered pathetically. 'I promise.'

I watched, wide-eyed and excited, as Jan raised the wooden spoon and then brought it down swiftly. A resounding smack filled the room, followed by a sharp yelp of pain from Delia. The red imprint of the spoon was clearly marked on her right buttock, the redness in stark contrast to the pale tones of her flesh. Such a small mark, an oval redness that probably stung unbearably. Before Delia had a chance to complain the spoon came down again, adding a second mark to her right bottom cheek.

I tried to resist the rush of pleasure I felt, watching Delia's behind being so soundly smacked, but I couldn't. My breath was short and I could feel the desire in the pit of my belly, so strong and so uncontrollable. I longed to grab the spoon from Jan's hand and to continue the punishment myself, to get my revenge for the tricks Delia had been playing on me.

Four, five, six strokes of the spoon all landed on Delia's right bottom cheek until she was squirming and groaning, rubbing her thighs together as though she could rub away the pain burning on her backside. Each stroke was hard and precise, forming a row of red ovals on her flesh, the skin raised where the stroke was hardest.

'Oh... it hurts, it hurts...' Delia wailed, her eyes filling with tears. Each time she squirmed, each time she moved, her panties went deeper into her pussy, exposing more of her soft flesh to the bite of punishment.

'Enough of that! You know I can't stand weakness!' Jan cried, her voice making me quiver with fear and silencing Delia's pathetic sobs instantly.

The arm went high again and Jan brought it down hard, switching to the left side. The twin globes of her bottom were ill-matched in colour; where her right side blazed pink and red her left was still white, apart from the first blush of the first stroke. I watched avidly, listening to the hiss as the spoon came down, the hard smack of impact and the whispers of pain that escaped from Delia's quivering lips.

Two strokes and then three, a pause while Jan stroked her hand across Delia's backside, and then four and five. I marvelled at how precise each stroke was, at how Jan seemed to measure every ounce of pain and punishment she so expertly inflicted. I had been so lucky to escape; I knew that such a punishment would have made me scream with horror.

There was no let up. When both of Delia's perfect bottom cheeks were tanned a deep and painful red, Jan switched target again, this time aiming her strokes at the top of the thighs. Delia cried out, she tried to push herself up but I stepped forward and held her down, pressing my breasts against her back as I made sure she couldn't move. The more Delia squirmed the more my nipples rubbed against her through the thin material of my top, making me sigh with pleasure at the tremors of ecstasy that were triggered inside me.

'I can see what you're doing,' Jan said quietly.

I looked up at her guiltily, realising I'd been caught out. I let go of Delia and stepped back, noting that my nipples were hard points poking against my top. My pleasure had been plain to see, only I had not realised it. Delia was still lying across the table, her bottom and her thighs patterned with ovals of pink and scarlet. I could almost feel the heat from her flesh, and could only dimly imagine the torment pulsing through her.

'Well?' Jan demanded, placing the wooden spoon on the table, only inches from Delia's face.

'I... I couldn't help it...' I whispered hesitantly. A sharp stab of fear tore through me, and with a sinking feeling I saw that I too was going to suffer the ordeal of chastisement that night.

'I expected more from you,' Jan told me, her voice emotionless. 'After the punishments you've suffered in the last two days I had hoped that you'd learned your lesson.'

'But I have,' I told her emphatically, hoping my obvious sincerity would win some mercy.

'But you haven't, my dear,' Jan said. 'It's time you had another lesson, and perhaps this time you'll not forget it so easily. I've finished with you for now,' she added, turning to look down upon Delia.

Delia pushed herself up slowly. I could see her wincing with pain as she straightened her lovely long legs. When she turned to me I saw the wetness between her thighs through the thin black lace that was pressed deep into her crotch.

'Please, Jan...' I started to beg, but one look from her told me I was only making things worse for myself. When Jan was angry there was no stopping her, she could be as strict and as ruthlessly as anybody.

'Take your top off and face me,' she commanded. I pulled my top off slowly, wondering why it was that I was to be spanked like this when Delia had been allowed to keep her bra on. My face was crimson with shame as I dropped my top to the floor; my chest was already flushed pink with the pleasure I had gained by rubbing against Delia.

'Delia, stand behind her and cup her breasts for me,' Jan ordered.

My mind was in turmoil as Delia stood behind me and passed her hands under my arms and cupped my breasts. She teased my erect nipples with her thumbs, making me sigh with pleasure, much as I hated to.

'Perhaps this is the most apt lesson you'll ever learn,' Jan told me, her clear blue eyes gazing at me steadfastly.

I swallowed hard and watched in horror as she picked up the spatula I had selected and raised it high into the air.

'No!' I cried, but it was too late. The blast of impact was unbearable as the flat wooden surface made contact with my breasts, slapping down and beating hard against my erect nipples. I squirmed and tried to turn away, but Delia held me in place.

The searing pain burst over me again as Jan brought the spatula down, spanking me with all the power and pleasure she had when punishing my posterior. I cried as it swept down again, marking my skin and biting hard at my nipples. The pain was intense, but with it there was something else, something I had not been expecting. Each stroke brought a surge of feeling, a powerful blast of sensation that seemed to connect with the pleasure deep between my thighs.

Like a dream I watched myself being punished, Delia's hands squeezing and moulding my breasts while they were spanked so painfully. And then, before I knew it, I was pressed across the table and the spanking was resumed on my bottom. As my burning nipples, bright red points that pulsed with fire, brushed the cool mahogany surface I shuddered and cried out my orgasm. Never had I felt such bitter ecstasy, so painful where the pleasure was so pure.

Jan beat me beautifully, using the hard flat spatula across the tight roundness of my behind. My white panties were pulled down around my knees, exposing the heat and the wetness of my quim, swimming in the juices of my pleasure. Each stroke across my reddened bottom sent spasms of sensuality throughout my body so that it felt as if my entire being were aflame.

All the time I was aware of Delia standing beside me, her greedy eyes drinking in the vision of my punishment just as I had watched her being punished. There was lust in her eyes also. I could see her fingers caressing her body as she watched, driven beyond endurance both by her own quivering backside and by the sight of mine.

At last it was over, the painful rhythm of chastisement had ended. Painfully, almost light-headed, I pushed myself from the table. I felt strange as I stood beside Delia, both of us in a state of undress and with our bodies marked by the force of our correction.

'I want the both of you upstairs in two minutes,' Jan told us, the excitement of her eyes reflected at last in her voice. 'It seems to me that both of you are in need of longer term treatment,' she added.

'But... Chris gets back tonight,' I whispered, remembering that my husband was due to return. Would it mean a return to normality for me?

'You wouldn't want Chris to find out about this, would you?' Jan warned.

'No, of course not,' I told her hurriedly. My backside was stinging horribly, the heat merging with the lava flow between my thighs.

'Good, in that case I think we can continue as we are,' Jan decided. 'From now on I shall expect the both of you to report to me regularly, and if for any reason I am unhappy with your behaviour I'll have no compunction in punishing you. Is that clear?'

I looked at Delia, and then at Jan. 'Yes, we understand,' Delia and I said, sighing together. My heart was racing with excitement; I had so much to learn and now I knew that Jan would continue to be my teacher.

'Good,' Jan smiled. 'Now, both of you upstairs, you've yet to thank me in the special way I like...'

My heart jumped. Secretly I was filled with a strange fear of what the future held, but that fear was part of an excitement that filled me completely. I turned towards the door, certain that my life would never ever be the same again.

Party Dress

Hasheeda sat on the edge of the bed and watched as Louise wriggled out of the jeans which were moulded to the tight curve of her backside. Faded blue and ripped at the knee, it sometimes seemed to Hasheeda that those jeans were the sexiest things in Louise's wardrobe. She watched as the jeans were inched down, gradually revealing the twin globes of Louise's bottom clad only in the minutest strip of lace, until finally Louise stepped out of the denim bundle on the floor.

'Come on,' Louise urged, turning to face Hasheeda.

Hasheeda let her eyes wander over her friend, now wearing nothing but skimpy white panties and a cropped top that bulged around her breasts. Louise's body was young and firm, with long, slender thighs, a prominent backside and full, pert breasts that always drew lots of attention. The contrast with Hasheeda's own body was striking. They had the same build but Hasheeda's dark skin, pouting lips and eyes of a brown so dark they almost looked black, meant that the two young women made a striking pair.

'Are you sure about this?' Hasheeda asked, realising that she had been staring. Although she and Louise had been sharing the flat for nearly six months she still found the difference between life at home with her family and life as a student very difficult to take sometimes.

Louise laughed. She came over and sat by Hasheeda, took her by the hand and looked at her earnestly. 'You don't have to do this if you don't want to,' she said quietly, gazing directly into Hasheeda's dark eyes.

'What if my mum and dad find out?' Hasheeda asked.

Louise's eyes were warm, blue-green and filled with concern.

'How?' she asked softly. 'Explain to me how they'll find out.'

Hasheeda looked down, her eyes scanning over Louise's smooth, glassy thighs and the white lacy panties pulled tightly between her thighs. Not for the first time she wondered what it would be like to touch Louise there, to slip her fingers under the lace, to trace the contours of her friend's sex…

'Well?' Louise asked.

The sharp tone jolted Hasheeda back to reality. 'I don't know,' she admitted.

'This is a private party,' Louise said, repeating herself for the umpteenth time. 'One of the lads at the halls of residence has organised it. All they want is a couple of girls to do a turn for some guy's birthday party.'

Hasheeda sighed. 'That's just the problem,' she explained, 'I really don't know what "do a turn" means.'

Louise leaned forward and kissed Hasheeda on the cheek. 'Don't be so uptight about things,' she urged. 'I told you, it'll be a laugh. We'll turn up as a couple of sexy schoolgirls, mess around a bit, grab the money and run. Come on, it'll be an adventure.'

It all sounded so simple, but Hasheeda couldn't bring herself to get into Louise's frame of mind. Things were never that simple…

Louise jumped up off the bed and went back to the wardrobe. 'I've got these,' she said, handing Hasheeda a bag full of clothes.

'Where from?'

'Charity shops,' Louise explained. 'It cost me a tenner,' she added, 'but Mike's promised us fifty each for doing this.'

The money was tempting; living away from home was a lot more expensive than Hasheeda had first imagined.

Especially with a flatmate like Louise around. She looked in the bag and saw a pleated blue skirt, a white blouse, a school tie and a pair of white cotton knickers. School uniform, of a type which no longer existed, except in the memories of the middle-aged and in old films.

Louise pulled her top off so that she was naked bar her panties. Her breasts were large and well shaped, peaked with reddish brown nipples that sometimes stood erect as she showered. Hasheeda liked to watch Louise taking a shower, there was something deeply attractive about it, and Louise didn't seem to mind chatting while Hasheeda watched. Once or twice Hasheeda had even been tempted to let Louise watch her while she bathed, but then her nerve had failed and she had carefully locked the bathroom.

The skirt Louise pulled on was way too short, it barely seemed to cover her backside. And the blouse was almost see-through; Louise's breasts were clearly discernible through it. The tie went on, skewed violently to one side, and with Louise's hair already arranged in a couple of untidy pigtails, it made her look like an insolent schoolgirl. The underwear went on last, replacing the wisp of white lace with old fashioned navy blue knickers that covered more than they revealed.

'Well, how do I look?' Louise asked, twisting round to face Hasheeda. Her eyes were bright with excitement, and the grin on her face seemed to carry a hint of innocence that was at odds with the outrageous image.

Hasheeda half smiled. Louise looked stunning; sexy, playful and completely desirable. 'You look good,' she said, avoiding her friend's eyes. Sometimes it was just so difficult coping with the conflicting feelings at war inside her head.

'Your turn now,' Louise declared.

Hasheeda stood up shyly. Undressing in front of another person always made her feel vulnerable. At home it was all so different… Louise was watching her, smiling still, her excitement infectious. There was nothing for it but to get changed, Hasheeda realised. She pulled off her baggy jumper and then tugged down her loose cotton trousers, so she was clad only in black bra and panties. Her skin was a soft, sugary brown, in contrast to the darker discs that tipped her breasts and which were visible through the lacy cups of the bra.

Louise smiled encouragement, her eyes roving freely over Hasheeda's near naked body. 'Come on,' she said, 'we'll have a good time, I promise.'

The bra came off first, though Hasheeda put her arm across her chest, covering her breasts as she leaned over to retrieve the white blouse from the carrier bag. She fumbled for a moment, conscious that she was being watched, her face burning slightly with embarrassment. She moved quickly and pulled the blouse on, buttoning it up hurriedly.

'Why do you always hide yourself when you get changed?' Louise asked as she watched. She sounded genuinely perplexed.

Hasheeda felt herself growing even more embarrassed, her face glowing with shame. 'I don't know,' she admitted.

'But you've got a lovely body,' Louise assured her. 'I mean, your boobs look fabulous and...'

'Please, don't,' Hasheeda whispered uncomfortably.

Louise shrugged. 'Okay, but I really don't understand it...'

Hasheeda pulled the skirt on and then turned to look at herself in the mirror. She smiled, surprised at the reflection that greeted her. The gymslip skirt was outrageously short, it barely covered her backside, and the white blouse did nothing to hide her breasts, the dark nipples clearly visible under the white cotton. Louise came up behind her and peered over her shoulder.

'You look good, don't you?'

Hasheeda smiled. 'I suppose so,' she admitted.

Louise reached round and started to undo the top buttons

of Hasheeda's blouse. Her arms brushed across Hasheeda's breasts, making the nipples stand out even more.

'Stop,' Hasheeda said, alarmed by the feel of Louise so close and by the amount of her cleavage now on display.

'Why?' Louise demanded. 'Look at you, look at how sexy you are.'

Hasheeda said nothing, and slipped out of Louise's embrace. Her face was still burning and now her heart was pounding. She felt so confused. On the one hand she felt excited by the way she and Louise were dressed, and the feel of Louise's touch was like heaven, but at the same time she knew her strict parents would be appalled at what she was doing, and even more disgusted to know that Hasheeda was responding to it.

She turned her back on Louise and then slipped her black panties off, aware of the sticky heat between her thighs and the tingling in the pit of her tummy. She quickly pulled on the virginal white panties Louise had given her, trying to ignore the fire burning inside her. It was wrong to feel such things, but from the moment she had first set eyes on Louise her feelings had been growing more and more confused.

'And the tie,' Louise reminded her, sitting on the bed to watch as Hasheeda finished readying herself. She leaned back and the short skirt rode up, revealing a gorgeous expanse of thigh and a glimpse of dark blue knickers pulled tight against her pussy.

Hasheeda gazed at her friend for a moment, her eyes drawn to the flesh on display, and then threaded the school tie on. She tied it in an untidy knot, doing just as Louise had done. When finished she turned once more to the mirror and looked at herself. Like Louise, she looked like an impertinent sixth-former, a bad girl up to no good.

'Let me look,' Louise cried impatiently.

Hasheeda, her smile wavering, turned to face her friend. 'Are you sure about this?' she asked once more.

Louise laughed. 'This is going to be fun, remember?'

'I still don't know what we have to do.'

Louise sighed. 'Look,' she suggested wearily, 'we'll go through it now, okay?'

'Okay.'

'Mike'll pick us up and drive us over to the party. We'll burst in and make lots of noise. We'll act up. Poke our tongues out, take the mick a bit, flash our knicks, that kind of thing. Okay?'

'No, not really,' admitted Hasheeda quietly.

Louise ignored the comment. 'Then we'll get into trouble somehow, we'll do something silly like knock a drink over. Once we're in trouble Mike'll get things going by saying that something needs to be done about it. That's when the birthday boy gets his treat.'

Hasheeda swallowed hard. 'What does that mean?' she demanded suspiciously.

'It means that one of us goes over his knee for a pretend spanking.'

Hasheeda's expression went from outright suspicion to complete horror. 'Louise! We… we just can't do it.'

Louise took Hasheeda's hand and pulled her down next to her on the bed. 'Come on,' she whispered, looking deeply into her friend's dark eyes, 'we *can* do it and we will. Think of the money…'

'But I can't…'

Louise touched Hasheeda's face softly, stroking the smooth skin of her cheek with her fingertips. She leaned forward slightly and kissed Hasheeda's dark lips. Hasheeda tensed. She knew she ought to push Louise away, but the sensuous feeling was too strong to resist. She opened her mouth and accepted Louise's tongue between her lips. They kissed slowly, letting it linger and the pleasure grow stronger.

'Please, baby,' Louise whispered, 'don't worry, I wouldn't let anything horrible happen to us.'

Hasheeda inhaled sharply. She was trembling, her heart pounding in her chest while she struggled to accept what had just happened. Louise smiled again and kissed her once more, merging their lips and pushing her tongue deeper into the velvety warmth of Hasheeda's mouth.

'You feel so good,' Louise sighed. She put a hand on Hasheeda's bare knee and then slid it up smoothly across the thigh, pressing her fingers across soft brown flesh. She stroked her hand back and forth until her fingers strayed under the short blue skirt.

'This is wrong…' Hasheeda managed to whisper, her eyes half closed with pleasure as she felt Louise's fingers stroking her inner thigh, moving ever higher. Her nipples were hard points of flesh and she knew her pussy was moist with arousal.

'No, baby,' Louise whispered, kissing Hasheeda's lips once more, 'this isn't wrong, it's beautiful.'

Hasheeda looked down at her smooth coffee-coloured skin that contrasted with the pale flesh of Louise's hand, moving so deliciously up and down. The sight caused a wave of pleasure to pulse through her, making her pussy feel hotter and wetter. She parted her thighs slightly, unable to resist the temptation.

'Let me do this,' Louise whispered, beginning to slowly unbutton Hasheeda's blouse.

Hasheeda held her breath, her heart pounding as Louise carefully undid each button in turn until she had worked her way most of the way down. Then Louise, half smiling, looked up and smiled as she pulled the blouse open, exposing voluptuous breasts, the smooth curves tipped with chocolate coloured nipples that were hard, bulging buds.

Louise showed no signs of hesitating. She cupped Hasheeda's breasts in her hands, closing her fingers over the fullness of flesh and brushing lightly against the most sensitive tissues. Hasheeda sighed and inched closer, pushing her breasts forward, her eyes half closed with pleasure. Her thighs were now parted and the skirt was in disarray over her lap, exposing the tight white cotton knickers pressed between her thighs.

Louise lifted Hasheeda's breasts, holding them tightly, moulding the flesh between her fingers so that the nipples bulged even more. She licked her lips, smiled, and then kissed each one slowly. Hasheeda moaned softly, the sound escaping involuntarily from her lips as she felt waves of bliss pass through her. Louise kissed again, closing her wet lips over each hard nipple in turn, caressing each with her tongue and being rewarded once more with little gasps of pleasure.

'Baby,' Louise whispered, 'I didn't know you liked girls...'

'I... I didn't either,' Hasheeda whispered. She was trembling, but the fear had given way to something far stronger. She looked down at Louise, gazing back at her adoringly, and smiled.

Louise sat up and kissed Hasheeda hotly on the mouth. 'God, if only I'd known,' she sighed, keeping her hands on Hasheeda's breasts. 'I'm never going to be able to keep my hands off you now...'

Hasheeda closed her eyes as she felt Louise's hand slide under her thigh. The feel of the other girl's fingers triggered echoes of pleasure that seemed to connect with the raging heat in her sex and the sensations in her breasts. Everything was joined, pleasure points connecting in all sorts of unexpected ways... She responded to the feel of Louise's fingers by parting her thighs still more, opening herself so that her nectar oozed from between her pussy lips and onto the white panties pressed deliciously against her clitoris.

She gasped as Louise pressed a finger against the panties, pushing the cotton deeper into the wet heat, deeper between pussy lips that ached with desire. She reached out for support, putting her arms around Louise's shoulder and falling forward. Louise kissed her on the lips and neck, pressing her mouth greedily as she continued to blindly explore Hasheeda's pussy.

'You're so wet…' Louise whispered excitedly as her fingers slipped under the panties and into the slick moisture that flowed like honey.

'No… no…' Hasheeda whispered, her body wracked by sudden spasms that started in her tummy and rippled through her. 'You mustn't…' she begged weakly.

Louise withdrew her fingers, now coated with Hasheeda's pussy juices. She smiled, licked them, and then offered them to Hasheeda. 'Taste yourself,' she suggested.

Hasheeda gazed at the two fingers offered to her, both of them glistening with her own sex juices. She opened her mouth and gingerly licked, secretly thrilled that her friend was willing to taste her. She closed her eyes and let Louise stroke her again, coating even more of the salty-sweet essence onto her fingers. She smiled as Louise licked them clean, clearly enjoying both the taste and the act itself.

'Louise… There's something you should know…'

Louise pressed her fingers under Hasheeda's panties once more, making Hasheeda sigh deliriously. 'Oh baby, you're just so wet…'

'Louise… You have to know… I… I've never had sex…'

Louise stopped suddenly. 'Never?' she asked, as though unable to believe what she had just heard.

'Never,' Hasheeda admitted shyly. 'And I can't…' she added, her voice trailing to nothing as Louise continued to use her fingers on her.

'What do you mean, you can't?' Louise asked, suddenly pulling the white panties to one side, exposing the dark triangle of hair that guarded the entrance to Hasheeda's sex.

Hasheeda was breathing hard as she looked down at her rudely exposed pussy, the dark hair contrasting with the softer tone of her skin and the darker tones of her pussy lips. She felt herself to be on the verge of the abyss, teetering on the edge as the pleasure ebbed and flowed through her.

'I can't,' Hasheeda repeated. 'It's a promise I made to my mum, and I can't break it. I can't…'

'You poor baby,' Louise whispered, and then kissed her, pushing her tongue in deep and hard and taking the last of Hasheeda's resolve. She drew back from the kiss and then knelt down between Hasheeda's thighs. She moved forward and touched her mouth to the other girl's exposed pussy.

Hasheeda clutched the bed as the excitement exploded inside her. She felt Louise's tongue press deeper into her body, lapping at the juices there before homing in on the apex of her sex. The feel of her friend's mouth on her clitoris, sucking on it eagerly, made her scream with pleasure. Her entire being responded as she gave herself at last, opening herself completely to Louise as orgasm overtook her.

Moments later, still in a daze, Hasheeda realised she could taste herself on Louise's mouth as they kissed again. The thought excited her, though she still felt breathless and slightly weak.

'Is it always that good?' she asked, lounging back on the bed.

'It is with me,' Louise responded, laughing. 'Baby, you're just *so* sexy it's untrue.'

Hasheeda smiled. 'I just can't believe what we just did…'

'My God!' Louise cried suddenly.

'What is it?'

'Look at the time… Mike's going to be here soon and we're not ready.'

After the high of her orgasm the reminder about the party brought Hasheeda down with a bump. 'Can't we forget that?' she asked. 'I mean, there's so much for us to learn about each other, and—'

'No,' Louise snapped insistently, 'we need to do this. Come on, baby,' she urged, stroking Hasheeda's breasts affectionately, 'do this for me, okay?'

'But I don't feel ready.'

'Let me show you,' Louise said softly, taking Hasheeda by the hand. 'Come on, across here,' she urged, rising and positioning her friend across the padded arm of the small sofa.

Hasheeda moved into place, her legs touching the floor, her bare breasts pressed against the seat and her bottom raised high over the padded arm. She looked up at Louise with dark eyes full of pleading, her excitement now diminished.

'You've been a bad girl!' Louise snapped suddenly, putting real fire into her voice.

'Not so loud,' Hasheeda said, alarmed by the loud stridency in Louise's normally gentle voice.

'Quiet, girl!' Louise cried. 'Obviously you need to be taught a lesson you'll not forget in a hurry.'

Hasheeda's eyes started to fill with tears. The game was not to her liking, especially not after what had only just happened. She still felt nervous and confused; she needed to be held and comforted, not shouted at and threatened. 'I don't like…' she started to say, pushing herself off the arm of the sofa.

Louise acted instantly. She pushed Hasheeda down and lifted her short skirt, exposing Hasheeda's pert backside, still clad in tight white knickers which were moist between the thighs. With her long brown legs fully displayed, the prone position made her seem even more frightened and vulnerable, the effect heightened by tear-filled eyes.

'I'm going to have to pull your knickers down, girl,' Louise warned coldly, 'and give you the sort of punishment that all bad girls deserve.'

Hasheeda was about to protest again when she saw the coldness in Louise's eyes. It might have been a game but her friend was not taking it lightly, she seemed to be totally intent on going through with it.

Louise hooked her fingers under Hasheeda's panties and

started to yank them down. Hasheeda felt humiliated to be across the sofa, her bottom exposed in the most undignified manner while her naked breasts brushed uncomfortably against the sofa. Soon her panties were down between her ankles, a white bundle still wet enough to betray her earlier arousal.

'This is to remind you that you've been a bad girl,' Louise said sternly. She stood by Hasheeda, her legs apart, dressed in a school uniform that did little to conceal the curves of her body. She raised her right arm and then brought it swiftly down, her open palm slapping hard on Hasheeda's naked backside.

'Quiet!' Louise hissed angrily as Hasheeda cried out with pain and shock. She lifted her hand again and brought it down violently, smacking Hasheeda on the other side of her bottom.

The pain of contact was sharp and sudden and Hasheeda squealed again with the third stroke. Her bottom was burning, she could feel the raw heat marked on her brown skin, the imprint of fingers and palm marked on her flesh. She tried to rise again but Louise pushed her down violently and spanked her again, with a force that made Hasheeda catch her breath. The heat of correction was intense, a fire on the skin that seemed to be spreading.

'Please… please stop,' she begged, the tears welling in her eyes so that everything was blurred. She didn't want to be smacked, she didn't need to be punished, and yet Louise was continuing, relentless and merciless. Each stroke seemed to merge into the last, a constant rhythm of punishment on the tight contours of her behind.

'If you don't be quiet now,' Louise warned, her voice a low, cold whisper, 'you'll get worse.'

'But I haven't done anything…' Hasheeda wailed.

'That's it!' Louise snapped. She grabbed Hasheeda and pulled her from the sofa onto the floor, forcing her onto hands and knees. The other girl tried to resist but Louise slapped her face hard and then grabbed a thick handful of jet-black hair. 'Will you do as you're told?' she demanded.

'Yes… yes…' Hasheeda sobbed. Her backside was smarting terribly, she could sense the redness imprinted on her flesh, and yet suddenly she felt something else. Her heart was pounding again and her nipples were hard…

'Anything?' Louise persisted, wrapping her hand in Hasheeda's hair ever tighter.

'Yes, yes,' Hasheeda whispered, realising with mounting horror that she was becoming aroused by the harsh treatment. Her nipples were erect and the heat was there between her thighs and in the pit of her tummy.

Louise smacked her again, bringing her hand down with full force so that the smack resounded around the room. Hasheeda moaned, unable to endure the pain of her chastisement even though it seemed to be merging with the excitement burning in her pussy. She closed her eyes, expecting the punishment to continue, but instead she sighed as she felt Louise's fingers stroke the inside of her thigh. Instinctively she arched her back, lifting her punished bottom higher, offering herself completely to her friend. Louise responded by stroking slowly between Hasheeda's pussy lips, drawing out the honey from within and making Hasheeda shudder with pleasure.

'You're just *so* wet,' Louise whispered, obviously delighted by the fact.

Hasheeda looked over her shoulder at her punished bottom, her soft brown skin marked a vivid red where she had been spanked the hardest. She sighed softly as Louise teased and stroked her between the thighs, making her whimper with excitement.

'It seems to me,' Louise whispered wickedly, 'that you like me to be rough with you.'

'I… I like whatever you do to me,' Hasheeda whispered nervously, unable to deny that the harsh punishment had given her pleasure as well as a certain, delicious kind of pain. Her nipples were aroused, rigid and sensitive, and when Louise squeezed them the sudden burst of pain brought a cry to Hasheeda's lips and a rush of ecstatic sensation.

Louise, kneeling down, moved into place behind Hasheeda. She slapped her several more times, this time more playfully but still hard enough to make Hasheeda wince with pain. Hasheeda's bottom was high in the air, perfectly displayed, her bottom cheeks partially splayed to reveal both the deep channel between them, the dark button of her anus and the puffy, sensitive folds of her pussy. She was open and vulnerable, every inch of her most intimate parts there to be looked at and played with.

'Baby, how am I ever going to keep my hands off you?' Louise asked, gently pulling Hasheeda's buttocks further apart. She gazed adoring at the tense anal opening and the sweet flesh between the dark-skinned pussy lips, and then she brought her mouth to Hasheeda's sex. She pushed her tongue deep between the pussy lips, delighting in the wet heat and the taste of her friend.

Hasheeda knew she was going to climax again soon, despite the throbbing pain that still smarted on her behind. She lay still, allowing the other girl to do as she pleased, content to be used and to take her pleasure from it. Louise's tongue was a torment, flicking expertly from tracing the contours of Hasheeda's pussy lips to lapping wetly at her bulging clitoris.

'And look at this…' Louise whispered, shifting her attentions slightly higher. She flicked her tongue across Hasheeda's anal hole, making the girl gasp with delight. 'You like that?'

'Yes,' Hasheeda replied breathlessly, unable to believe that having her anus licked could be so pleasurable.

'Bad girl!' Louise laughed and smacked her hand across Hasheeda's thigh.

The momentary pain subsided into a warm tingle that

merged with the pleasure of being tongued. Hasheeda closed her eyes as Louise began to use her mouth again.

Louise licked across Hasheeda's anal crack, tracing every contour with the tip of her tongue before settling against the tight entrance. She pushed in a little way and was gratified to find Hasheeda squirming with delight. She paused momentarily to wet her fingers inside Hasheeda's soaking pussy, and then kissed the girl's anus, gently penetrating with her tongue.

Hasheeda moaned and pushed her bottom higher, wanting the other girl to suck and lick, to penetrate her from behind. The feel of Louise's tongue against her bottom hole was indescribable, edging her closer and closer to orgasm.

'Are you a bad girl?' Louise teased.

'Yes, I'm a bad girl...' Hasheeda whispered.

Louise sat up and then pushed her pussy-soaked finger gently into Hasheeda's well-lubricated anal hole.

Hasheeda cried out, but made no move to get away as Louise's finger went deeper. She hardly dared move or breathe, but she felt a strange sense of pride as Louise's finger moved in and out. It felt so dirty to be violated in that way, it was at once humiliating and yet immensely exciting.

'You're just so tight,' Louise said, straining to kiss Hasheeda on the mouth as she continued to frig her anally.

The sudden knock on the door caused both of them to look up sharply. They had both forgotten about the party again, but the impatient rap at the door brought everything sharply into focus. Hasheeda looked at Louise, hoping once more for a reprieve.

'Please,' she begged, 'I'm just not ready for any more...'

Louise looked at her, and then back towards the door. 'But you said you'd do anything I asked,' she reminded her friend, turning back to her.

Hasheeda sat heavily on the floor, her bare bottom on the carpet, her skirt in total disarray, her breasts fully displayed and her panties a damp bundle around her ankles. She looked at herself and then stood up shakily. 'I can't,' she whispered and then, stepping out of her panties, she ran to her bedroom, tears streaming from her big dark eyes.

'Wait!' Louise called after her, but it was too late.

Hasheeda slammed the door of her room and then crawled to the top of her bed. The tears fell freely as the realisation came to her of all she had done. She had allowed herself to be dressed like a petulant schoolgirl. She had swapped hot kisses and caresses with another young woman. Her breasts had been sucked, her pussy stroked and fingered until she had screamed her orgasm like a whore. She had even been punished, spanked like a recalcitrant child, and then fingered anally. And everything, no matter how demeaning, how perverse and humiliating, had given her pleasure. Now, as she sat silently in her room, the full enormity of it all dawned. All the promises to her parents were broken. She had gone from being a shy virgin who had never even undressed in front of another person to a dirty little whore who had taken her pleasure from the pain of punishment and the rituals of humiliation.

She sat in silence, brooding on what she had done, whilst trying to listen to the hurried conversation going on in the other room. Mike's voice she recognised at once, a deep growl that filtered through the room, but there were other voices also. Other men, though Hasheeda could not hear clearly enough to place them. She hoped fervently that Louise was making up some excuse, giving them a plausible story so they wouldn't have to turn up at the party.

Moments later the door opened a crack and Louise, with her school uniform in sexy disarray, slipped into the room. She came over at once, concern writ clear on her face. 'Are you all right?' she asked softly, sitting on the edge of the bed.

'Have they gone?' Hasheeda asked hopefully, glad for Louise's evident consideration.

Louise took Hasheeda's hand and kissed it softly. 'We're not going to the party,' she reported, and then pulled Hasheeda towards her. They kissed passionately, their lips merging together as Louise pushed her tongue into Hasheeda's mouth.

Hasheeda's breasts were still bared, and when Louise stroked them the nipples were gloriously erect and responsive. 'I'm so glad,' Hasheeda whispered between kisses, parting her thighs so Louise could stroke her there.

'We're not going to the party,' Louise whispered in return, 'but now you have to show me that you really are going to do as you're told.'

Hasheeda froze. 'What do you mean?'

'We're not going to the party,' Louise told her again, 'but the party's come here.'

Louise stood up and went to the door immediately. She opened it a fraction and called to Mike. Hasheeda was too stunned to say anything. Instead she huddled nervously at the top of the bed, curling up tight to cover herself as much as possible. She was aware that the short skirt did little to hide her smoothly tanned limbs, and she had no time to button the blouse, which was open to the waist so she had only her arms to cover her breasts.

'This is *my* nasty girl,' Louise announced to Mike proudly, 'and she's going to show me just how much of a nasty girl she is, aren't you?'

Hasheeda could not look either Louise or Mike in the eye. 'Yes,' she whispered, her throat dry.

'And does your nasty girl have a taste for hard cock?' Mike asked, his voice carrying a cruel note that made Hasheeda feel even more frightened.

'She doesn't yet,' Louise replied, walking back to the bed, 'but she will have.'

Hasheeda huddled up tighter, trying desperately to think of a way out of the awful situation. Louise crawled up onto the bed and then squeezed into the space behind

Hasheeda, gazing meaningfully into her eyes, as though willing her to comply.

'Don't make me punish you in front of Mike,' Louise warned. Hasheeda thought back to the chastisement she had already received, and shuddered. She knew another spanking would hurt, but that having Mike witness it would redouble the humiliation and the excitement. The prospect was both appalling and appealing.

Hasheeda allowed herself to be pulled back so that she was sitting with her legs curled under her, the short skirt thankfully covering the tops of her thighs. Her arms were still crossed over her chest, but Louise reached from behind and took each hand in turn and lowered it. Hasheeda looked away, unable to face Mike, who was gazing at the swell of her breasts, his eyes fixed on the dark nipples. Her breasts were framed on either side by the crisp white shirt and delineated by the knotted tie which dangled between them.

Louise reached round and cupped Hasheeda's breasts, her pale fingers massaging the darker flesh, making the nipples stand out more. She kissed Hasheeda gently on the back of the neck before speaking to Mike. 'Isn't she gorgeous?' she said.

Hasheeda flushed, her face was burning but there was no denying the thrill she felt on hearing Louise speaking about her in such a manner. She dared to look up at Mike, and saw he was undressing. A spasm of fear passed through her; she had never seen a naked man before and the prospect frightened her.

'Don't be nervous,' Louise whispered, kissing her on the neck.

Hasheeda sighed as her nipples were stroked and teased. Her pussy was wet and she could feel her juices oozing deliciously from between her sex lips. When Louise urged her forward she complied, getting up on hands and knees obediently. Her breasts swayed free and, glancing back over her shoulder, she saw that her skirt was being pushed over her waist.

Mike finished undressing and climbed onto the bed. Hasheeda gazed at the erect flesh jutting from its bed of dark, curly hair. It was thickly veined and tipped with a bulbous head, leaking a wet jewel of liquid.

'Oh, baby,' Louise exclaimed, 'your first cock…'

Mike drew closer and took his hardness in his hand. 'Well, just how nasty are you?' he demanded.

Louise crawled forward immediately. 'Like this,' she told Hasheeda, reaching out to stroke Mike's thick cock. She took it in her hand, wrapping her fingers around the base and then leaning forward to touch her lips to the reddish-coloured glans.

Hasheeda watched, wide-eyed with excitement, as Louise first kissed the glans and then smoothed her lips down along the full length of Mike's rod. She smiled as she did so, enjoying the look on Hasheeda's face as well as enjoying the feel of hard cock on her lips. She used her tongue to trace the thick vein from the base to the tip. Then she closed her lips around the head, taking it slowly into her mouth, sucking gently.

'That's good…' Mike whispered, pressing forward so that his hardness went deeper into Louise's welcoming mouth. She closed her eyes and worked her head up and down, taking his cock down deep into her throat and then releasing it slowly so that just the very tip remained between her lips.

Hasheeda watched in silence, and then Louise turned to her. They kissed, a deep, passionate embrace that Louise broke when she moved away. 'Now you,' she whispered, still holding Mike's hardness in her hand.

Hasheeda touched her lips to Mike's cock, half afraid he would pull away from her. She kissed him slowly, letting her tongue run up and down the smooth flesh. Gaining a little in confidence she let Louise guide the reddish tip of his maleness to her lips. She let her tongue travel across the little slit so she could taste the clear fluid that leaked from it.

'Take it all now,' Mike urged impatiently.

Louise flicked her tongue over Mike's cock one last time and then kissed Hasheeda on the lips. 'Good girl,' she whispered as she withdrew.

Hasheeda opened her mouth and let Mike push into her. She closed her lips tightly over his length, letting him enter her deeply, her tongue sliding across the thick muscle. He took her by the hair and started to thrust his cock in and out of her mouth slowly, fucking her deeply while she remained on hands and knees for him.

'Baby,' Louise whispered, 'you suck cock so beautifully…'

Hasheeda gasped as she felt Louise's fingers press into her wetness. She parted her thighs still more, opening herself to Louise's fingers and tongue. Her orgasm was so close, she was on the edge, enjoying the cock in her mouth and fingers and tongue in her pussy and toying with her anus.

Louise lay under Hasheeda, alternately sucking on her firm breasts hanging down or else pushing her tongue into Hasheeda's dark pussy and savouring the juices that poured so freely. She wet her fingers in her own pussy juices and then pressed a finger deep into Hasheeda's rear hole.

It seemed to Hasheeda that she was nothing but pleasure. Every inch of her being was alive with ecstasy, every sensation amplified and merging until it seemed that a finger brushing her nipple connected directly with the tongue lapping at her pussy, or with Mike's hardness pressed deep into her mouth.

'Baby, you need this too,' Louise whispered.

Hasheeda opened her eyes and looked up. Two other men had joined them. She knew Jack and Phil by sight; Phil, an ebony-skinned black student, smiled at her while Jack, a slim blond, looked at her with pure lust in his eyes. Both men were naked and moving towards her. Her eyes strayed down to their hard cocks, and she knew she wanted them both.

Louise sat up on the bed. 'You need a cock here,' she said, pushing her finger into Hasheeda's anus again.

Hasheeda gasped, she could hardly contain herself. She was ready to come, to scream her pleasure at the top of her lungs.

'And I need a cock too,' Louise added, smiling at Phil.

Before Hasheeda knew what was happening Jack had moved into position. His erection jutted obscenely from between his thighs as he took her by the waist. He smiled at her and then, taking his cock in his hand, he guided himself into place. She held her breath as he pushed the engorged tip to her tight rear opening. She was wet; her own juices had been slicked there by Louise, who had lubricated her well using her fingers and tongue. There was a feeling of discomfort as his hard flesh pushed through her tight anal ring, but there was pleasure too as he started to penetrate her.

Hasheeda looked nervously over her shoulder. She tensed, but Louise kissed her and told her to relax. Slowly she was sodomised, the rigid column slipping inch by inch into her rectum. At last she dared to breathe again. She moved slightly from side to side, stimulated further by the feel of Jack's long, hard cock inside her.

'Good girl,' Louise whispered, evidently proud with what she had engineered.

She closed her eyes and took Mike's hardness in her mouth once more. It was difficult not to picture herself as she was: on hands and knees with a cock in her mouth and another buried deep between her bottom cheeks. The man behind her started to fuck her using long, slow strokes, his cock sliding deep into her behind while he used his hands to gently pull her buttocks apart.

When she opened her eyes she saw Louise lying beside

her. Her skirt was off and her legs were widely parted, her sex fully displayed. Phil had her by the waist and he pressed his massive dark cock into her pussy. She was shuddering and moaning as she was fucked, her pleasure somehow merging with Hasheeda's. When their eyes met they managed to smile before each was engulfed by yet another wave of pleasure. She tensed suddenly and cried out as a wave of orgasm swept through her, taking the strength from her and leaving her gasping for breath.

Louise sat up on her knees and, taking Hasheeda away from Mike's glistening hardness, kissed her on the mouth. 'Baby,' she whispered, 'oh baby, see, I told you this would be good, didn't I?'

Hasheeda moaned as Jack slammed his cock into her behind with sharp, violent strokes. 'And… and I'm still a virgin…' she whispered, astounded by the realisation.

'Your pussy's for me only,' Louise told her.

Phil nudged his way forward and offered his thick black cock to Hasheeda. She looked up at him deliriously, and then closed her lips around his flesh. He filled her mouth, so she closed her eyes and moved her head to accommodate his length. Beside her she was aware that Louise was now on hands and knees, her mouth a warm velvety pocket for Mike to fuck.

Hasheeda opened her eyes again when she felt Phil slowing down. She held his cock in her hand, her fingers nestling in jet-black pubic hair. His length glistened, his flesh darker than her own. She turned and saw that Jack had moved over and was using his mouth to wet Louise's anus, licking her excitedly so that her hole was wet and ready.

'You need this now,' Mike told her.

'Let Mike fuck you,' Louise instructed, her voice a soft murmur as Jack started to fuck her anally.

Mike smoothed his hands up and down her thighs and across her bottom, as though marvelling at the soft flesh offered up to him. His fingers slipped into her pussy and she sighed, her eyelids fluttering as the sensations drew her towards another orgasm. He continued to stroke her pussy lips as he pushed his cock into the welcoming groove of her rear hole. She relaxed, letting him fill her completely with his erect cock.

Phil took Hasheeda's face in his hands and kissed her slowly, pressing his tongue where his cock had been only moments earlier.

'This is for us,' Louise whispered.

Hasheeda turned and kissed Louise. They were positioned side by side, school uniforms in disarray, bottoms exposed, and a cock taking them anally. The two girls turned to Phil. They both began to kiss and suck his cock, moving sinuously to give him pleasure, sharing his hardness as though it were a prize.

'I'm coming…' Phil whispered urgently.

'Now you're going to learn what it is to take a man's come and swallow it,' Louise told her. Louise gave way and Hasheeda took the length deep between her lips. She gasped and struggled for breath as thick jets of jism were pumped into her mouth. She sucked hard, wanting every drop of his fluid, wanting it greedily. He released her a second later and sat back on the bed. Hasheeda looked at him and swallowed hard, taking his seed just as he had demanded. She smiled shyly, secretly thrilled at what she had just done.

Mike started to fuck her harder. A moment later he tensed and uttered a strangled cry as he pressed his cock deep into her backside. She lifted her bottom higher, pushing back to meet his hard thrusts. His abdomen slammed against her bottom and it seemed as though his cock was growing bigger and harder, filling her completely. At last he too climaxed, and this time Hasheeda cried out her own orgasm. Nothing had ever prepared her to feel such an intense sensation; it was more than pleasure, it was a blissful feeling that took her out of herself completely.

She rolled back instinctively, eyes closed, sated, her body jewelled with beads of perspiration. However, she had hardly taken a breath when she felt something between her thighs. She opened her eyes to find that Louise was on hands and knees between them. She was still being fucked from behind, her partner's hands gripping her bottom tightly as he pounded into her.

'Baby, I love you…' Louise whispered, and then she knelt lower and pressed her lips to Hasheeda's pussy.

Hasheeda lay back and let the pleasure take her again.

La Tempête

He liked the look of her as soon as she came in, wide-eyed and hesitant. She looked young; if she was over eighteen it had to be by a matter of months and not years.

Smartly dressed in fashionably long black boots, short skirt and white blouse, she saw Nick sitting at the corner table and flashed him a shy smile.

'Mr Moore?' she asked hopefully, her dark eyes meeting his for only an instant before turning away.

'And you must be Carole,' he guessed, rising from his seat to offer her a place at the table.

'I know I'm early,' she apologised, 'but the bus came early and the traffic wasn't as bad as...'

'Don't apologise,' Nick laughed. 'Arriving early for a job interview never did anyone any harm.'

She allowed herself a smile, her lips parting to reveal straight white teeth. Her round face was perfect, when she smiled it seemed to light up her eyes, making her seem even more pretty. When she sat down, opposite Nick, she smoothed her skirt in a gesture of modesty that was entirely natural to her.

'Is the job still open then?' she asked, a sigh of relief clear in her voice.

'Yes, but only just,' he admitted. Word of the excellent salary had gone round quickly and Nick had been inundated with calls, and there had been many potential applicants who had sounded perfect. Of the ten vacancies only one now remained unfilled, though he knew that Carole looked perfect for the part.

'Thank God for that,' she sighed. 'I was sure you'd get someone else.'

'No, I don't work like that. If I've promised you an interview I'm not going to give the job to someone else while you're still waiting.'

'I really appreciate that, Mr Moore,' she beamed.

The conversation was interrupted by a harsh metallic screech that filled the entire room. Nick waited for it to die down, glad to see that the builders had resumed work after yet another coffee break. 'As you can hear,' he explained to Carole, 'there's still a lot to finish before we open.'

She nodded. The dining area was almost totally finished, the tables and chairs set in secluded alcoves, the walls decorated with *fin de siècle* scenes of Paris. There was still an atmosphere of spit and sawdust, the inevitable result of all the redecorating, but already the underlying ambience was beginning to appear.

'I think it looks really good,' she said approvingly.

'There's still a lot to do, but I agree with you, it's beginning to look the part. Which brings me neatly back to you.'

'I'm very keen Mr Moore, you must realise that,' she assured him earnestly. The top few buttons of her blouse were undone, giving a glimpse of smooth white skin without a hint of cleavage. One more button undone and it would have been coquettish, but there was something instinctively modest about her and he was certain it wasn't put on for his benefit. Some of the girls he'd interviewed had been practically naked, flaunting themselves shamelessly in the hope that he'd take an interest, to no avail. The restaurant he had in mind was sophisticated and classy, the last thing he wanted was a staff young and loud.

'Tell me Carole, how many times have you been to Paris?' he asked, formally marking the start of the interview.

'Four times, two weekends and two longer holidays,' she said.

'And your French?'

'I couldn't be an interpreter, but I do speak the language.

I have my certificates at home if you want me to bring them in...'

He smiled, and slid a leather-bound menu across the table to her. 'Read from this,' he said, leaning back in his seat.

She opened it carefully and scanned through it. It was all in French of course, with no English translation; there was a separate menu for that. He listened closely as she began to read, fluently and with a pronunciation that was perfect. There was no doubt that she knew what she was reading as well, she was practically licking her lips as she went through the main courses.

'Very good,' he said, interrupting her in mid-sentence. 'I am impressed. You sound like you enjoy your food as well.'

She smiled shyly. 'Thank you, Mr Moore. I've got my figure to think about,' she added, 'but I do like my food.'

'Good, I like that, there's nothing worse than being served by someone who has no understanding of food.'

'I only wish I could afford to eat at places like this,' she sighed, handing back the menu.

He nodded. The prices in the menu were not cheap, there was no denying that, but then again *La Tempête* was not going to be just another French restaurant.

'Tell me what you know about the job,' he suggested.

She took a deep breath before beginning. 'This is going to be a very special French restaurant, very different to all the others. You've got an excellent chef, even I've heard of him,' she paused momentarily, but there was no reassuring smile from Nick. 'It won't be the sort of place you come to on a whim. Every place has to be booked in advance, they'll even be someone at the door to stop undesirables from barging in from the pub and that sort of thing.'

'It's not so much people from the pub I'm worried about,' he said, clarifying the point for her. 'It's just that I don't want crowds of drunken hoorays turning up and spoiling the atmosphere. Do you know the kind of atmosphere I'm after?'

'I think so,' she said uncertainly. 'Parisian sophistication, I think. You know, very elegant, smart. Am I right?'

'Partly. The missing word in your description is decadent. Visiting *La Tempête* will be an experience in more than the culinary sense. Was that not explained to you?'

'Yes, Mr Moore,' she said quickly, her eyes widening with the fear that she had just messed up her chances of working there.

'Part of that decadent ambience will be created by the girls who'll work here. *La serveuse* will be a central character, she will embody the elegant and the decadent, both in the way she looks and in the way she acts. You do understand that, don't you?'

For a moment he was certain she was going to shake her head or burst into tears. 'I think so, Mr Moore,' she agreed softly, her voice barely a whisper of indecision.

'As you know, the salary I'm offering is far higher than the norm, but that salary has to be earned. Of course you'll have the added perk of enjoying some of the finest cuisine this side of the channel.'

'Yes, I hadn't thought of that,' she agreed, her smile returning slowly. Her eyes were still full of uncertainty, as though she were struggling with herself and could not make a decision.

'I like you Carole,' he told her, smiling properly for the first time. 'You have excellent French and, even better, an appreciation of the finer things in life. If it were up to me then the job would be yours, however, there are the final formalities before I can make that offer.'

She looked at him eagerly, the chance of a job clearing the indecision. 'What do I have to do?'

'There's the uniform to try on,' he explained.

'The uniform?'

He laughed. 'I thought you knew. There is indeed a special uniform for the waitresses, very French and very naughty. That's what I meant about helping to create that special ambience.'

'I hadn't realised,' she said, sounding crestfallen.

'It's a French maid's outfit,' he told her, deciding to be blunt rather than trying to break it gently. 'Very enticing and sexy, in a light-hearted way. If the uniform looks good on you then the job is practically yours. So far the other girls have loved it.'

She looked at him dubiously, the suspicion clouding her dark eyes. 'I wasn't really expecting this...' she started to mumble. The screech of the electric drill drowned out the rest of her words, but the look on her face told its own story.

'May I suggest that you try it on, and if you feel uncomfortable about it then we can talk about finding you some other job?'

She hesitated for a moment, weighing up the possibilities, and then nodded reluctantly. 'Okay, I'll try it on, but I have to say that I wasn't really expecting anything like this.'

'The staff changing room is currently the scene of all that banging and screeching, I'm afraid. It's the last part of the building to be finished. However, if you don't mind changing in the kitchen today...'

She looked shocked. 'The kitchen? But... Isn't there some...'

Nick glared at her. 'Are you always so difficult?' he demanded, suddenly angered by her obvious distrust. None of the other girls had been so suspicious, even though the uniform was a surprise for most of them too.

'I'm sorry,' she mumbled, her pretty face flushing pink with embarrassment. 'If it's private I'll change in the kitchen,' she agreed.

Nick sighed. 'If it wasn't private I wouldn't have asked you to change in there. Now, please be a good girl and go and try your uniform out. It's there waiting for you, hanging behind the door. There's no mirror I'm afraid, but if you give me a shout when you're ready I'll tell you how you look.'

It was obvious that she was unhappy about the whole idea, but she did as she was told. He watched her cross the length of the restaurant and enter the kitchen, noting the way her long black boots accentuated the shape of her legs, and the way the tight skirt clung to her well-shaped behind. She was tall and slim but with curves in all the right places, which was just what he was looking for.

Finding the right sort of girl had proved to be a far bigger problem than he had anticipated. There were lots of pretty girls of the right age around, but few of them had the intelligence, the elegance, or the personality to carry off the roles he had assigned them. Luckily, once he had recruited the first four they had helped him find the others. Carole had been recommended by one of the other girls, and so far he was impressed by her looks and by her knowledge of French, however he was not so enamoured by her personality. If she were only a little more trusting, or perhaps a little more relaxed, then he'd be certain.

His ruminations were interrupted by one of the builders, a burly monster of a man, striding purposely towards the kitchen. 'Where do you think you're off too?' Nick demanded, rising quickly from his seat.

'There's something needs seeing to in there,' the builder announced, his broad grin splitting his face in two.

'Very funny,' Nick sighed. 'Now isn't there some real work for you to be getting on with?'

The builder look offended, the grin replaced by a sullen frown. 'I was only having a laugh,' he complained. 'A fella's got to have a laugh sometimes. Pretty bit of skirt like that appreciates a joke, I can tell.'

'She might appreciate the joke, I certainly don't. Now, if you don't mind...'

The builder glared at Nick for a moment, then turned and marched back the way he had come, muttering a litany of complaints as a salve to his injured pride. It was no surprise; the lure of pretty young women was certainly going to be one of the main attractions of the restaurant, but it was also going to be one of the problems. A strict door policy sounded like financial suicide for a new restaurant, but it was the only way Nick could think of having some control over the clientele. It was a gamble, and the thought always caused a shudder of fear to pass through him. His house, savings and a substantial loan from the bank were all riding on the success of *La Tempête*, which promised to be as stormy as its name.

'I'm ready,' she cried from the kitchen, her voice lacking in any form of enthusiasm.

She looked gorgeous. The black satin and white frills complementing her dark good looks and soft white skin. It was a perfect fit, from the towering black high heels to the seamed stockings, to the low cut of the uniform to the lace cap which banded her dark hair. When she moved the skirt swished slightly and he was treated to an enticing glimpse of flesh above the thick black stocking tops. The deep cleavage of her breasts was emphasised by the constricting tightness, and the apron tied at her waist served to draw attention to the roundness of her backside.

The effect was spoilt by the pensive expression on her face, her eyes flitting from side to side nervously, her lips pursed as though stifling her anger. She was standing straight, hands together in front of her, balanced finely on the high heels.

'What is it, girl?' he demanded, annoyed by her obvious discomfort. If it wasn't enough worrying about the opening of the restaurant, he had to contend with the antics of silly teenage girls.

'I'm sorry, Mr Moore,' she whispered, her face flaring red once again, 'but I don't think I can handle this.'

He exhaled heavily. 'Handle what, exactly?' he asked, not bothering to hide his exasperation.

'All of this,' she explained, rubbing a hand down the smooth satin uniform. 'I mean it'll hurt, won't it?'

He looked at her quizzically. 'The shoes?' he asked.

'No, not that, I can handle the stilettos all right. No, I mean, you know... The punishment when I'm naughty.'

By now her face was bright red and her eyes were fixed at a point six inches in front of her toes. Her voice had become a strained whisper. 'I don't understand,' Nick admitted, hardly daring to let his imagination get ahead of him.

'The decadence thing... You said you wanted us to be all decadent and naughty...' she tried to explain, but seemed to have trouble finding the right words. 'With the high heels and everything I suppose we'll always be spilling things and so on... It'll hurt, won't it, afterwards.'

'You mean when you make mistakes, when you're naughty, as you put it,' he looked to her for the nod of confirmation, 'you expect to be punished – physically.'

'Like in those magazines,' she added, helpfully.

He nodded sagely. Those magazines. She looked so young and naïve, but obviously her education extended down to *those* magazines. He could follow her train of thought – maid's uniform, decadence, naughtiness, correction. 'Yes, I suppose it will hurt. But unless you try it how will you know?'

'I know the other girls have accepted... Did they try it first?'

He suppressed the smile. 'Yes, they were all punished by me, but only after they'd put the uniform on first. In your case I'm inclined to be extra strict, you're being very difficult about this. You either want this job or you don't.'

'But I do,' she insisted forcefully.

'In that case I think you should be a good girl and bend over the counter there,' he pointed to one of the worktops, smooth steel polished like a mirror.

She hesitated, and he could see the arguments raging

inside her. There was doubt there, and denial, but there was also excitement and a curiosity that could not be suppressed. Hesitantly she turned round, took the two steps to the appointed place, and stopped. For a moment she stared at her reflection in the cold steel, allowing him the chance to appreciate how she looked from behind. Long straight legs, beautifully shaped by the shiny black heels, slim waist but a well proportioned rear, long black hair held in place by the frilly lace cap.

When she bent over at the waist the skirt raised at the back, lifting clear of the stocking tops and displaying the black suspenders which pressed firmly into the flesh of her thighs. She pressed her face and chest against the worktop, wriggling slightly in an effort to get comfortable.

'Lift your skirt completely,' he ordered, enjoying the view. When the skirt was raised he saw the tiny black briefs were pulled up between the round globes of her bottom, the thin wisp of lace delineating the rear cleavage to her advantage. She looked good, there was no denying the enticing image her primly offered backside made.

'How many?' she asked, almost breathless with fear and anticipation.

'Six, with my hand.'

She made no reply. Instead she arched her back slightly, offering a rounder target. He stepped forward, hardly daring to believe what was happening. He touched her softly, running his fingertips over her backside, from one side to the other. She hardly dared to breathe, her eyes were half closed and her fists were clenched tightly.

The first smack was hard, landing flat on her left buttock, making a resounding slapping sound that seemed to fill the kitchen completely. She uttered a strangled gasp but did not cry or make any movement. His fingers were clearly imprinted on her white flesh, a red badge of pain that he swore was warm to the touch. He lifted his arm and brought it down again, on the same bottom cheek and with the same force. She inched forward, her knuckles white as she gripped the edge of the worktop. Her skin marked easily, white flesh running to pink and then red at the site of impact. He touched her again, able to feel the distinct mark as well as see it.

The third stroke, and then the fourth. She cried out but, biting her lip and gripping hard, she did not move out of position. There was determination in her eyes, but with it the misting over of pain and pleasure. Her left bottom cheek was red, patterned from the top of the thigh and above. A fifth stroke, as hard and as painful as the first four. She seemed to draw her stomach down and raise her bottom higher, offering him her derriere for punishment as though it were his to do with as he wished. The wisp of lace between her thighs was drawn tightly into her flesh, a black band against white skin turning pink.

The last stroke was the hardest of all, the sound of it matched by a squeal of pain that she uttered despite her best efforts. His own hand was buzzing, throbbing with pain, and yet he knew it was only a pale echo of the sensations she was experiencing. When he touched, stroking her punished left buttock, he let his fingers slip lower, brushing against the sticky warmth of her sex.

'Have we finished?' she asked, hardly able to speak clearly. The contrast between the two sides of her rear end was plain to see; on the left a pattern of red finger marks and the shadow of his hand on her flesh, on the right the pure unblemished softness of her skin.

'Not yet,' he told her firmly. 'There's the other side to do as well.'

She sighed, her breath misting on the cold steel upon which her face rested. He looked around quickly, searching for the right implement in a kitchen full of them. There were a dozen different wooden spoons, and a number of small pans which looked ideal for tanning the hide of a silly girl. The spatula looked perfect however; long, slightly curved, very strong and easy to handle.

'Six strokes,' he informed her.

'With that?' she cried, clearly alarmed by the wooden implement he had to hand.

'Seven strokes for that,' he decided. She fell silent, resigned to the facts of her punishment.

He was careful with the first stroke, bringing it down flat against the unmarked skin of her right buttock. The sound was impressive and the solid red mark it created looked good. Her eyes were wide, and he could tell that the spatula was indeed a more effective instrument of correction than his bare hand.

The next few strokes fell in quick succession, each delivered firmly and with a resounding crack. She was panting, breathing heavily, making little sobbing sounds as he administered her chastisement.

He stopped at number four and examined her closely, comparing each bottom cheek, touching her intimately without a murmur of dissent from her lovely lips. She was undoubtedly aroused. When he touched a finger to her sex she seemed to melt, a sigh issuing from her lips as she closed her eyes to the pleasure. He resumed the punishment, smacking hard the final strokes, the last delivered squarely between her buttocks.

The punishment over, he stepped back for a moment. She seemed dazed, hardly able to move, as though she too was welded to the cold steel worktop. It gave him a chance to savour the image of her, bent beautifully over, her uniform up around her waist, long legs stretched tautly, bottom perfectly displayed in all it's pink, punished glory.

'You can stand up now,' he told her, finally.

She seemed to wake suddenly. She pushed herself up and modestly brushed down her uniform, hiding from view the evidence of her punishment. Her chest was flushed pink, her white skin mottled by the evidence of her pleasure just as her bottom had been mottled by her chastisement.

'Do you still want the job?' he asked, his manner cool and professional, despite the raging desire he felt.

'Will it get any worse than that?' she asked, swallowing hard.

'Only if you're really bad,' he told her. 'Don't worry though, most nights of the week you'll just be on display, looking pretty to keep our clients happy until the food arrives. However, the uniform and the punishment are reserved for special nights, when only the most select of our clients are invited.'

'You mean this,' she clutched her uniform, 'is for the special clients only? Other nights we wear something else?'

He smiled. 'That's right. Other nights you'll wear a more respectable uniform, still pretty and sexy, but not like this. On our special nights, however, you'll have to be extra careful not to make a mistake and earn a spanking from our customers.' He paused. The entire business plan had just been rewritten, but he knew it made more sense. Act as a normal French restaurant for most nights, but offer the privilege of punishing the girls on certain special occasions – and charge prices accordingly. 'So,' he finished, 'what do you say?'

She reached down and rubbed her bottom surreptitiously, as though the stinging was too powerful to ignore. 'What if I make mistakes on the other nights?' she asked.

'I reserve the right to punish you when required, my girl.'

She nodded at once. 'Yes, Mr Moore. When do I start?'

He smiled. 'You've already started. If I were you I'd change and get home for a good night of rest. You've got a long day ahead of you tomorrow.'

'But the restaurant doesn't open for...'

'It's all right,' he said, stopping her mid-sentence. 'It's just that I have nine other girls to re-interview,' he announced, smiling.

Let Me Be Your…

I liked Andy Gale almost as soon as I met him. He was the sort of young man that most people liked, and when he joined my team I felt naturally drawn to him. I was his supervisor then, but we were soon friends rather than just work colleagues. It was just the way he was; easy going, personable, and with a sharp, irreverent sense of humour. A few weeks after he'd started, by which time we were well on the way to becoming good friends, I noticed the picture of Philipa on his desk.

Andy saw me looking at the framed photo. His young wife, she looked to be in her early twenties, was smiling, her long blonde hair swept back to reveal a round face, with shining blue-green eyes and prominent lips glossed an eye-catching scarlet.

'She's a bit of a looker,' I remarked casually, then handed him the thick sheaf of papers I wanted him to go through.

He took the file and made a face. 'Thanks,' he said, weighing it all in his hand. 'You haven't met Philipa yet, have you?'

I shook my head. 'Not yet,' I said, standing up, 'but I'm sure that one day we'll get round to going out for a drink, the three of us.'

'Yes, that'd be good,' Andy agreed.

And that was the end of it for a while. At the time it was just a bit of idle chatter, the sort of meaningless small-talk that goes on in offices all the time. I really doubted that I would ever meet Andy and Philipa outside the work environment; the most I could have expected would be to swap a few words with her at our Christmas party. Not that I would have turned that down, the young woman in the photograph was extremely attractive. There was no doubt in my mind that Andy was an extremely lucky man to be married to her.

It was at least a month before Andy raised the subject again. Perhaps he had seen me glancing at Philip's photograph a few times more, or perhaps he'd been thinking things through. In any case, late one afternoon he came over to my office to talk through some sales projections he'd prepared for me. The conversation was long and tedious, but halfway through he casually asked me if I had any plans for the following Friday evening. I hadn't; since splitting up with my wife many of my evenings were spent slumped in front of the television with nothing but a frozen meal and a bottle for company.

'What've you got in mind,' I asked, imagining that he was about to ask me to join him for a post-work drink or two at one of the local pubs.

'I wondered whether you'd want to come out for a meal and a drink with me and Philipa,' he said. 'I mean, if you can't make it then it's no big deal.'

'That'll be great,' I assured him hastily.

'Good,' he said. 'We fancied a curry, is that okay?'

'No problem. Now,' I said, trying not to show just how grateful I felt for the invitation, 'if you think we can forget about these,' I slid the projections back across my desk towards him, 'then you're wrong.'

He laughed. 'Damn, does that mean we've got to carry on?'

'Afraid so.'

By the time Friday had arrived I was really looking forward to going out. I was certain that Andy and Philipa would be good company, and in the event I was not disappointed. As soon as I set eyes on Philipa I realised that the photograph I'd seen did her no justice. Her eyes sparkled and her smile was warm and friendly, which perfectly described her personality. Although not very tall, she had a good figure and her petite frame had curves in all the right places. She was wearing a little black dress that clung sensuously to her curves and was short enough to give me a good view of her lithe, well-shaped legs.

Andy did the introductions as soon as I arrived at the restaurant and soon we were seated, the three of us around a circular table. We took our time ordering, but the discussion about the food provided a neutral subject to get the conversations started.

During the meal Andy tried to talk about work a couple of times, but this was vetoed first by Philipa and then by me. It was soon apparent that there was a real spark between the three of us, the conversation flowed freely and time sped by.

'Well, this has been a great evening,' I sighed, just as the last of the coffee arrived. To be honest, I was feeling more relaxed than I had for a long time. I suppose since Jan and I had split up I'd been getting more and more uptight. Although I don't mind my own company, I suppose I was forgetting what it was like to be sociable.

'Yes, it's been good,' Philipa agreed, beaming me a bright smile. Her eyes met mine for an instant, lingered, and then she looked away. It wasn't the only time it had happened that evening, and each time my heart raced a little bit faster.

'We'll have to do this again,' Andy said, joining in. I noticed he was looking at Philipa, and then he turned back to me. Something had passed between them, I knew it instantly. Had he picked up on the way Philipa and I had been looking at each other?

I avoided Andy's eyes guiltily. The last thing I wanted him to think was that I had somehow been flirting with his young wife. 'Please,' I said, 'I know it was you who invited me out, but it's on me. Okay?'

'Oh, come on,' Andy retorted. 'You've been a great help to me at work, this is the least I can do.'

I shook my head. 'No way, Andy,' I insisted. 'I'm paying,

and that's the end of it. Clear?'

'No, it's our treat,' Philipa said, taking her husband's hand in hers.

Andy clasped her hand and looked directly at me. 'I tell you what,' he decided, 'why don't you come back to our place for a drink?'

Philipa smiled invitingly. 'Yes, that's a great idea, what do you say?'

Her eyes were on mine again and this time it was no accident. I looked up and saw that Andy was unconcerned, he was sitting forward waiting for my answer. 'Only if I get to pay the bill here,' I said.

Philipa's smile broadened further. 'Good,' she enthused, 'I'm glad that's settled.'

I swallowed hard. For a second I was certain I was imagining things, that the eye contact and her smiles were entirely innocent. Perhaps it was the drink or the effect of too many lonely nights on my part. And then, when I caught her eye again, I became certain that there was definitely something else going on.

I called for the bill and Philipa decided she needed to freshen up before we left. I watched her walk across the restaurant, the tight-fitting dress clinging to her curves, the black velvet contrasting with the golden tan of her skin. She was delicious, there was no doubting that.

'You still think she looks good?' Andy asked me, as though reading my mind.

I had been staring at his wife openly. If he was angry there was no sign of it in his voice. I avoided his eyes. 'I'm not going to say she's ugly, am I?' I responded, hoping I could joke my way out of a tricky situation.

He smiled. 'Well, you could,' he said, 'but you'd be talking crap.'

The waiter arrived bearing the credit card slip for me to sign. My hand was shaky as I scrawled my signature.

'It's getting late,' I said after the waiter had finished,

'why don't you just drop me off home?'

'Our company not good enough for you?' Andy demanded. His tone was jokey, bantering like he did in the office, but there was something else going on. He was edgy, but perhaps he was picking that off me.

'No, of course not,' I said uncomfortably.

We both fell silent as we watched Philipa returning. Her black high heels shaped her legs, making every sinew and muscle taut. Her arms were crossed in front of her as she clutched a black velvet handbag which matched the dress. She was smiling, her lips parted over white teeth, her eyes sparkling with excitement.

'Are we ready?' she asked.

She took Andy's arm as we left the restaurant, holding him tight, her body close to his. They were a couple; young, happy, and a painful reminder of where I had once been. I chided myself for feeling bitter; my marriage had dissolved itself, I was at once an innocent party and an injured victim.

Her heels clicked on the pavement, echoing across dark streets as we walked back to their car. There was no conversation between us, but out in the open the silence was not as strained as it would have been in the confines of the restaurant.

'Shall I drive?' she offered as we drew up to Andy's black BMW. The car was his pride and joy; under the streetlights it gleamed like some dark, menacing creature.

'Let you drive this?' he asked, winking at me. 'Come on darling, I love you deeply and all that, but no way.'

'Huh! You'd let me drive, wouldn't you?' she asked, turning to me for support.

I smiled encouragingly. 'Not a bloody chance,' I told her.

Andy's laughter filled the street and he was still laughing as he slipped into the driving seat. Philipa shrugged and walked over to the passenger side. I watched her get into the car, my eye drawn to the line of her breasts and to the smoothness of her soft skin. I hesitated for a moment, trying to get a grip on myself. The night air was cool and it felt good as I sucked it deep into my lungs.

'Still with us?' Andy remarked sharply as I finally took the back seat.

'Listen, Cole,' I snapped, 'don't forget who signs your pay cheque at the end of the month.'

There was a stunned silence in the car for a moment, and then he started to laugh. I did too, a heartbeat later.

'Yes, boss,' he said, gunning the car into life.

'You don't have to sign his cheque,' Philipa told me, turning round in her seat to look at me.

'I know I don't,' I agreed, 'but I'm a sucker for sad cases. I think of it as charity.'

'You could always sign the cheque to me,' she suggested sweetly.

'I've got no problem with that,' I mused, as though giving the idea some consideration.

'And what exactly do you propose to do to earn the dosh?' Andy asked, glancing round at the two of us. His hands were tight on the wheel, in control.

'I'm sure we can come to some arrangement,' Philipa suggested, and then she laughed, getting an echo of it from Andy too.

'Well, boss,' Andy said, 'what about it? Philipa gets the wages.'

I wanted to kill the topic stone dead, there was something underlying the humour and it made me feel uncomfortable. 'Sure,' I said finally, 'but she gets the car too.'

'No way!' snapped Andy. 'The deal's off. No one drives this baby but me.'

'Oh well,' Philipa sighed, 'at least I don't have to sweat blood making up my commission every month.'

'You don't have to do that,' Andy responded, our eyes meeting in the rear-view mirror.

'Oh, yes?' she asked on cue.

'No,' he continued expansively, 'you just get the boss's job and make everyone else sweat blood…'

I laughed. He was a reckless bastard at times; the mood I was in it was more than likely I would have taken offence, but he didn't care. The fact that he took risks was what made him good at his job.

Their place was on one of those box-like estates of geometric houses with parking spaces out front and a square of grass masquerading as a front garden. The houses were stamped from a single template, and in the darkness it was hard to tell one bijou residence from the next. The streetlights cast a pale orange glow and my breath misted as I stepped out of the car.

It was cold, colder than it had been for a long time. Philipa shivered as Andy strode to the front door. My eyes were drawn to her as she waited in the darkness. She turned and our eyes met. She half smiled, and then the door was open and the warmth inside drew her away.

'Come on,' Andy urged me, an outstretched arm pointing the way inside.

I entered and he followed me in, a step behind.

'Through here,' Philipa called from the front room.

I walked along thickly carpet floor, a couple of steps through the hall and then a right turn into the room. Further along the hall there were stairs going up, and beyond that the darkness of the kitchen. Philipa was standing by the window, her back to it, her bottom pressed against a radiator. She was standing absolutely straight, her feet side by side, thighs together, arms down at her sides.

'Nice place you've got here,' I remarked, a barefaced lie but it seemed an appropriate thing to say.

'What're you drinking?' Andy asked me, clapping his hands together as he entered the room.

'Anything,' I said.

'Water, then?'

'Only if you want me to go home now,' I said.

'Scotch all right?'

'I'll take it neat,' I decided.

Philipa broke away from the window. 'I'll get it,' she said.

'Make mine a whiskey too,' Andy told her.

She stopped in the doorway. 'It's okay,' she told me, 'you can sit down.'

I nodded stupidly. A three-seater sofa faced a brick fireplace, to the left of it there was a matching armchair which directly faced the TV and video. I hesitated, and then decided to go for the armchair. Andy sat on the sofa, in the place nearest to me.

'It wasn't a bad meal, was it?' he remarked conversationally. His face was slightly flushed and his eyes darted from me to Philipa, returning with the drinks.

She came over to me first, a silver tray in her hands. I took my glass and thanked her, keeping my eyes off her as she moved to Andy. She sat beside her husband, knees together, leaning forward, drink cradled in her hands. Her long nails were painted red.

I took a sip of my drink and enjoyed the burning in the back of my throat. It was good Scotch. 'I'm obviously paying you too much,' I said, breaking the awkward silence.

'It's a good drop of booze,' Andy agreed, swishing his Scotch and water round his glass.

'Is there anything I can get you?' Philipa asked softly. She looked at me coyly, her face lowered slightly and her blue eyes tilted up at me. I looked at her and my heart was pounding in my chest. There was no mistaking that look, no mistaking the allure in her voice and the slight pursing of her lips. I was erect just looking at her.

Andy slid his hand up and down her smooth thighs, stroking her soft skin as I watched. 'Do you want her?' he asked me, his voice low, almost a whisper.

I looked at him. What the fuck was going on? He smiled but said no more. There was nothing I could say so the

226

question hung in the air, filling the room with its tension. At last Philipa turned to Andy and kissed him softly on the mouth. She placed her drink on the carpet and then walked towards me, keeping her eyes averted.

She stopped beside the armchair. Her perfume mingled with the alcohol as I took another drink. She was so close I could feel the heat from her body. I looked up at her.

'Let me be your slut,' she said huskily.

I moved away, looking beyond her to her husband. 'Andy? What the—'

'You heard her,' he said, 'she wants to be a slut for you.'

'Please,' she added. 'I'll do anything you want me to.'

'Touch her,' Andy suggested.

I stood up. 'What sort of screwed up—'

She took my arm and kissed me softly on the cheek. It was such an innocent, chaste kiss that for a moment I was completely thrown. Then she lowered her head and started to lift the hem of her black dress. I was transfixed as inch by inch she revealed herself, exposing the curve of her upper thighs and then the swell of her sex. She was shaven, her pussy bare, bulging labia clean, a glimpse of pink flesh within.

'I'll be your girl,' she whispered, looking up at me with pure desire in her sweet baby blue eyes.

'Treat her badly,' Andy told me. 'She likes it, she likes to be handled rough. Don't you?' he demanded of her, his voice a cruel sneer.

'I want whatever you want,' she whispered, holding her dress up so I could feast my eyes on her sex.

'And you?' I demanded, stepping away from Philipa to face Andy.

He shrugged and downed the last of his drink. 'She's a slut who needs cock,' he said, 'what can I do?'

It was bizarre. 'Don't you care?'

'I told you,' he repeated, 'she's a slut. I give her what she needs but sometimes it's not enough. Now, you want to take her or not?'

I looked from him to her. Her eyes were full of pleading. For a moment I had no answer, but then I nodded. 'I want her,' I whispered.

She looked happy; she wet her lips with the tip of her tongue and smiled. At last she released the dress and once more she was modest: young, pure and pretty.

'Why don't you go upstairs and wait?' Andy suggested, speaking to his wife.

She started to go but then stopped. 'Is that what you want me to do?' she asked me.

'Yes, go and wait,' I told her.

Andy and I waited for her to go before speaking again.

'I know what you're thinking,' he told me, standing up.

'Do you? Then you know I think you're crazy.'

He shook his head sadly. 'No, mate, you don't understand this at all.'

'Don't I?' I hissed angrily.

'She might look all sweet and innocent on the outside, but believe me, she's a slut. There's no other word to describe her.'

'What does that make you then?'

He laughed derisively. 'Look, you either want her or you don't. She wants you, that's clear enough. Take her, do what you want to her, anything.'

'What if I beat her?' I demanded, wanting to shock some sense into him.

'Then she'll be even wetter for you. She'll love you for it. Go on, beat her, screw her in the arse. She's yours, in any way you want.'

I sat down heavily. 'How often do you do this?'

He swallowed the last of his drink. 'What difference does that make? Look,' he snapped, his face reddening, 'last year I watched her being fucked by three guys at once and she loved it. The dirty whore loved every second of it. By the time they'd finished with her she was covered in sweat and spunk. Fuck it, one of them even pissed on her, and she was delirious.'

I listened, astounded. The scenario he was describing repelled and excited me in equal measure. 'And you watched?' I whispered.

He nodded. 'I watched, and once they'd finished I fucked her again until she screamed her climax.'

'It turned you on,' I said, appalled.

He laughed. 'It did,' he admitted. 'Now you know what a sick bastard I am what're you going to do? Go upstairs, or do I call a cab for you?'

'You know I can't leave,' I said.

He looked relieved. 'She wants to be your slut,' he reminded me.

I stood and walked to the door. He was pouring himself another drink when I looked back. There was nothing else for me to say. I shut the door and walked to the stairs. My mouth was suddenly dry as I headed up.

There were a number of doors at the top of the stairs, but only one of them leaked any light. I was about to knock when I stopped myself. I pushed the door open and stepped in. Philipa was sitting on the bed, wearing a pair of skimpy black knickers and a matching lacy bra. She was on her knees, tilted forward slightly so her breasts were thrust forward.

'I'll be good for you,' she promised huskily.

'You'd better be,' I warned her.

'I will… I will,' she promised.

I could see that my harsh tone was exactly what she wanted. 'And if I beat you? Will you still be good?'

She nodded eagerly. 'If that's what you want, then I'll be good.'

I edged to the end of the bed and reached for her. She stretched forward and rubbed her face against my open palm, her lips kissing me softly. Her skin was so soft and warm. I ran my fingers through her long fine hair and she smiled. I stroked her hair and the back of her neck and she responded with an almost feline purr of pleasure.

'Is this what you want?' I asked, taking her hand and touching it to the bulge etched in my trousers. Her fingers traced the outline of my hard cock, and then she looked up and nodded.

'And what will you do to get it?' I whispered hoarsely.

'Anything…'

'You have to earn it first,' I told her through gritted teeth.

'But… but…'

I grabbed her hair and yanked her head back. She cried out, as much from the shock as the pain, I guessed. Her lips were open, a look of fear in her eyes. 'You dirty bitch,' I whispered softly into her ear.

'I am… I'm dirty…' she responded, gasping when I yanked her hair harder.

'You've made a mistake,' I told her, using my free hand to stroke the smooth flesh of her inner thighs. She felt good, her skin so soft and warm and responsive. I knew she'd be wet, there was no need to touch her there – yet.

'A mistake?' she echoed, trying to look me in the eye.

I let go of her hair, and as she turned towards me I slapped her face, hard. She winced and pulled away. Tears filled her eyes as she rubbed the shocking pain from her cheek. My fingers tingled where I'd slapped her.

'A mistake,' I confirmed.

There was confusion in her eyes. All she needed to do was to tell me to stop, to ask me to leave. Instead she nursed her face and looked up at me with wide blue eyes that begged for more. 'I'll do whatever you want me to,' she whispered.

I smiled. 'I know.'

The look in my eyes made her turn away for a second.

'Shall I undress for you?' she asked quietly.

I reached for her again and she crawled along the bed towards me. I touched her face where I'd smacked her, stroking my fingers over the reddened skin. I knew it was all true; I could do as I liked to her and she wouldn't resist. The thought made my cock harden once more. I sat beside her and pulled her closer, halfway across my lap so I could kiss her. She put her arms around me, holding tightly while I pushed my tongue between her lips.

As we kissed I stroked her back, enjoying the feel of her warmth, marvelling at the smoothness of her skin. With my other hand I began to rub the inside of her thigh, moving it slowly up and down. She moved round slightly but I moved my hand no higher; I wanted to take my time with her.

She moved back a little when I stopped kissing her. Her breasts bulged in her tight black bra and I could see her nipples were hard, pressing tightly against the lace. I brushed the back of my fingers across her nipples and she sighed softly.

I made her sit up for me so I could squeeze her breasts, holding them in my hands, cupping her flesh so it bulged even more. I brushed my thumbs back and forth over the springy flesh, making the nipples harder still while she sighed her pleasure. She reached round suddenly and unclipped her bra, letting it fall away so that her breasts were exposed.

I slapped her hard across the thigh, making her yelp with surprise. 'I didn't tell you to do that,' I admonished angrily.

'I'm sorry—'

I slapped her again, making her cry out loudly. Already I could see my hands imprinted along her thigh. Her skin marked well, the red flush of pain merging attractively with the gold of her tan. I kissed her hotly on the mouth and then reached for one of her breasts. She squealed as I grabbed a handful of flesh, crushing the nipple in my palm as my fingers tightened. I kissed her again while I squeezed, and her moans of complaint were breathed into my mouth as soft sighs of pleasure. I eased up a bit and then homed in on the nipple, my fingers closing on the erect bud until her whimpers made me stop.

I started to suck on her injured flesh, my mouth closing around the rosy flesh. I held her nipple between my lips and swept my tongue across it. I only vaguely listened to her murmurs of pleasure. I sucked harder, using my teeth to bite and then my lips to soothe, and she moaned louder. When I slid my hand under her thighs she moved to open herself, but again I only touched her halfway up her thigh.

I rolled away from her for a moment and started to undress. She watched me greedily, her eyes sparkling with desire. 'Get on the floor,' I ordered, aware of the urgency of her need.

I stripped off quickly while she watched from her position on the floor, on her knees like a supplicant. My cock was hard, jutting powerfully from the dark curls between my thighs. It was what she wanted, it was where her attention was focused.

'Well, slut, is this what you want?' I teased her, gripping my cock at the base.

She looked at me and nodded slowly. I beckoned and she crawled towards me, her breasts swaying tightly from side to side. She crawled between my thighs and started to kiss me there, her lips planting soft caresses as she worked her way towards my hardness. I wrapped my hand in her hair again and pulled her forward. She looked up at me, and then closed her lips around the tip of my erect cock. She sucked softly, her tongue passing the gentlest of caresses under the glans as I pushed myself deeper into the velvety embrace of her mouth.

I leaned back as she took more of my shaft into her mouth. The girl loved it, that was for sure. She knew exactly how to kiss and suck to give maximum pleasure. I released her hair and she began to wind herself up and down, moving so her lips barely covered my glans before swooping down to close her lips around the base. Each time it felt as though

I was in heaven, and I knew she was working me perilously close to orgasm.

I sat back up and watched her as she sucked me; eyes half closed, her lips so full and red stretched tightly, her cheeks hollowed as she sucked. Her hands held my balls, holding gently, a finger outstretched and rubbing under my thigh. I was close to coming but I resisted the urge to stand and slam my hardness into the back of her throat.

She looked like a child who'd lost a favourite toy when I pulled her away from my cock. She sat up again, her eyes wide as she gazed at the glistening rod of flesh inches from her lips. I sat back on the bed and gestured for her to join me. She climbed up in a single, sinuous movement that emphasised the shape of her body. I touched her breasts again, flicking my thumbs over her large, responsive nipples.

'Don't you want to come in my mouth?' she asked, pouting.

I kissed her moist lips, putting my tongue where my cock had just been. 'I haven't decided where I'm going to spunk into you, yet,' I told her.

'I'm wet,' she said, rubbing a finger against the outside of her black panties.

I stroked the inside of her thigh again, this time sliding my hand high so that my thumb brushed against the warmth of her knickers. I could feel she was wet, and by the way she moved I knew she was desperate for me to touch her there. I toyed with her for a few moments, enjoying the feel of the soft flesh of her inner thigh and the look of consternation on her face.

'Please…' she said at last, her voice filled with urgency, 'I need…'

'Listen, you're a dirty whore,' I said nastily. 'I don't care what you need. Clear?'

She swallowed hard and nodded. 'Yes…'

'Yes, what?'

'Yes, sir?' she said, taking a guess at the magic word that would please me.

I shook my head. 'You call me Mr Crane,' I whispered.

'Yes, Mr Crane,' she said, closing her eyes as I scraped my fingers across her panties.

'Why are you wet?'

'Because I need your cock, Mr Crane,' she said. 'I need it… Please…'

I kissed her again as my hands closed over her pert breasts. I was going to make her wait, I was going to make the bitch wait so long she would scream in frustration. She threw her head back as I started to suck on her nipples again, moving from one to the other in turn, wetting the nipples and then sucking hard so that she sighed her pleasure.

'I'm going to beat you,' I whispered, as though it were a sweet endearment.

'Please… fuck me first…' she begged, taking my face in her hands so I could see the desperation in her eyes. I slapped her hands away and went back to her breasts, using my lips and tongue on the hard fleshy points that protruded deliciously the more I played with them.

She squirmed and writhed as I mouthed her nipples. Occasionally I touched her pussy, fleeting touches across the wet panties that made her moan and shudder. Her wordless whispers were part incantation of pleasure and part litany of frustration.

'Please…'

I suddenly saw the snaking of her fingers down between her thighs. I sat up instantly and grabbed her hand. She looked at me blindly, fear in her eyes as she registered my displeasure. I smacked her across the thigh again, a hard open-handed smack that echoed around the room and made her cry out.

'Well, it looks like you're such a dirty bitch you can't wait,' I hissed.

'I'm sorry… It's just that you're making me feel so horny and I need to—'

'Shut up!'

She fell silent instantly. I looked around the room. If she wanted to play rough then that was exactly what the slut was going to get. My trousers were on the floor next to the bed. I picked them up and started to unthread my black leather belt. She watched silently, her eyes fixed on the belt as I unravelled it slowly.

'Let's just see how much you want some cock,' I told her, standing up. I looped the belt once and then gripped it tightly. 'This is your choice. If you're the slut you say you are then you'll take the belt to show me how much you want my cock.'

'I want your cock,' she said quietly.

My reaction was instantaneous. I grabbed her by the arm and pulled her across the bed, pushing her down flat on her stomach. I was rough with her but she made no complaint. I feasted my eyes on her flawlessly smooth back, her trim waist and the curve of her bottom delineated by the thin strip of her black knickers. I raised my arm and brought the belt down with one swift movement. It snapped across the top of her thighs and she let out a startled cry.

For a second I was certain Andy was going to come running into the room to investigate. It amazed me that he had left us to it for so long, and I could not imagine that he could sit back and let me thrash Philipa so violently. Her skin was marked scarlet where the belt had licked her, and I could only guess at the pain it had caused her on impact. There was not a sound outside; it beggared belief, but Andy was not going to come to her rescue.

'Well?' I challenged, standing over her, the belt dangling from my hand like a noose.

She touched the livid weal raised below her backside. 'I need cock,' she whispered, looking from her marked flesh to me.

I beat her again, bringing the leather belt down hard across the top of her thighs. Again, and again. She let out a sharp breath with each stroke and I could see her hands gripping her pillow tightly. I leaned over her and pulled her panties down to her knees, exposing the globes of her behind. My hand accidentally brushed against her pussy lips and she moaned softly, the fire of her desire undiminished.

I striped her backside several times, the belt sweeping down in a tight arc that snapped satisfyingly. She writhed, twisting from side to side, unintentionally giving me a better view of her hairless pussy and the graceful curves of her bottom.

At last I was ready to stop. I dropped the belt and pulled her round to face me. Her eyes were full of tears and for a moment she couldn't speak. I kissed her once on the lips and found that she responded instantly. I pushed her head down and forced my hard cock into her mouth.

She sucked me gratefully, holding the base of my cock with one hand and cradling my balls with the other. Her eyes were closed blissfully as her mouth worked up and down my length. She was on hands and knees and I could see the marks imprinted deeply on her behind, but her pain did nothing to distract from what she was doing.

I lay back and she continued, planting soft kisses up and down my cock before sucking it deep into her mouth once more. Her breasts brushed against my thigh, her nipples hard and responsive and adding to my excitement. I took a handful of hair and pulled her away from my cock again.

'Please…' she complained.

I reached for my belt and looped it around her neck before threading it through the buckle and pulling so it tightened like a leash. The black leather contrasted nicely with her golden curls and tanned skin.

'Like a bitch,' I explained, pulling her across the bed.

'Your bitch, Mr Crane,' she told me, the shadow of a

proud smile forming on the fullness of her lips.

Her panties were still down around her knees. I had her kneel in front of me, her hands behind her back so that her breasts were pushed forward enticingly. My eyes moved over her, surveying her body as though critical. In truth there was nothing to criticise; she was what any man would have desired. I smacked one of her breasts hard, wanting to see her eyes cloud with pain, wanting to colour her flesh and then see her desire redoubled.

I slipped my hand down between her thighs and closed my fingers over her sex, squeezing her pussy lips together. She moaned urgently, grabbing hold of me as though she needed support. I held her for a moment, breathing in her scent and enjoying the feeling of total mastery.

'Please…' she repeated once more, her wide eyes filled with desperation.

'I want to hear what a slut you are,' I told her, keeping hold of her pussy with one hand while caressing her breasts with the other.

'I am a slut… I am…' she whispered weakly.

'Tell me,' I insisted, 'I want to hear it all.'

'I love cock… I need it…'

The door opened at that instant and Andy came in. I looked up at him and felt a thrill of pleasure pass through me. Here I was, with his gorgeous young wife desperate for my cock, and now he was going to witness it too. If this is what they wanted then I was not going to disappoint them.

'Tell him about our last holiday,' Andy suggested, standing awkwardly in the doorway. He still had a drink to hand but his voice sounded clear, as though he'd been taking it nice and slow rather than hitting the bottle hard.

'We were in Cyprus,' she began, 'staying in this hotel near the sea in Ayia Napa. The waiters were all over me, you could see they all fancied me… And I fancied them…'

'How many of them had you?' I demanded.

'All of them…' she replied breathlessly. 'Every night Andy would choose which ones would have me. Sometimes it was just a couple, but on our last night he invited five of them back to our room. I was stripped down to nothing and on my hands and knees for them… I took their cocks in my mouth, my pussy, in my arse… They did what they liked to me, fucking me hard, egging each other on until I was covered in spunk and begging for more.'

I slipped my fingers into her pussy, letting her juices run down them, pushing myself into her wet heat. She shuddered and cried out, collapsing onto my chest as she climaxed suddenly. I pushed her back onto the bed and parted her thighs quickly, moving into place. She sighed as I pushed my cock deep into her sex. She moaned as I started to fuck her furiously. She moved with me, writhing furiously to match the violent rhythm of my strokes.

'Is this what you want?' I hissed through gritted teeth.

She pulled me down, holding me tightly, her nails digging into my back. 'Yes… Fuck me… Fuck me hard…'

It took every ounce of self-control but I stopped suddenly, thrusting my cock deep into her and then holding it there. She looked at me breathlessly, confused by my sudden stop.

'Not yet,' I told her, smiling.

She started to grind her hips against me. I pushed myself off her and rolled to one side, my heart pounding in my chest. My erection was smeared liberally with her juices, glistening thickly on my skin.

'You've dirtied me,' I told her.

She understood what that meant. In seconds she was on hands and knees beside me, licking her taste from my erection. She worked diligently, her tongue seeking out every drop, from my glans right down in the tangle of my pubic hair. She licked and kissed and then she opened her mouth and took my length again. Her fingers curled around the base and she held me tight as she sucked deeply.

'Doesn't she know how to suck cock?' Andy asked,

watching her dispassionately.

'Her mouth's made for it,' I sighed, lying back as the pleasure surged through me. She began to swoop up and down, her mouth tight, a perfect pussy, her tongue caressing all the while.

'Suck it, bitch!' I gasped, and pressed her head down, holding her in place. She struggled for a moment and then, as she gagged, I pumped deep into her throat. I cried out as I jetted thick spurts of come into her mouth. My orgasm swept through me, blissful, ecstatic.

I relaxed and lay back, momentarily dazed, but she continued to suck, swallowing every drop of come as it seeped from my semi-erect penis. At last she sat up, smiling, her lips were swollen, bruised almost. I had never seen a woman look so wanton or so desirable.

'Can I?' Andy asked. I turned, suddenly remembering he was there too. He must have seen the momentary confusion on my face.

'She's yours tonight,' he reminded me. 'If you want me to leave then say so.'

I hesitated, then said, 'She needs something more.'

Andy walked to the side of the bed and from a drawer he pulled out a selection of sex toys. Vibrators, a gag, a few wispy items of lingerie and a long, thick dildo of black and gold.

'I want that,' I decided instantly, pointing to the immense dildo.

Andy handed it over. Long and heavy, with a wide base and a long smooth body, it looked more like a weapon of pain than an instrument of pleasure. Bigger than any man, the thing felt strange in my hand. I could see from the hesitation in Philipa's eyes that she feared what I would do with it.

'And me?' Andy asked.

I looked at him and then at her. 'Take her mouth,' I suggested, feeling magnanimous. He smiled, almost pathetically grateful.

'Fuck her hard,' I added, indicating to her that she should position herself on the edge of the bed, on hands and knees.

Andy undressed quickly, shedding his clothes untidily on the floor while I stroked his wife. Her skin was warm, slightly clammy, but her nipples were still swollen and sensitive as I raked my nails across them. I kissed her on the mouth and tasted my come there, misted on her breath like a perfume.

'Will you fuck me again?' she asked softly.

My cock was becoming hard again, swelling nicely as I touched her. 'If you're good,' I teased.

She kissed me and then turned to Andy. His cock was hard, marbled with veins and jutting from his fist. He took her by the chin and pulled her towards him. I watched, fascinated, as her lips slid smoothly over his flesh, her mouth engulfing his hardness in its wet warmth. She moved slowly at first, teasing him until he grabbed her by the hair and forced himself deep inside.

I moved behind her and was treated to a rear view of her swollen pussy lips. Her bottom was rounded, cleaved deeply but offering an enticing glimpse of her anus. I traced the round end of the dildo up and down her inner thigh, marvelling at the contrast between her smooth skin and the flawless black plastic. As I stroked her she pushed her stomach down and her bottom up, opening herself slightly. Her juices glistened from between her pussy lips and I leant over to gently kiss her there. She responded by moving back, pushing her buttocks towards me. I pressed my tongue into her pussy and lapped at her juices.

I started to use my fingers on her sex, pressing deep and then smearing her juices over her pussy and along her anal crack. She half turned towards me, keeping her mouth closed over Andy's cock. I smacked her backside hard, and she yelped.

'She needs to be beaten again,' I told Andy.

He wrapped his hand in her hair and nodded. 'It's okay,' he said, 'I'll make sure she doesn't complain too loudly.'

He thrust hard into her mouth and I watched her eyes flicker with excitement. The slut liked it rough. She needed a cock in her mouth while she was beaten, that much was clear.

I got up on my knees behind her and pushed my erection against her pussy. She moved against me, her hand sneaking down to part her pussy lips in preparation. I watched her open herself, her fingers slipping slightly into her sex so that they came out wet. I took my cock in hand and rubbed it against her, moving it back and forth so that she wriggled urgently against me.

'Such a greedy bitch,' I murmured.

She cried out when I smacked her. My hand came swinging down powerfully onto her bottom. Her skin was marked instantly with the vivid red imprint of my fingers. I moved back and started to spank her slowly, each stroke aimed perfectly, executed methodically. Six strokes in and her bottom cheeks were patterned with the livid bas-relief of my fingers. I held her with my free hand as I continued, aiming for the tops of her thighs as well as the globes of her backside.

All the while Andy continued to fuck her in the mouth. He was the one in control; I could see she moved at his command. He held her with both hands, moving her mouth back and forth as he thrust into her powerfully. She could barely keep up, and the whispers of complaint as I punished her were lost as he fucked her brutally.

I picked up the black dildo and pushed it against her pussy lips. It seemed impossible that an object so big and hard could penetrate the delicate folds. I pressed it in slowly, excited by the sight of the black phallus entering her body. It went in slowly but surely, stretching her sex, filling her up. She bucked and writhed but I couldn't tell whether that was the dildo or the way the she was being fucked in the mouth.

She climaxed suddenly, her whole body convulsing as it burst from within her. I pushed the dildo in almost completely while she whimpered and gasped. Andy grunted once and forced his hardness to the back of her throat as he climaxed. She sucked on it instinctively, swallowing his seed as it burst into the back of her mouth.

Moments later she collapsed on the bed, sprawling forward on her stomach, her limbs unable to support her any longer. The dildo was still buried inside her, the thick round base of it pushing against her pussy lips. Andy sat on the end of the bed, his cock still leaking droplets of come.

'I've not finished with you yet,' I whispered into her ear.

She turned to me and I saw a dribble of come leaking from her lips. Her eyes were half closed and she seemed lost to the world. I crawled back across the bed until I was behind her and then yanked her up by the waist. She was only halfway up, her face and chest were still flat on the bed, but her backside was lifted high and her thighs were nicely parted. I traced the outline of the black dildo, my fingers caressing her bulging sex.

Slowly I eased the dildo from her, the plastic surface dappled with jewels of her juices. I wet my fingertip in her pussy and then touched it to the puckered hole that was her anus. She began to sigh, softly at first but louder as I alternated between stroking her pussy and then wetting her anal hole. With my free hand I passed her the dildo, offering it to her insistently.

'Suck it,' I ordered.

'Go on, bitch,' Andy added, watching her excitedly as she pursed her red lips and touched them to the end of the dildo. Her mouth looked so small beside the black beast which had filled her cunt.

I pushed my finger into her rear hole and she gasped. 'Suck it clean for me,' I told her.

She opened her mouth and took in the first few inches of hard black plastic. She licked and sucked and cleansed it of her pussy juices. She looked up at me coyly as she took the dildo deeper. It distended her cheek and stretched her mouth. Her eyes fluttered as I began to finger-fuck her arsehole, pushing in and out while I watched her suck on that immense phallus.

'Isn't that what you want?' I taunted.

'Yes... I need cock...' she responded, letting her tongue traverse the length of the dildo. The bitch was turning herself on again, and making me boil with desire.

I took the monster from her and pushed the end of it against her tightly puckered anal hole. Her eyes widened as I started to push. She arched her back and gasped as I penetrated, making it distend the tight ring of muscle. Her eyes had that glazed look and I knew she was edging towards orgasm once more.

She parted her thighs again and pressed her backside higher, opening herself still more. My fingers were still wet with her juices and when I tracked the rim of the dildo in her anus she sighed and moaned softly, her pleasure clearly expressed. I started to sodomise her with the implement, moving it out slowly then pushing it in forcefully, so that she cried out with pleasure and pain.

Andy was watching, his eyes wide with excitement. His cock was reawakened and I knew he'd want to take her again.

I moved round, so I was at her side rather than directly behind her. 'Well, bitch?' I demanded.

She twisted towards me and reached for my hardness. Her mouth was soft and warm as it slipped over my cock. I caught my breath as she began to suck me again. I swear she could do things with her mouth that I'd never experienced before. She licked and suckled and moved, and in seconds I was ready to explode in her mouth again.

I pushed the dildo deeper into her anus and then took her

face in my hands. I thrust into her mouth again and again, fucking her hard. I was breathing fast and my excitement was building towards another explosive orgasm.

'Slow down,' I warned, smacking her across the backside again.

She did as she was told, wrapping her elegant fingers around my cock as she did so. She glanced up at me, her eyes playful as she withdrew my cock to lap her tongue around the glans.

I kissed her, aware that her mouth had already taken two lots of seed. How many other cocks had she taken in the past? How many in one night? Suddenly I understood what drove Andy on. I understood the excitement and the pleasure, the perverse pride in watching his wife take other men's cocks.

When I moved round to her behind she reached back and started to play with her pussy. I smacked her hand away instantly. She still needed to learn a lesson.

'Take her mouth again,' I snapped to Andy.

'Please…' she started to complain, but Andy grabbed her hair and slapped her face at the same time. She looked at him sulkily, but he ignored her and forced her mouth around his cock again.

I withdrew the dildo from her rear hole and let it drop onto the bed. Her pussy and anus were there for me, waiting to be used and abused. I pushed my fingers into her cunt and she rocked with pleasure. I fingered her for a while and was rewarded with another flood of her pussy juices. I used them to wet my cock, making it glisten with her honey.

Her backside was still red with my handprints, and I smacked her again a few times until she whimpered around her husband's gnarled stalk. I positioned my cock against the dark ring of her anal opening. I held her bottom cheeks apart and pressed down. She cried out as my cock entered her behind. I held my breath until my stomach was pressed tight against her backside. Her anal ring gripped my cock tightly and I was in heaven.

'Take her cunt now,' I told Andy suddenly.

He smiled and slid under her. She made way for him and then he worked his limbs between hers and mine. Somehow in the tangle of arms and legs he moved into place. I felt her move down on him and then, through her body, I felt his hardness enter her sex.

I started to fuck her immediately, holding her by the waist as I thrust into her bottom. Andy was moving too, thrusting upwards into the depths of her cunt. She was sighing and moaning, her eyes closed as the pleasure soared through her body.

I paused momentarily and grabbed the dildo. I held it for a moment and then passed it to her.

'Let's see what a slut you are,' I taunted. 'Suck it.'

She hesitated. 'But that's been…'

'Suck it!'

Andy stopped too. I felt my cock stiffen even more inside her as she took the black monster to her lips. It had been buried deep in her anus and now she kissed the tip gingerly, almost reverently. She looked at me and I knew she was the perfect slut. Her lips closed tightly over the smooth plastic as she took it deeper into her mouth.

I grabbed her by the waist again and started to fuck her, hard. She writhed and rocked, moving herself intricately as two throbbing cocks filled her body. I uttered a strangled cry and started to come, my orgasm bursting in waves of thick seed. A moment later, with the dildo still in her mouth, Andy thrust upwards one last time and I felt his climax echoed by her own.

My body felt drained as I lay back. I was bathed in sweat. Philipa crawled towards me and kissed my hand gratefully.

'Am I a bad girl?' she asked me.

Our eyes locked and I knew I was in love with her.

'No,' I whispered.

Andy stroked her back lazily. 'You're a slut,' he told

her, his voice filled with affection, 'and I love you for it.'

'I'll be your slut again,' she promised me, and then, with my cock hardening again, she began to kiss me.

More exciting titles available from Chimera

1-901388-55-7*	Slave to Cabal	*McLachlan*
1-901388-57-3*	Forbidden Fantasies	*Gerrard*
1-901388-58-1*	Chain Reaction	*Pope*
1-901388-60-3*	Sister Murdock's House of Correction	*Angelo*
1-901388-61-1*	Moonspawn	*McLachlan*
1-901388-59-X*	The Bridle Path	*Eden*
1-901388-62-X*	Ruled by the Rod	*Rawlings*
1-901388-63-8*	Of Pain and Delight	*Stone*
1-901388-65-4*	The Collector	*Steel*
1-901388-66-2*	Prisoners of Passion	*Dere*
1-901388-67-0*	Sweet Submission	*Anderssen*
1-901388-69-7*	Rachael's Training	*Ward*
1-901388-71-9*	Learning to Crawl	*Argus*
1-901388-36-0*	Out of Her Depth	*Challis*
1-901388-68-9*	Moonslave	*McLachlan*
1-901388-72-7*	Nordic Bound	*Morgan*
1-901388-80-8*	Cauldron of Fear	*Pope*

* * *

1-901388-73-5*	Managing Mrs Burton *(Feb)*	*Aspen*
1-901388-74-3*	In Too Deep *(Feb)*	*Beaufort*
1-901388-75-1*	Lucy *(Mar)*	*Culber*
1-901388-77-8*	The Piano Teacher *(Mar)*	*Elliot*

* * *

All **Chimera** titles are/will be available from your local bookshop or newsagent, or direct from our mail order department. Please send your order with a cheque or postal order (made payable to *Chimera Publishing Ltd*) to: **Chimera Publishing Ltd., PO Box 152, Waterlooville, Hants, PO8 9FS**. If you would prefer to pay by credit card, email us at: **chimera@fdn.co.uk** or call our **24 hour telephone/fax credit card hotline: +44 (0)23 92 783037** (Visa, Mastercard, Switch, JCB and Solo only).

To order, send: Title, author, ISBN number and price for each book ordered, your full name and address, cheque or postal order for the total amount, and include the following for postage and packing:
UK and BFPO: £1.00 for the first book, and 50p for each additional book to a maximum of £3.50.
Overseas and Eire: £2.00 for the first book, £1.00 for the second and 50p for each additional book.

*Titles £5.99. All others £4.99

For a copy of our free catalogue please write to:

Chimera Publishing Ltd
Readers' Services
PO Box 152
Waterlooville
Hants
PO8 9FS

Or visit our Website for details of all our superb titles
www.chimerabooks.co.uk

Sales and Distribution in the USA and Canada:

LPC Group
1436 West Randolph Street
Chicago
IL 60607
(800) 626-4330

***